Recollections of
Dante Gabriel Rossetti

T. Hall Caine

Contents

RECOLLECTIONS OF
DANTE GABRIEL ROSSETTI

BY

T. Hall Caine

PREFACE.

One day towards the close of 1881 Rossetti, who was then very ill, said to me:

"How well I remember the beginning of our correspondence, and how little did I think it would lead to such relations between us as have ensued! I was at the time very solitary and depressed from various causes, and the letters of so young and ardent a well-wisher, though unknown to me personally, brought solace."

"Yours," I said, "were very valuable to me."

"Mine to you were among the largest bodies of literary letters I ever wrote, others being often letters of personal interest."

"And so admirable in themselves," I added, "and so free from the discussion of any but literary subjects that many of them would bear to be printed exactly as you penned them."

"That," he said, "will be for you some day to decide."

This was the first hint of any intention upon my part of publishing the letters he had written to me; indeed, this was the first moment at which I had conceived the idea of doing so. Nothing further on the subject was said down to the morning of the Thursday preceding the Sunday on which he died, when we talked together for the last time on subjects of general interest,--subsequent interviews being concerned wholly with solicitous inquiries upon my part, in common with other anxious friends, as to the nature of his sufferings, and the briefest answers from him.

"How long have we been friends?" he said.

I replied, between three and four years from my first corresponding with him.

"And how long did we correspond?"

"Three years, nearly."

"What numbers of my letters you must possess! They may perhaps even yet be useful to you."

From this moment I regarded the publication of his letters as in some sort a trust; and though I must have withheld them for some years if I had consulted my own wishes simply, I yielded to the necessity that they should be published at once, rather than run any risk of their not been published at all.

What I have just said will account for the circumstance that I, the youngest and latest of Rossetti's friends, should be the first to seem to stand towards him in the relation of a biographer. I say *seem* to stand, for this is not a biography. It was always known to be Rossetti's wish that if at any moment after his death it should appear that the story of his life required to be written, the one friend who during many of his later years knew him most intimately, and to whom he unlocked the most sacred secrets of his heart, Mr. Theodore Watts, should write it, unless indeed it were undertaken by his brother William. But though I know that whenever Mr. Watts sets pen to paper in pursuance of such purpose, and in fulfilment of such charge, he will afford us a recognisable portrait of the man, vivified by picturesque illustration, the like of which few other writers could compass, I also know from what Rossetti often told me of his friend's immersion in all kinds and varieties of life, that years (perhaps many years) may elapse before such a biography is given to the world. My own book is, I trust, exactly what it purports to be: a volume of Recollections, interwoven with letters and criticism, and preceded by such a summary of the leading facts in Rossetti's life as seems necessary for the elucidation of subsequent records. I have drawn Rossetti precisely as I found him in each stage of our friendship, exhibiting his many contradictions of character, extenuating nothing, and, I need hardly add, setting down naught in malice. Up to this moment I have never inquired of myself whether to those who have known little or nothing of Rossetti hitherto, mine will seem to be on the whole favourable or unfavourable portraiture; but I have trusted my admiration of the poet and affection for the friend to penetrate with kindly and appreciative feeling every comment I have had to offer. I was attracted to Rossetti in the first case by ardent love of his genius, and retained to him ultimately by love of the man. As I have said in the course of these Recollections, it was largely his unhappiness that held me, with others, as by a spell, and only too sadly in this particular did he in his last year realise his own picture of

Dante at Verona:

> Yet of the twofold life he led
> In chainless thought and fettered will
> Some glimpses reach us,--somewhat still
> Of the steep stairs and bitter bread,--
> Of the soul's quest whose stern avow
> For years had made him haggard now.

I am sensible of the difficulty and delicacy of the task I have undertaken, involving, as it does, many interests and issues; and in every reference to surviving relatives as well as to other persons now living, with whom Rossetti was in any way allied, I have exercised in all friendliness the best judgment at my command.

Clement's Inn, October 1882.

*** It has not been thought necessary to attach dates to the
letters printed in this volume, for not only would the
difficulty of doing so be great, owing to the fact that
Rossetti rarely dated his letters, but the utility of dates
in such a case would be doubtful, because the substance of
what is said is often quite impersonal, and, where
otherwise, is almost independent of the time of production.
It may be sufficient to say that the letters were written in
the years 1879,1880, and 1881.

CHAPTER I.

D ante Gabriel Rossetti was the eldest son of Gabriele Rossetti and Frances Polidori, daughter of Alfieri's secretary, and sister of the young physician who travelled with Lord Byron. Gabriele Rossetti was a native of Yasto, in the district of the Abruzzi, kingdom of Naples. He was a patriotic poet of very considerable distinction; and, as a politician, took a part in extorting from Ferdinand I. the Constitution of 1820. After the failure of the Neapolitan insurrection, owing to the treachery of the King (who asked leave of absence on a pretext of ill-health, and returned with an overwhelming Austrian army), the insurrectionists were compelled to fly. Some of them fell victims; others lay long in concealment. Rossetti was one of the latter; and, while he was in hiding, Sir Graham Moore, the English admiral, was lying with an English fleet in the bay. The wife of the admiral had long been a warm admirer of the patriotic hymns of Rossetti, and, when she learned his danger, she prevailed with her husband to make efforts to save him. Sir Graham thereupon set out with another English officer to the place of concealment, habited the poet in an English uniform, placed him between them in a carriage, and put him aboard a ship that sailed next day to Malta, where he obtained the friendship of the governor, John Hookham Frere, by whose agency valuable introductions were procured, and ultimately Rossetti established himself in England. Arrived in London about 1823, he lived a cheerful life as an exile, though deprived of the advantages of his Italian reputation. He married in 1826, and his eldest son was born May 12, 1828, in Charlotte Street, Portland Place, London. He was appointed Professor of Italian at King's College, and died in 1854. His house was for years the constant resort of Italian refugees; and the son used to say that it was from observation of these visitors of his father that he depicted the principal personage of his *Last Confession*. He did not live to see the returning glories of his country or the consummation we have witnessed of that great movement founded upon the principles for which he fought and suffered. His present position in Italy as a poet and patriot is a high one, a medal having been struck in his honour. An effort is even now afoot to erect a statue to him in his native place, and one of the last occasions upon which the son put pen to paper was when trying to make a reminiscent rough portrait for the use of the sculptor. Gabriele Rossetti spent his last years in the study of Dante, and his works on the subject are unique, exhibiting a peculiar view of Dante's conception of Beatrice, which he believed to be purely ideal, and employed solely for purposes of speculative and political disquisition. Something of this interpretation was fixed undoubtedly upon the personage by Dante himself in his later writings, but whether the change were the result of a maturer and more complicated state of thought, and whether the real and ideal characters of Beatrice may not be compatible, are questions which the poetic mind will not consider it possible to decide. Coleridge, no doubt, took a fair view of Rossetti's theory when he said: "Rossetti's view of Dante's meaning is in great part just, but he has pushed it beyond all bounds of common sense. How could a poet--and such a poet as Dante--have written the details of the allegory as conjectured by Rossetti? The boundaries between his allegory and his pure picturesque are plain enough, I think, at first reading." It was, doubtless, due to his devotion to studies of the Florentine that Gabriele Rossetti named after him his eldest son.

Dante Gabriel Rossetti, whose full baptismal name was Gabriel Charles Dante, was educated principally at King's College School, London, and there attained to a moderate proficiency in the ordinary classical school-learning, besides a knowledge of French, which throughout life he spoke well. He learned at home some rudimentary German; Italian he had acquired at a very early age. There has always been some playful mention of certain tragedies and translations upon which he exercised himself from the ages of five to fifteen years; but it is hardly necessary to say that he himself never attached value to these efforts of his precocity; he even displayed, occasionally, a little irritation upon hearing them spoken of as remarkable youthful achievements.

One of these productions of his adolescence, Sir Hugh the Heron, has been so frequently alluded to, that it seems necessary to tell the story of it, as the author himself, in conversation, was accustomed to do. At about twelve years of age, the young poet wrote a scrap of a poem under this title, and then cast it aside. His grandfather, Polidori, had seen the fragment, however, and had conceived a much higher opinion of its merits than even the natural vanity of the young author himself permitted him to entertain. It had then become one of the grandfather's amusements to set up an amateur printing-press in his own house, and occupy his leisure in publishing little volumes of original verse for semi-public circulation. He urged his grandson to finish the poem in question, promising it, in a completed state, the dignity and distinction of type. Prompted by hope of this hitherto unexpected reward, Rossetti--then thirteen to fourteen years of age--finished the juvenile epic, and some bound copies of it got abroad. No more was thought of the matter, and in due time the little bard had forgotten that he had ever done it. But when a genuine distinction had been earned by poetry that was in no way immature, Rossetti discovered, by the gratuitous revelation of a friend, that a copy of the youthful production--privately printed and never published--was actually in the library of the British Museum. Amazed, and indeed appalled as he was by this disclosure, he was powerless to remedy the evil, which he foresaw would some day lead to the poem being unearthed to his injury, and printed as a part of his work. The utmost he could do to avert the threatened mischief he did, and this was to make an entry in a commonplace-book which he kept for such uses, explaining the origin and history of the poem, and expressing a conviction that it seemed to him to be remarkable only from its entire paucity of even ordinary poetic promise. But while this was indubitably a just estimate of these boyish efforts, it is no doubt true, as we shall presently see, that Rossetti's genius matured itself early in life.

Whilst still a child, his love of literature exhibited itself, and a story is told of a disaster occurring to him, when rather less than nine years of age, which affords amusing proof of the ardour of his poetic nature. Upon going with his brother and sisters to the house of his grandfather, where as children they occupied themselves with sports appropriate to their years, he proposed to improvise a part of a scene from *Othello*, and cast himself for the principal *role*. The scene selected was the closing one of the play, and began with the speech delivered to Lodovico, Montano, and Gratiano, when they are about to take Othello prisoner. Rossetti used to say that he delivered the lines in a frenzy of boyish excitement, and coming to the words--

Set you down this:
And say, besides,--that in Aleppo once,
Where a malignant and a turban'd Turk
Beat a Venetian, and traduced the state,
I took by the throat the circumcised dog,
And smote him--thus!--

he snatched up an iron chisel, that lay somewhere at hand, and, to the consternation of his companions, smote himself with all his might on the chest, inflicting a wound from which he bled and fainted.

He is described by those who remember him, at this period, as a boy of a gentle and affectionate nature, albeit prone to outbursts of masterfulness. The earliest existent portraits represent a comely youth, having redundant auburn hair curling all round the head, and eyes and forehead of extraordinary beauty. It is said that he was brave and manly of temperament, courageous as to personal suffering, eminently solicitous of the welfare of others, and kind and considerate to*such as he had claims upon. This is no doubt true portraiture, but it must be stated (however open to explanation, on grounds of laudable self-depreciation), that it is not the picture which he himself used to paint of his character as a boy. He often described himself as being destitute of personal courage when at school, as shrinking from the amusements of schoolfellows, and fearful of their quarrels; not wholly without generous impulses, but, in the main, selfish of nature and reclusive in habit of life. He was certainly free from the meaningless affectation--for such it too frequently is-- of representing his school-days as the happiest of his life. If, after so much undervaluing of himself, it were possible to trust his estimate of his youthful character, he would have had you believe that school was to him a place of semi-purgatorial probation,--which nothing but love of his mother, and desire to meet her wishes, prevented him, as an irreclaimable antischoliast, from obstinately renouncing at a time when he had learned little Latin, and less Greek.

Having from childhood shown a propensity towards painting, the strong inclination was fostered by his parents, and art was looked upon as his future profession. Upon leaving school about 1843, he studied first at an art academy near Bedford Square, and afterwards at the Eoyal Academy Antique School, never, however, going to the Eoyal Academy Life School. He appears to have been an assiduous student. In after life when his habit of late rising had become a stock subject of banter among his intimate friends, he would tell with unwonted pride how in earlier years he used to rise at six A.M. once a week in order to attend a life-class held before breakfast. On such occasions he was accustomed, he would say, to purchase a buttered roll and cup of coffee at some stall at a street corner, so as not to dislocate domestic arrangements by requiring the servants to get up in the middle of the night. He left the Academy about 1848 or 1849, and in the latter year exhibited his picture entitled the ***Girlhood of Mary Virgin***. This painting is an admirable example of his early art, before the Gothicism of the early Italian painters became his quest. Better known to the public than the picture is the sonnet written upon it, containing the beautiful lines--

An angel-watered lily, that near God
Grows and is quiet.

While Rossetti was still under age he associated with J. E. Millais, Holman Hunt, Thomas Woolner, James Collinson, F. G. Stephens, and his brother, W. M. Rossetti, in the movement called pre-Raphaelite. At the beginning of his career he recognised, in common with his associates, that the contemporary classicism had run to seed, and that, beyond an effort after perfection of ***technique***, the art of the period was all but devoid of purpose, of thought, imagination, or spirituality. At such a moment it was matter for little surprise that ardent young intellects should go back for inspiration to the Gothicism of Giotto and the early painters. There, at least, lay feeling, aim, aspiration, such as did not concern itself primarily with any question of whether a subject were painted well or ill, if only it were first of all a subject at all--a subject involving manipulative excellence, perhaps, but feeling and invention certainly. This, then, stated briefly, was the meaning of pre-Raphaelitism. The name (as shall hereafter appear) was subsequently given to the movement more than half in jest. It has sometimes been stated that Mr. Ruskin was an initiator, but this is not strictly the case. The company of young painters and writers are said to have been ignorant of Mr. Ruskin's writings when they began their revolt against the current classicism. It is a fact however, that, after perhaps a couple of years, Mr.

Ruskin came to the rescue of the little brotherhood (then much maligned) by writing in their defence a letter in the ***Times***. It is easy to make too much of these early endeavours of a company of young men, exceptionally gifted though the reformers undoubtedly were, and inspired by an ennobling enthusiasm. In later years Rossetti was not the most prominent of those who kept these beginnings of a movement constantly in view; indeed, it is hardly rash to say that there were moments when he seemed almost to resent the intrusion of them upon the maturity of aim and handling which, in common with his brother artists, he ultimately compassed. But it would be folly not to recognise the essential germs of a right aspiration which grew out of that interchange of feeling and opinion which, in its concrete shape, came to be termed pre-Raphaelitism. Rossetti is acknowledged to have taken the most prominent part in the movement, supplying, it is alleged, much of the poetic impulse as well as knowledge of mediaeval art. He occupied himself in these and following years mainly in the making of designs for pictures--the most important of them being ***Dante's Dream, Hamlet and Ophelia, Cassandra, Lucretia Borgia, Giotto painting Dante's Portrait, The First Anniversary of the Death of Beatrice Mary Magdalene at the Door of Simon the Pharisee, The Death of Lady Macbeth, Desdemona's Death-song*** and a great subject entitled ***Found***, designed and begun at twenty-five, but left incomplete at death.

All this occurred between the years 1849-1856, but three years before the earlier of these dates Rossetti, as a painter, had come under an influence which he was never slow to acknowledge operated powerfully on his art. In 1846, Mr. Ford Madox Brown exhibited designs in the Westminster competition, and his cartoons deeply impressed Rossetti The young painter, then nineteen years of age, wrote to the elder one, his senior by no more than seven years, begging to be permitted to become a pupil. An intimacy sprang up between the two, and for a while Rossetti worked in Brown's studio; but though the friendship lasted throughout life the professional relationship soon terminated. The ardour of the younger man led him into the-brotherhood just referred to, but Brown never joined the pre-Raphaelites, mainly, it is said, from dislike of coterie tendencies.

About 1856, Rossetti, with two or three other young painters, gratuitously undertook to paint designs on the walls of the Union Debating Hall at Oxford, and about the time he was engaged upon this task he made the acquaintance of Mr. William Morris, Mr. Burne Jones, and Mr. Swinburne, who were undergraduates at the University. Mr. Burne Jones was intended for a clerical career, but due to Rossett's intercession Holy Orders were abandoned, to the great gain of English art. He has more than once generously allowed that he owed much to Rossetti at the beginning of his career, find regarded him to the last as leader of the movement with which his own name is now so eminently and distinctively associated. Together, and with the co-operation of Mr. William Morris and Canon Dixon, they started and carried on for about a year a monthly periodical called *The Oxford and Cambridge Magazine*, of which Canon Dixon, as one of the projectors, shall presently tell the history. At a subsequent period Mr. Burne Jones and Rossetti, together with Mr. Madox Brown and some three others, associated with Mr. Morris in establishing, from the smallest of all possible beginnings, the trading firm now so well known as Morris and Co., and they remained partners in this enterprise down to the year 1874, when a dissolution took place, leaving the business in the hands of the gentleman whose name it bore, and whose energy had from the first been mainly instrumental in securing its success.

It may be said that almost from the outset Rossetti viewed the public exhibition of pictures as a distracting practice. Except the *Girlhood of Mary Virgin*, the *Annunciation* was almost the only picture he exhibited in London, though three or four water-colour drawings were at an early period exhibited in Liverpool, and of these, by a curious coincidence, one was the first study for the *Dante's Dream*, which was purchased by the corporation of the city within a few months of the painter's death. To sum up all that remains at this stage to say of Rossetti as a pictorial artist down to his thirtieth year, we may describe him (as he liked best to hear himself described) simply as a poetic painter. If he had a special method, it might be called a distinct poetic abstraction, together with a choice of mediaeval subject, and an effort after no less vivid rendering of nature than was found in other painters. With his early designs (the outcome of such a quest as has been indicated) there came, perchance, artistic crudities enough, but assuredly there came a great spirituality also. By and by Rossetti perceived that he must make narrower the stream of his effort if he would have it flow deeper; and then, throughout many years, he perfected his technical methods by abandoning complex subject-designs, and confining himself to simple three-quarter-length pictures. More shall be said on this point in due course. Already, although unknown through the medium of the public picture-gallery, he was recognised as the leader of a school of rising young artists whose eccentricities were frequently a theme of discussion. He never invited publicity, yet he was rapidly attaining to a prominent position among painters.

His personal character in early manhood is described by friends as one of peculiar manliness, geniality, and unselfishness. It is said that, on one occasion, he put aside important work of his own in order to spend several days in the studio of a friend, whose gifts were quite inconsiderable compared with his, and whose prospects were all but hopeless,--helping forward certain pictures, which were backward, for forthcoming exhibition. Many similar acts of self-sacrifice are still remembered with gratitude by those who were the recipients of them. Rossetti was king of his circle, and it must be said, that in all that properly constituted kingship, he took care to rule. There was then a certain determination of purpose which occasionally had the look of arbitrariness, and sometimes, it is alleged, a disregard of opposing opinion which partook of tyranny: but where heart and not head were in question, he was assuredly the most urbane and amiable of monarchs. In matters of taste in art, or criticism in poetry, he would brook no opposition from any quarter; nor did he ever seem to be conscious of the unreasonableness of compelling his associates to swallow his opinions as being absolute and final. This disposition to govern his circle co-existed, however, with the most lavish appreciation of every good quality displayed by the members of it, and all the little uneasiness to which his absolutism may sometimes have given rise was much more than removed by constantly recurring acts of good-fellowship,--indeed it was forgotten in the presence of them.

A photograph which exists of Rossetti at twenty-seven conveys the idea of a nature rather austere and taciturn than genial and outspoken. The face is long and the cheeks sunken, the whole figure being attenuated and slightly stooping; the eyes have the inward look which belonged to them in later life, but the mouth, which is free from the concealment of moustache or beard, is severe. The impression conveyed is of a powerful intellect and ambitious nature at war with surroundings and not wholly satisfied with the results. It ought to be added that, at the period in question, health was uncertain with Rossetti: and this fact, added to the circumstance of his being at the time in the very throes of those difficulties with his art which he was soon to surmount, must be understood to account for the austerity of his early portrait. Rossetti was not in a distinct sense a humourist, but there came to him at intervals, in earlier manhood, those outbursts of volatility, which, to serious natures, act as safety-valves after prolonged tension of all the powers of the mind. At such moments of levity he is described as almost boyish in recklessness, plunging into any madcap escapade that might be afoot with heedlessness of all consequences. Stories of misadventures, quips and quiddities of every kind, were then his delight, and of these he possessed a fund which no man knew better how to use. He would tell a funny story with wonderful spirit and freshness of resource, always leading up to the point with watchful care of the finest shades of covert suggestion or innuendo, and, when the climax was reached, never denying himself a hearty share in the universal laughter. One of his choicest pleasures at a dinner or other such gathering was to improvise rhymes on his friends, and of these the fun usually lay in the improvisatore's audacious ascription of just those qualities which his subject did not possess. Though far from devoid of worldly wisdom, and indeed possessed of not a little shrewdness in his dealings with his buyers (often exhibiting that rarest quality of the successful trader, the art of linking one transaction with another), he was sometimes amusingly deficient in what is known as common sense. In later life he used to tell with infinite zest a story of a blunder of earlier years which might easily have led to serious if not fatal results. He had been suffering from nervous exhaustion and had been ordered to take a preparation of nux vomica. The dose was to be taken three times daily: in the morning, at noon, and in the evening. One afternoon he was about to start out for the house of a friend with whom he had promised to lunch, when he remembered that he had not taken his first daily dose of medicine. He forthwith took it, and upon setting down the glass, reflected that the second dose was due, and so he took that also. Putting on his hat and preparing to sally forth he further reflected that before he could return the third dose ought in ordinary course to be taken, and so without more deliberation he poured himself a final portion and drank it off. He had thereupon scarcely turned himself about, when to his horror he discovered that his limbs were growing rigid and his jaw stiff. In the utmost agitation he tried to walk across the studio and found himself almost incapable of the effort. His eyes seemed to leap out of their sockets and his sight grew dim. Appalled and in agony, he at length sprang up from the couch upon which he had dropped down a moment before, and fled out of the house. The violent action speedily induced a copious perspiration, and this being by much the best thing that could have happened to him, carried off the poison and so saved his life. He could never afterwards be induced to return to the drug in question, and in the last year of his life was probably more fearfully aghast at seeing the present writer take a harmless dose of it than he would have been at learning that 50 grains of chloral had been taken.

He had, in early manhood, the keenest relish of a funny prank, and one such he used to act over again in after life with the greatest vivacity of manner. Every one remembers the story told by Jefferson Hogg how Shelley got rid of the old woman with the onion basket who took a place beside him in a stage coach in Sussex, by seating himself on the floor and fixing a tearful, woful face upon his companion, addressing her in thrilling accents thus--

For heaven's sake, let us sit upon the ground,
And tell sad stories of the death of kings.

Rossetti's frolic was akin to this, though the results were amusingly different. It would appear that when in early years, Mr. William Morris and Mr. Burne Jones occupied a studio together, they had a young servant maid whose manners were perennially vivacious, whose good spirits no disaster could damp, and whose pertness nothing could banish or check. Rossetti conceived the idea of frightening the girl out of her complacency, and calling one day on his friends, he affected the direst madness, strutted ominously up to her and with the wildest glare of his wild eyes, the firmest and fiercest setting of his lower lip, and began in measured and resonant accents to recite the lines--

Shall the hide of a fierce lion
Be stretched on a couch of wood,
For a daughter's foot to lie on,
Stained with a father's blood?

The poet's response is a soft "Ah, no!" but the girl, ignorant of course of this, and wholly undisturbed by the bloodthirsty tone of the question addressed to her, calmly fixed her eyes on the frenzied eyes before her, and answered with a swift light accent and rippling laugh, "It shall if you like, sir!" Rossetti's enjoyment of his discomfiture on this occasion seemed never to grow less.

His life was twofold in intellectual effort, and of the directions in which his energy went out the artistic alone has thus far been dealt with. It has been said that he early displayed talent for writing as well as painting, and, in truth, the poems that he wrote in early youth are even more remarkable than the pictures that he painted. His poetic genius developed rapidly after sixteen, and sprang at once to a singular and perfect maturity. It is difficult to say whether it will add to the marvel of mature achievement or deduct from the sense of reality of personal experience, to make public the fact that *The Blessed Damozel* was written when the poet was no more than nineteen. That poem is a creation so pure and simple in the higher imagination, as to support the contention that the author was electively related to Fra Angelico. Described briefly, it may be said to embody the meditations of a beautiful girl in Paradise, whose lover is in the same hour dreaming of her on earth. How the poet lighted upon the conception shall be told by himself in that portion of this book devoted to the writer's personal recollections.

The Blessed Damozel is a conception dilated to such spiritual loveliness that it seems not to exist within things substantially beautiful, or yet by aid of images that coalesce out of the evolving memory of them, but outside of everything actual It is not merely that the dream itself is one of ideal purity; the wave of impulse is pure, and flows without taint of media that seem almost to know it not. The lady says:--

> We two will lie i' the shadow of
> That living mystic tree
> Within whose secret growth the Dove
> Is sometimes felt to be,
> While every leaf that His plumes touch
> Saith His Name audibly.

Here the love involved is so etherealised as scarcely to be called human, save only on the part of the mortal dreamer, in whose yearning ecstasy the ear thinks it recognises a more earthly note. The lover rejoins.--

> (Alas! We two, we two, thou say'st!
> Yea, one wast thou with me
> That once of old. But shall God lift
> To endless unity
> The soul whose likeness with thy soul
> Was but its love for thee?)

It is said of the few existent examples of the art of Giorgione that, around some central realisation of human passion gathers always a landscape which is not merely harmonised to it, but a part of it, sharing the joy or the anguish, lying silent to the breathless adoration, or echoing the rapturous voice of the full pleasure of those who are beyond all height and depth more than it. Something of this passive sympathy of environing objects comes out in the poem:

> Around her, lovers, newly met
> 'Mid deathless love's acclaims,
> Spoke evermore among themselves
> Their rapturous new names;
> And the souls mounting up to God
> Went by her like thin flames.

> And still she bowed herself and stooped
> Out of the circling charm;
> Until her bosom must have made
> The bar she leaned on warm,
> And the lilies lay as if asleep
> Along her bended arm.

The sense induced by such imagery is akin to that which comes of rapt contemplation of the deep em-blazonings of a fine stained window when the sun's warm gules glides off before the dim twilight. And this sense as of a thing existent, yet passing stealthily out of all sight away, the metre of the poem helps to foster. Other metres of Rossetti's have a strenuous reality, and rejoice in their self-assertiveness, and seem, almost, in their resonant strength, to tell themselves they are very good; but this may almost be said to be a disembodied voice, that lives only on the air, and, like the song of a bird, is gone before its accents have been caught. Of the four-and-twenty stanzas of the poem, none is more calmly musical than this:

> When round his head the aureole clings,
> And he is clothed in white,
> I 'll take his hand and go with him
> To the deep wells of light;
> We will step down as to a stream,
> And bathe there in God's sight.

Perhaps Rossetti never did anything more beautiful and spiritual than this little work of his twentieth year; and more than once in later life he painted the beautiful lady who is the subject of it, with the lilies lying along her arm.

A first draft of ***Jenny*** was struck off when the poet was scarcely more than a boy, and taken up again years afterwards, and almost entirely re-written--the only notable passage of the early poem that now remains being the passage on lust. It is best described in the simplest phrase, as a man's meditations on the life of a courtesan whom he has met at a dancing-garden and accompanied home. While he sits on a couch, she lies at his feet with her head on his knee and sleeps. When the morning dawns he rises, places cushions beneath her head, puts some gold among her hair, and leaves her. It is wisest to hazard at the outset all unfavourable comment by the frankest statement of the story of the poem. But the ***motif*** of it is a much higher thing. ***Jenny*** embodies an entirely distinct phase of feeling, yet the poet's root impulse is therein the same as in the case of ***The Blessed Damozel***. No two creations could stand more widely apart as to outward features than the dream of the sainted maiden and the reality of the frail and fallen girl; yet the primary prompting and the ultimate outcome are the same. The ardent longing after ideal purity in womanhood, which in the one gave birth to a conception whereof the very sorrow is but excess of joy found expression in the other through a vivid presentment of the nameless misery of unwomanly dishonour:--

> Behold the lilies of the field,
> They toil not neither do they spin;
> (So doth the ancient text begin,--
> Not of such rest as one of these Can share.)
> Another rest and ease
> Along each summer-sated path
> From its new lord the garden hath,
> Than that whose spring in blessings ran
> Which praised the bounteous husbandman,
> Ere yet, in days of hankering breath,
> The lilies sickened unto death.

It was indeed a daring thing the author proposed to himself to do, and assuredly no man could have essayed it who had not consciously united to an unfailing and unshrinking insight, a relativeness of mind such as right-hearted people might approve. To take a fallen woman, a cipher of man's sum of lust, befouled with the shameful knowledge of the streets, yet young, delicate, "apparelled beyond parallel," unblessed, with a beauty which, if copied by a Da Vinci's hand, might stand whole ages long "for preachings of what God can do," and then to endow such a one with the sensitiveness of a poet's own mind, make her read afresh as though by lightning, and in a dream, that story of the old pure days--

> Much older than any history
> That is written in any book,

and lastly, to gather about her an overwhelming sense of infinite solace for the wronged and lost, and of the retributive justice with which man's transgressions will be visited--this is, indeed, to hazard all things in the certainty of an upright purpose and true reward.

Shall no man hold his pride forewarn'd
Till in the end, the Day of Days,
At Judgment, one of his own race,
As frail and lost as you, shall rise,--
His daughter with his mother's eyes!

Yet Rossetti made no treaty with puritanism, and in this respect his *Jenny* has something in common with Hawthorne's *Scarlet Letter*--than which nothing, perhaps, that is so pure, without being puritanical, has reached us even from the land that gave *Evangeline* to the English tongue. The guilty love of Hester Prynne and Arthur Dimmesdale is never for an instant condoned, but, on the other hand, the rigorous severity of the old puritan community is not dwelt upon with favour. Relentless remorse must spend itself upon the man before the whole measure of his misery is full, and on the woman the brand of a public shame must be borne meekly to the end. But though no rancour is shown towards the austere and blind morality which puts to open discharge the guilty mother whilst unconsciously nourishing the yet more guilty father, we see the tenderness of a love that palliates the baseness of the amour, and the bitter depths of a penitence that cannot be complete until it can no longer be concealed. And so with Jenny. She may have transient flashes of remorseful consciousness, such as reveal to her the trackless leagues that separate what she was from what she is, but no effort is made to hide the plain truth that she is a courtesan, skilled only in the lures and artifices peculiar to her shameful function. No reformatory promptings fit her for a place at the footstool of the puritan. Nothing tells of winter yet; on the other hand, no virulent diatribes are cast forth against the society that shuts this woman out, as the puritan settlement turned its back on Hester Prynne. But we see her and know her for what she is, a woman like unto other women: desecrated but akin.

This dramatic quality of sitting half-passively above their creations and of leaving their ethics to find their own channels (once assured that their impulses are pure), the poet and the romancer possess in common. If there is a point of difference between their attitudes of mind, it is where Rossetti seems to reserve his whole personal feeling for the impeachment of lust;--

Like a toad within a stone
Seated while Time crumbles on;
Which sits there since the earth was cursed
For Man's transgression at the first;
Which, living through all centuries,
Not once has seen the sun arise;
Whose life, to its cold circle charmed,
The earth's whole summers have not warmed;
Which always--whitherso the stone
Be flung--sits there, deaf, blind, alone;--
Ay, and shall not be driven out
Till that which shuts him round about
Break at the very Master's stroke,
And the dust thereof vanish as smoke,
And the seed of Man vanish as dust:--
Even so within this world is Lust.

Sister Helen was written somewhat later than *The Blessed Damozel* and the first draft of *Jenny*, and probably belonged to the poet's twenty-fourth or twenty-fifth year. The ballad involves a story of witchcraft A girl has been first betrayed and then deserted by her lover; so, to revenge herself upon him and his newly-married bride, she burns his waxen image three days over a fire, and during that time he dies in torment In *Sister Helen* we touch the key-note of Rossetti's creative gift. Even the superstition which forms the basis of the ballad owes something of its individual character to the invention and poetic bias of the poet. The popular superstitions of the Middle Ages were usually of two kinds only. First, there were those that arose out of a jealous Catholicism, always glancing towards heresy; and next there were those that laid their account neither with orthodoxy nor unbelief, and were purely pagan. The former were the offspring of fanaticism; the latter of an appeal to appetite or passion, or fancy, or perhaps intuitive reason directed blindly or unconsciously towards natural phenomena. The superstition involved in *Sister Helen* partakes wholly of neither character, but partly of both, with an added element of demonology. The groundwork is essentially catholic, the burden of the ballad showing that the tragic event lies between Hell and Heaven:--

(O Mother, Mary Mother,
Three days to-day, between Hell and Heaven!)

But the superstructural overgrowth is totally undisturbed by any animosity against heresy, and is concerned only with a certain ultimate demoniacal justice visiting the wrongdoer. Thus far the elemental tissue of the superstition has something in common with that of the German secret tribunal of the steel and cord; with this difference, however, that whereas the latter punishes in secret, even *as the deity*, the former makes conscious compact with the powers of evil, that whatever justice shall be administered upon the wicked shall first be purchased by sacrifice of the good. Sister Helen may burn, alive, the body and soul of her betrayer, but the dying knell that tells of the false soul's untimely flight, tolls the loss of her own soul also:--

"Ah! what white thing at the door has cross'd,
Sister Helen?
Ah! what is this that sighs in the frost!"
"A soul that's lost as mine is lost,
Little brother!"
(O Mother, Mary Mother,
Lost, lost, all lost, between Hell and Heaven!)

Here lies the divergence between the lines of this and other compacts with evil powers; this is the point of Rossetti's departure from the scheme that forms the underplot of Goethe's *Faust*, and of Marlowe's *Faustus*, and was intended to constitute the plan of Coleridge's *Michael Scott*. It has been well said that the theme of the Faust is the consequence of a misology, or hatred of knowledge, resulting upon an original thirst for knowledge baffled. Faust never does from the beginning love knowledge for itself, but he loves it for the means it affords for the acquisition of power. This base purpose defeats itself; and when Faust finds that learning fails to yield him the domination he craves, he hates and contemns it. Away, henceforth, with all pretence to knowledge! Then follows the compact, the articles to which are absolute servility of the Devil on the one part, and complete possession of the soul of Faust on the other. Faust is little better than a wizard from the first, for if knowledge had given him what he: sought, he had never had recourse to witchcraft! Helen, however, partakes in some sort of the triumphant nobility of an avenging deity who has cozened hell itself, and not in vain. In the whole majesty of her great wrong, she loses the originally vulgar character of the witch. It is not as the consequence of a poison-speck in her own heart that she has recourse to sorcery. She does not love witchery for its own sake; she loves it only as the retributive channel for the requital of a terrible offence. It is throughout the last hour of her three-days' conflict, merely, that we see her, but we know her then not more for the revengeful woman she is than for the trustful maiden she has been. When she becomes conscious of the treason wrought against her, we feel that she suffers change. In the eyes of others we can see her, and in our vision of her she is beautiful; but hers is the beauty of fair cheeks, from which the canker frets the soft tenderness of colour, the loveliness of golden hair that has lost its radiance, the sweetness of eyes once dripping with the dews of the spirit, now pale, and cold, and lustreless. Very soon the wrongdoer shall reap the harvest of a twofold injury: this day another bride shall stand by his side. Is there, then, no way to wreak the just revenge of a broken heart? *That* suggests sorcery. Yes, the body and soul of the false lover may melt as before a flame; but the price of vengeance is horrible. Yet why? Has not love become devilish? Is not life a curse? Then wherefore shrink? The resolute wronged woman must go through with it. And when the last hour comes, nature itself is portentous of the virulent ill. In the wind's wake, the moon flies through a rack of night clouds. One after one the suppliants crave pardon for the distant dying lover, and last of these comes the three-days' bride.

In addition to the three great poems just traversed, Rossetti had written, before the completion of his twenty-sixth year, ***The Staff and Scrip, The Burden of Nineveh, Troy Town, Eden Bower*** and ***The Last Confession***, as well as a fragment of ***The Bride's Prelude***, to which it will be necessary to return. But, with a single exception, the poems just named may be said to exist beside the three that have been analysed, without being radically distinct from them, or touching higher or other levels, and hence it is not considered needful to dwell upon them at length. ***The***

Last Confession covers another range of feeling, it is true, whereof it may be said that the nobler part is akin to that which finds expression in the pure and shattered love of Othello; but it is a range of feeling less characteristical, perhaps less indigenous and appreciable.

In the years 1845-49 inclusive, Rossetti made the larger part of his translations (published in 1861) from the early Italian poets, and though he afterwards spoke of them as having been the work of the leisure moments of many years, of their subsequent revision alone, perhaps, could this be altogether true. The *Vita Nuova*, together with the many among Dante's *Lyrics* and those of his contemporaries which elucidate their personal intercourse; were translated, as well as a great body of the sonnets of poets later than Dante.[1] This early and indirect apprenticeship to the sonnet, as a form of composition, led to his becoming, in the end, perhaps the most perfect of English sonnet-writers. In youth, it was one of his pleasures to engage in exercises of sonnet-skill with his brother William and his sister Christina, and, even then, he attained to such proficiency, in the mere mechanism of sonnet structure, that he could sometimes dash off a sonnet in ten minutes--rivalling, in this particular, the impromptu productions of Hartley Coleridge. It is hardly necessary to say that the poems produced, under such conditions of time and other tests, were rarely, if ever, adjudged worthy of publication, by the side of work to which he gave adequate deliberation. But several of the sonnets on pictures--as, for example, the fine one on a Venetian pastoral by Giorgione--and the political sonnet, Miltonic in spirit, *On the Refusal of Aid between Nations*, were written contemporaneously with the experimental sonnets in question.

As *The House of Life* was composed in great part at the period with which we are now dealing (though published in the complete sequence nearly twenty-five years later), it may be best to traverse it at this stage. Though called a full series of sonnets, there is no intimation that it is not fragmentary as to design; the title is an astronomical, not an architectural figure. The work is at once Shakspearean and Dantesque. Whilst electively akin to the *Vita Nuova*, it is broader in range, the life

---

1   Rossetti often remarked that he had intended to translate
    the sonnets of Michael Angelo, until he saw Mr. Symonds's
    translation, when he was so much impressed by its excellence
    that he forthwith abandoned the purpose.

involved being life idealised in all phases. What Rossetti's idea was of the mission of the sonnet, as associated with life, and exhibiting a similitude of it, may best be learned from his prefatory sonnet:--

A Sonnet is a moment's monument,--
Memorial from the Soul's eternity
To one dead deathless hour. Look that it be,
Whether for lustral rite or dire portent,
Of its own arduous fulness reverent:
Carve it in ivory or in ebony,
As Day or Night may rule; and let Time see
Its flowering crest impearled and orient.
A Sonnet is a coin; its face reveals
The soul,--its converse, to what Power 'tis due:--
Whether for tribute to the august appeals
Of Life, or dower in Love's high retinue,
It serve; or 'mid the dark wharfs cavernous breath,
In Charon's palm it pay the toll to Death.

Rossetti's sonnets are of varied metrical structure; but their intellectual structure is uniform, comprising in each case a flow and ebb of thought within the limits of a single conception. In this latter respect they have a character almost peculiar to themselves among English sonnets. Rossetti was not the first English writer who deliberately separated octave and sestet, but he was the first who obeyed throughout a series of sonnets the canon of the contemporary structure requiring that a sonnet shall present the twofold facet of a single thought or emotion. This form of the sonnet Rossetti was at least the first among English writers entirely to achieve and perfectly to render. *The House of Life* does not contain a sonnet which is not to some degree informed by such an intellectual and musical wave; but the following is an example more than usually emphatic:

Even as a child, of sorrow that we give
dead, but little in his heart can find,

Since without need of thought to his clear mind
Their turn it is to die and his to live:--
Even so the winged New Love smiles to receive
Along his eddying plumes the auroral wind,
Nor, forward glorying, casts one look behind
Where night-rack shrouds the Old Love fugitive.

There is a change in every hour's recall,
And the last cowslip in the fields we see
On the same day with the first corn-poppy.
Alas for hourly change! Alas for all
The loves that from his hand proud youth lets fall,
Even as the beads of a told rosary!

The distinguishing excellence of craftsmanship in Rossetti's sonnets was early recognised; but the fertility of thought, and range of emotion compassed by this part of his work constitute an excellence far higher than any that belongs to perfection of form, rhythm, or metre. Mr. Palgrave has well said that a poet's story differs from a narrative in being in itself a creation; that it brings its own facts; that what we have to ask is not the true life of Laura, but how far Petrarch has truly drawn the life of love. So with Rossetti's sonnets. They may or may not be "occasional." Many readers who enter with sympathy into the series of feelings they present will doubtless insist upon regarding them as autobiographical. Others, who think they see the stamp of reality upon them, will perhaps accept them (as Hallam accepted the Sonnets of Shakspeare) as witnesses of excessive affection, redeemed sometimes by touches of nobler sentiments--if affection, however excessive, needs to be redeemed. Others again will receive them as artistic embodiments of ideal love upon which is placed the imprint of a passion as mythical as they believe to be attached to the autobiography of Dante's early days. But the genesis and history of these sonnets (whether the emotion with which they are pervaded be actual or imagined) must be looked for within. Do they realise vividly Life representative in its many phases of love, joy, sorrow, and death? It must be conceded that *he House of Life* touches many passions and depicts life in most of its changeful aspects. It would afford an adequate test of its comprehensiveness to note how rarely a mind in general sympathy with the author could come to its perusal without alighting upon something that would be in harmony with its mood. To traverse the work through its aspiration and foreboding, joy, grief, remorse, despair, and final resignation, would involve a task too long and difficult to be attempted here. Two sonnets only need be quoted as at once indicative of the range of thought and feeling covered, and of the sequent relation these poems bear each to each.

By thine own tears thy song must tears beget,
Singer! Magic mirror thou hast none
Except thy manifest heart; and save thine own
Anguish or ardour, else no amulet.

Cisterned in Pride, verse is the feathery jet
Of soulless air-flung fountains; nay, more dry
Than the Dead Sea for throats that thirst and sigh,
That song o'er which no singer's lids grew wet.

The Song-god--He the Sun-god--is no slave
Of thine: thy Hunter he, who for thy soul
Fledges his shaft: to the august control
Of thy skilled hand his quivered store he gave:
But if thy lips' loud cry leap to his smart,
The inspired record shall pierce thy brother's heart.

This is not meant to convey the same idea as Shelley's "learn in suffering," etc., but merely that a poem must move the writer in its composition if it is to move the reader.

With the following *The House of Life* is made to close:

When vain desire at last and vain regret
Go hand in hand to death, and all is vain,
What shall assuage the unforgotten pain

And teach the unforgetful to forget?

Shall Peace be still a sunk stream long unmet,--
Or may the soul at once in a green plain
Stoop through the spray of some sweet life-fountain,
And cull the dew-drenched flowering amulet?

Ah! when the wan soul in that golden air
Between the scriptured petals softly blown
Peers breathless for the gift of grace unknown,--
Ah! let none other alien spell soe'er
But only the one Hope's one name be there,--
Not less nor more, but even that word alone.

A writer must needs be loath to part from this section of Rossett's work without naming some few sonnets that seem to be in all respects on a level with those
to which attention has been drawn. Of such, perhaps, the most conspicuous are:--A
Day of Love; Mid-Rapture; Her Gifts; The Dark Glass; True Woman; Without Her;
Known in Vain; The Heart of the Night; The Landmark; Stillborn Love; Lost Days.
But it would be difficult to formulate a critical opinion in support of the superiority
of almost any of these' sonnets over the others,--so balanced is their merit, so equal
their appeal to the imagination and heart. Indeed, it were scarcely rash to say that
in the language (outside Shakspeare) there exists no single body of sonnets characterised by such sustained excellence of vision and presentment. It must have been
strange enough if the all but unexampled ardour and constancy with which Rossetti
pursued the art of the sonnet-writer had not resulted in absolute mastery.

In 1850 *The Germ* was started under the editorship of Mr. William Michael
Rossetti, and to the four issues, which were all that were published of this monthly
magazine (designed to advocate the views of the pre-Raphaelite brotherhood), Rossetti contributed certain of his early poems--The Blessed Damozel among the number. In 1856 he contributed many of the same poems, together with others, to *The
Oxford and Cambridge Magazine*, of which Canon Dixon has kindly undertaken
to tell the history. He says:

My knowledge of Dante Gabriel Rossetti was begun in connection with ***The Oxford and Cambridge Magazine***, a monthly periodical, which was started in January 1856, and lasted a year. The projectors of this periodical were Mr. William Morris, Mr. Ed. Burne Jones, and myself. The editor was Mr. (now the Rev.) William Fulford. Among the original contributors were the late Mr. Wilfred Heeley of Cambridge, Mr. Faulkner, now Fellow of University College, Oxford, and Mr. Cormel Price. We were all undergraduates. The publishers of the magazine were the late firm of Bell and Daldy. We gradually associated with ourselves several other contributors: above all, D. G. Rossetti.

Of this undertaking the central notion was, I think, to advocate moral earnestness and purpose in literature, art, and society. It was founded much on Mr. Ruskin's teaching: it sprang out of youthful impatience, and exhibited many signs of immaturity and ignorance: but perhaps it was not without value as a protest against some things. The pre-Raphaelite movement was then in vigour: and this Magazine came to be considered as the organ of those who accepted the ideas which were brought into art at that time; and, as in a manner, the successor of ***The Germ***, a small periodical which had been published previously by the first beginners of the movement. Rossetti, in many respects the most memorable of the pre-Raphaelites, became connected with our Magazine when it had been in existence about six months: and he contributed to it several of the finest of the poems that were afterwards collected in the former of his two volumes of poems: namely, ***The Burden of Nineveh, The Blessed Damozel, and The Staff and Scrip***. I think that one of them, ***The Blessed Damozel***, had appeared previously in ***The Germ***. All these poems, as they now stand in the author's volume, have been greatly altered from what they were in the Magazine: and, in being altered, not always improved, at least in the verbal changes. The first of them, a sublime meditation of peculiar metrical power, has been much altered, and in general happily, as to the arrangement of stanzas: but not always so happily as to the words. It is, however, pleasing to notice that in the alterations some touches of bitterness have been effaced. The second of these pieces has been brought with great skill into regular form by transposition: but again one repines to find several touches gone that once were there. The last of them, ***The Staff and Scrip***, is, in my judgment, the finest of all Rossetti's poems, and one of the most glorious writings in the language. It exhibits in flawless perfection the gift that he had above all other writers, absolute beauty and pure action. Here again it is not possible to see without regret some of the verbal alterations that have been made in the poem as it now stands, although the chief emendation, the omission of one stanza and the insertion of another, adds clearness, and was all that was wanted to make the poem perfect in structure.

I saw Rossetti for the first time in his lodgings over Blackfriars Bridge. It was impossible not to be impressed with the freedom and kindness of his manner, not less than by his personal appearance. His frank greeting, bold, but gentle glance, his whole presence, produced a feeling of confidence and pleasure. His voice had a great charm, both in tone, and from the peculiar cadences that belonged to it I think that the leading features of his character struck me more at first than the characteristics of his genius; or rather, that my notion of the character of the man was formed first, and was then applied to his works, and identified with them. The main features of his character were, in my apprehension, fearlessness, kindliness, a decision that sometimes made him seem somewhat arbitrary, and condensation or concentration. He was wonderfully self-reliant. These moral qualities, guiding an artistic temperament as exquisite as was ever bestowed on man, made him what he was, the greatest inventor of abstract beauty, both in form and colour, that this age, perhaps that the world, has seen. They would also account for some peculiarities that must be admitted in some of his works, want of nature, for instance. I heard him once remark that it was "astonishing how much the least bit of nature helped if one put it in;" which seemed like an acknowledgment that he might have gone more to nature. Hence, however, his works always seem abstract, always seem to embody some kind of typical aim, and acquire a sort of sacred character.

I saw a good deal of Rossetti in London, and afterwards in Oxford, during the painting of the Union debating-room. In later years our personal intercourse was broken off through distance; though I saw him occasionally almost to the time of his lamented death, and we had some correspondence. My recollection of him is that of greatness, as might be expected of one of the few who have been "illustrious in two arts," and who stands by himself and has earned an independent name in both. His work was great: the man was greater. His conversation had a wonderful ease, precision, and felicity of expression. He produced thoughts perfectly enunciated with a deliberate happiness that was indescribable, though it was always simple conversation, never haranguing or declamation. He was a natural leader because he was a natural teacher. When he chose to be interested in anything that was brought before him, no pains were too great for him to take. His advice was always given warmly and freely, and when he spoke of the works of others it was always in the most generous spirit of praise. It was in fact impossible to have been more free from captiousness, jealousy, envy, or any other form of pettiness than this truly noble man. The great painter who first took me to him said, "We shall see the greatest man in Europe." I have it on the same authority that Rossetti's aptitude for art was considered amongst painters to be no less extraordinary than his imagination. For example, that he could take hold of the extremity of the brush, and be as certain of his touch as if it had been held in the usual way; that he never painted a picture without doing something in colour that had never been done before; and, in particular, that he had a command of the features of the human face such as no other painter ever possessed. I also remember some observations by the same assuredly competent judge, to the effect that Rossetti might be set against the great painters of the fifteenth century, as equal to them, though unlike them: the difference being that while they represented the characters, whom they painted, in their ordinary and unmoved mood, he represented his characters under emotion, and yet gave them wholly. It may be added, perhaps, that he had a lofty standard of beauty of his own invention, and that he both elevated and subjected all to beauty. Such a man was not likely to be ignorant of the great root of power in art, and I once saw him very indignant on hearing that he had been accused of irreligion, or rather of not being a Christian. He asked with great earnestness, "Do not my works testify to my Christianity?" I wish that these imperfect recollections may be of any avail to those who cherish the memory of an extraordinary genius.

Besides his contributions to **The Germ**, and to **The Oxford and Cambridge Magazine**, Rossetti contributed **Sister Helen**, in 1853, to a German Annual. Beyond this he made little attempt to publish his poetry. He had written it for the love of writing, or in obedience to the inherent impulse compelling him to do so, but of actual hope of achieving by virtue of it a place among English poets he seems to have had none, or next to none. In later life he used to say that Mr. Browning's greatness and the splendour of Mr. Tennyson's merited renown seemed to him in those early years to render all attempt on his part to secure rank by their side as hopeless as presumptuous. This, he asserted, was the cause that operated to restrain him from publication between 1853 and 1862, and after that (as will presently be seen), another and more serious obstacle than self-depreciation intervened. But in putting aside all hope of the reward of poetic achievement, he did not wholly banish the memory of the work he had done. He made two or more copies of the most noticeable of the poems he had written, and sent them to friends eminent in letters. To Leigh Hunt he sent **The Blessed Damozel**, and received in acknowledgment a letter full of appreciative comment, and foretelling a brilliant future. His literary friends at this time were Mr. Ruskin, Mr. and Mrs. Browning; he used to see Mr. Tennyson and Carlyle at intervals, and was in constant intercourse with the younger writers, Mr. Swinburne and Mr. Morris, whose reputations had then to be made; Mr. Arnold, Sir Henry Taylor, Mr. Aubrey de Vere, Mr. E. Brough, Mr. J. Hannay, and Mr. Monckton Milnes (Lord Houghton), he met occasionally; Dobell he knew only by correspondence. Though unpublished, his poems were not unknown, for besides the semi-publicity they obtained by circulation "among his private friends," he was nothing loath to read or recite them at request, and by such means a few of them secured a celebrity akin in kind and almost equal in extent to that enjoyed by Coleridge's **Christabel** during the many years preceding 1816 in which it lay in manuscript. Like Coleridge's poem in another important particular, certain of Rossetti's ballads, whilst still unknown to the public, so far influenced contemporary poetry that when they did at length appear they had all the appearance to the uninitiated of work imitated from contemporary models, instead of being, as in fact they were, the primary source of inspiration for writers whose names were earlier established.

Towards the beginning of his artistic career Rossetti occupied a studio, with residential chambers, at Black-friars Bridge. The rooms overlooked the river, and the tide rose almost to the walls of the house, which, with nearly all its old surroundings, has long disappeared.

A story is told of Rossetti amidst these environments which aptly illustrates almost every trait of his character: his impetuosity, and superstition especially. It was his daily habit to ransack old book-stalls, and carry off to his studio whatever treasures he unearthed, but when, upon further investigation, he found he had been deceived as to the value of a book that at first looked promising, he usually revenged himself by throwing the volume through a window into the river running below--a habit which he discovered (to his amusement, and occasionally to his distress), that his friends, Mr. Swinburne especially, imitated from him and practised at his rooms on his behalf. On one occasion he discovered in some odd nook a volume long sought for, and having inscribed it with his name and address, he bore it off joyfully to his chambers; but finding a few days later that in some respects it disappointed his expectations, he flung it through the window, and banished all further thought of it. The tide had been at the flood when the book disappeared, and when it ebbed, the offending volume was found by a little mud-lark imbedded in the refuse of the river. The boy washed it and took it back to the address it contained, expecting to find it eagerly reclaimed; but, impatient and angry at sight of what he thought he had destroyed, Rossetti snatched the book out of the muddy hand that proffered it and flung it again into the Thames, with rather less than the courtesy which might have been looked for as the reward of an act that was meant so well. But the haunting volume was not even yet done with. Next morning, an old man of the riverside labourer class knocked at the door, bearing in his hands a small parcel rudely made up in a piece of newspaper that was greasy enough to have previously contained his morning's breakfast. He had come from where he was working below London Bridge: he had found something that might have been lost by Mr. Rossetti. It was the tormenting volume: the indestructible, unrelenting phantom that would not be laid! Rossetti now perceived that higher agencies were at work: it was ***not meant*** that he should get rid of the book: why should he contend against the inevitable? Reverently and with both hands he took the besoiled parcel from the brown palm of the labourer, placed half-a-crown there instead, and restored the fearful book to its place on his shelf.

And now we come to incidents in Rossetti's career of which it is necessary to treat as briefly as tenderly. Among the models who sat to him was Miss Elizabeth Eleanor Siddal, a young lady of great personal beauty, in whom he discovered a natural genius for painting and a noticeable love of the higher poetic literature. He felt impelled to give her lessons, and she became as much his pupil as model. Her water-colour drawings done under his tuition gave proof of a wonderful eye for colour, and displayed a marked tendency to style. The subjects, too, were admirably composed and often exhibited unusual poetic feeling. It was very natural that such a connection between persons of kindred aspirations should lead to friendship and finally to love.

Rossetti and Miss Siddal were married in 1860. They visited France and Belgium; and this journey, together with a similar one undertaken in the company of Mr. Holman Hunt in 1849, and again another in 1863, when his brother was his companion, and a short residence on the Continent when a boy, may be said to constitute almost the whole sum of Rossetti's travelling. Very soon the lady's health began to fail, and she became the victim of neuralgia. To meet this dread enemy she resorted to laudanum, taking it at first in small quantities, but eventually in excess. Her spirits drooped, her art was laid aside, and much of the cheerfulness of home was lost to her. There was a child, but it was stillborn, and not long after this disaster, it was found that Mrs. Rossetti had taken an overdose of her accustomed sleeping potion and was lying dead in her bed. This was in 1862, and after two years only of married life. The blow was a terrible one to Rossetti, who was the first to discover what fate had reserved for him. It was some days before he seemed fully to realise the loss that had befallen him, and then his grief knew no bounds. The poems he had written, so far as they were poems of love, were chiefly inspired by and addressed to her. At her request he had copied them into a little book presented to him for the purpose, and on the day of the funeral he walked into the room where the body lay, and, unmindful of the presence of friends, he spoke to his dead wife as though she heard, saying, as he held the book, that the words it contained were written to her and for her, and she must take them with her for they could not remain when she had gone. Then he put the volume into the coffin between her cheek and beautiful hair, and it was that day buried with her in Highgate Cemetery.

CHAPTER II.

It was long before Rossetti recovered from the shock of his wife's sudden death. The loss sustained appeared to change the whole course of his life. Previously he had been of a cheerful temperament, and accustomed to go abroad at frequent intervals to visit friends; but after this event he seemed to become for a time morose, and by nature reclusive. Not a great while afterwards he removed from Blackfriars Bridge, and after a temporary residence in Lincoln's Inn Fields, he took up his abode in the house he occupied during the twenty remaining years of his life, at 16 Cheyne Walk, Chelsea. This home of Rossetti's shall be fully described in subsequent personal recollections. It was called Tudor House when he became its tenant, from the tradition that Elizabeth Tudor had lived in it, and it is understood to be the same that Thackeray describes in **Esmond** as the home of the old Countess of Chelsey. A large garden, which recently has been cut off for building purposes, lay at the back, and, doubtless, it was as much due to the attractions of this piece of pleasant ground, dotted over with lime-trees, and enclosed by a high wall, that Rossetti went so far afield, for at that period Chelsea was not the rallying ground of artists and men of letters. He wished to live a life of retirement, and thought the possession of a garden in which he could take sufficient daily exercise would enable him to do so. In leaving Blackfriars he destroyed many things associated with his residence there, and calculated to remind him of his life's great loss. He burnt a great body of letters, and among them were many valuable ones from almost all the men and women then eminent in literature and art. His great grief notwithstanding, upon settling at Chelsea he began almost insensibly to interest himself in furnishing the house in a beautiful and novel style. Old oak then became for a time his passion, and in hunting it up he rummaged the brokers' shops round London for miles, buying for trifles what would eventually (when the fashion he started grew to be general) have fetched large sums. Cabinets of all conceivable superannuated designs--so old in material or pattern that no one else would look at them--were unearthed in obscure corners, bolstered up by a joiner, and consigned to their places in the new residence. Following old oak, Japanese furniture became Rossetti's quest, and following this came blue china ware (of which he had perhaps the first fine collection made), and then ecclesiastical and other brasses, incense-burners, sacramental cups, crucifixes, Indian spice boxes, mediaeval lamps, antique bronzes, and the like. In a few years he had filled his house with so much curious and beautiful furniture that there grew up a widespread desire to imitate his methods; and very soon artists, authors, and men of fortune having no other occupation, were found rummaging, as he had rummaged, for the neglected articles of the centuries gone by. What he did was done, as he used to say, less from love of the things hunted for, than from love of the pursuit, which, from its difficulty, gave rise to a pleasurable excitement. Thus did he grieve down his loss, and little did they think who afterwards followed the fashion he set them, and carried his passion for antique furniture to an excess at which he must have laughed, that his' primary impulse was so far from a desire to "live up to his blue ware," that it was more like an effort to live down to it.

It was during the earlier years of his residence at Chelsea that Rossetti formed a habit of life which clung to him almost to the last, and did more than aught else to blight his happiness. What his intimate friend has lately characterised in **The Daily News** as that great curse of the literary and artistic temperament, insomnia, had been hanging about him since the death of his wife, and was becoming each year more and more alarming. He had tried opiates, but in sparing quantities, for had he not the most serious cause to eschew them? Towards 1868 he heard of the then newly found drug chloral, which was accredited with all the virtues and none of the vices of other known narcotics. Here then was the thing he wanted; this was the blessed discovery that was to save him from days of weariness and nights of misery and tears. Eagerly he procured it, took it nightly in single small doses of ten grains each, and from it he received pleasant and refreshing sleep. He made no concealment of his habit; like Coleridge under similar conditions, he preferred to talk of it. Not yet had he learned the sad truth, too soon to force itself upon him, that the fumes of this dreadful drug would one day wither up his hopes and joys in life: deluding him with a short-lived surcease of pain only to impose a terrible legacy of suffering from which there was to be no respite. Had Rossetti been master of the drug and not mastered by it, perhaps he might have turned it to account at a critical juncture, and laid it aside when the necessity to employ it had gradually been removed. But, alas! he gave way little by little to the encroachments of an evil power with which, when once it had gained the ascendant, he fought down to his dying day a single-handed and losing fight.

It was not, however, for some years after he began the use of it that chloral produced any sensible effects of an injurious kind, and meantime he pursued as usual his avocation as a painter. Mention has been made of the fact that Rossetti abandoned at an early age subject designs for three-quarter-length figures. Of the latter, in the period of which we are now treating, he painted great numbers: among them, produced at this time and later, were ***Sibylla Palmifera and The Beloved*** (the property of Mr. George Rae), ***La Pia and The Salutation of Beatrice*** (Mr. F. E. Leyland), ***The Dying Beatrice*** (Lord Mount Temple), ***Venus Astarte*** (Mr. Fry), ***Fiammetta*** (Mr. Turner), ***Proserpina*** (Mr. Graham). Of these works, solidity may be said to be the prominent characteristic. The drapery of Rossetti's pictures is wonderfully powerful and solid; his colour may be said to be at times almost matchable with that of certain of the Venetian painters, though different in kind. He hated beyond most things the "varnishy" look of some modern work; and his own oil pictures had so much of the manner of frescoes in their lustreless depth, that they were sometimes mistaken for water-colours, while, on the other hand, his water-colours had often so much depth and brilliancy as sometimes to be mistaken for oil. It is alleged in certain quarters that Rossetti was deficient in some qualities of drawing, and this is no doubt a just allegation; but it is beyond question that no English painter has ever been a greater master of the human face, which in his works (especially those painted in later years) acquires a splendid solemnity and spiritual beauty and significance all but peculiar to himself. It seems proper to say in such a connexion, that his success in this direction was always attributed by him to the fact that the most memorable of his faces were painted from a well-known friend.

Only one of his early designs, the ***Dante's Dream***, was ever painted by Rossetti on a scale commensurate with its importance, and the solemnity and massive grandeur of that work leave only a feeling of regret that, whether from personal indisposition on the part of the painter or lack of adequate recognition on that of the public, the three or four other finest designs made in youth were never carried out. As the picture in question stands alone among Rossetti's pictorial works as a completed conception, it may be well to devote a few pages to a description of it.

It is essential to an appreciation of **Dante's Dream**, that we should not only fully understand the nature of the particular incident depicted in the picture, but also possess a general knowledge of the lives and relations of the two principal personages concerned in it. What we know, to most purpose, of the early life and love of Dante, we learn from the autobiography which he entitled **La Vita Nuova**. Boccaccio, however, writing fifty years after the death of the great Florentine, affords a more detailed statement than is furnished by Dante himself of the circumstances of the poets first meeting with the lady he called Beatrice. He says that it was the custom of citizens in Florence, when the time of spring came round, to form social gatherings in their own quarters for purposes of merry-making; that in this way Folco Portinari, a citizen of mark, had collected his neighbours at his house upon the first of May, 1274, for pastime and rejoicing: that amongst those who came to him was Alighiero Alighieri, father of Dante Alighieri, who lived within fifty yards; that it was common for children to accompany their parents at such merrymakings, and that Dante, then scarce nine years old, was in the house on the day in question engaged in sports, appropriate to his years, with other children, amongst whom was a little daughter of Folco Portinari, eight years old. The child is described as being, even at this period, in aspect extremely beautiful, and winning and graceful in her ways. Not to dwell upon these passages of childhood, it may be sufficient to say that the boy, young as he was, is said to have then conceived so deep a passion for the child that maturer attachments proved powerless to efface it. Such was the origin of a love that grew from childlike tenderness to manly ardour, and, surviving all the buffetings of an untoward fate, is known to us now and for all time in a record of so much reality and purity, as seems to every right-hearted nature to be equally the story of his personal attachment as the history of a passion that in Florence, six centuries ago, for its mortal put on immortality.

The Portinari and Alighieri were immediate neighbours, yet it does not appear that the young Dante encountered the lady in any marked way until nine years later, and then, in the first bloom of a gracious womanhood, she is described as affording him in the street a salutation of such unspeakable courtesy that he left the place where for the instant he had stood sorely abashed, as one intoxicated with a love that now at first knew itself for what it was. The incidents of the attachment are few in facts; numerous only in emotions, and therein too uncertain and liable to change to be counted. In order not to disclose a passion, which other reasons than those given by the poet may have tempted him to conceal, Dante affects an attachment to another lady of the city, and the rumour of this brings about an estrangement with the real object of his desires, which reduces the poet to such an abject condition of mind, as finally results in his laying aside all counterfeiting. Portinari, the father, now dies, and witnessing the tenderness with which the beautiful Beatrice mourns him, Dante becomes affected with a painful infirmity, wherein his mind broods over his enfeebled body, and, perceiving how frail a thing life is, even though health keep with it, his brain begins to travail in many imaginings, and he says within himself, "Certainly it must some time come to pass that the very gentle Beatrice will die." Feeling bewildered, he closes his eyes, and, in a trance, he conceives that a friend comes to him, and says, "Hast thou not heard? She that was thine excellent lady has been taken out of life." Then as he looks towards Heaven in imagination, he beholds a multitude of angels who are returning upwards, having before them an exceedingly white cloud; and these angels are singing, and the words of their song are, "Osanna in excelsis." So strong is his imagining, that it seems to him that he goes to look upon the body where it has its abiding-place.

> The sun ceased, and the stars began to gather,
> And each wept at the other;
> And birds dropp'd at midflight out of the sky;
> And earth shook suddenly;
> And I was 'ware of one, hoarse and tired out,
> Who ask'd of me: 'Hast thou not heard it said--
> Thy lady, she that was so fair, is dead?
>
> Then lifting up mine eyes, as the tears came,
> I saw the angels, like a rain of manna
> In a long flight flying back Heavenward,
> Having a little cloud in front of them,

After the which they went, and said 'Hosanna;'
And if they had said more, you should have heard.

Then Love said, 'Now shall all things be made clear:
Come, and behold our lady where she lies
These 'wildering phantasies
Then carried me to see my lady dead.
Even as I there was led,
Her ladies with a veil were covering her;
And with her was such very humbleness
That she appeared to say, 'I am at peace.'
(Dante and his Circle.)

The trance proves to be a premonition of the event, for, shortly after writing the poem in which his imaginings find record, Dante says, "The Lord God of Justice called my most gracious lady unto Himself."

It is with the incidents of the dream that Rossetti has dealt. The principal personage in the picture is, of course, Dante himself. Of the poet's face, two old and accredited witnesses remain to us--the portrait of Giotto and the mask supposed to be copied from a similar one taken after death. Giotto's portrait represents Dante at the age of twenty-seven. The face has a feminine delicacy of outline, yet is full of manly beauty; strength and tenderness are seen blended in its lineaments. It might be that of a poet, a scholar, a courtier, or yet a soldier; and in Dante it is all combined.

Such, as seen in Giotto, was the great Florentine when Beatrice beheld him. The familiar mask represents that youthful beauty as somewhat saddened by years of exile, by the accidents of an unequal fortune, and by the long brooding memory of his life's one, deep, irreparable loss. We see in it the warrior who served in the great battle of Campaldino: the mourner who sought refuge from grief in the action and danger of the war waged by Florence upon Pisa: the magistrate whose justice proved his ruin: the exile who ate bitter bread when Florence banished the greatest of her sons. The mask is as full as the portrait of intellect and feeling, of strength and character, but it lacks something of the early sweetness and sensibility. Rossetti's portraiture retains the salient qualities of both portrait and mask. It represents Dante in his twenty-seventh year; the face gives hint of both poet and soldier, for behind clear-cut features capable of strengthening into resolve and rigour lie whole depths of tenderest sympathy. The abstracted air, the self-centred look, the eyes that seem to see only what the mind conceives and casts forward from itself; the slow, uncertain, half-reluctant gait,--these are profoundly true to the man and the dream.

Of Beatrice, no such description is given either in the **Vita Nuova** or the **Commedia** as could afford an artist a definite suggestion. Dante's love was an idealised passion; it concerned itself with spiritual beauty, whereof the emotions excited absorbed every merely physical consideration. The beauty of Beatrice in the **Vita Nuova** is like a ray of sunshine flooding a landscape--we see it only in the effect it produces. All we know with certainty is that her hair was light, that her face was pale, and that her smile was one of thoughtful sweetness. These hints of a beautiful person Rossetti has wrought into a creation of such purity that, lovely as she is in death, as in life, we think less of her loveliness than of her loveableness.

The personage of Love, who plays throughout the **Vita Nuova** a mystical part is not the Pagan Love, but a youth and Christian Master, as Dante terms him, sometimes of severe and terrible aspect. He is represented in the picture as clad in a flame-coloured garment (for it is in a mist of the colour of fire that he appears to the lover), and he wears the pilgrim's scallop-shell on his shoulder as emblem of that pilgrimage on earth which Love is.

The chamber wherein the body of Beatrice has its abiding-place is, to Dante's imaginings, a chamber of dreams. Visionary as the mind of the dreamer, it discloses at once all that goes forward within its own narrow compass, together with the desolate streets of the city of Florence, which, to his fancy, sits silent for his loss, and the long flight of angels above that bear away the little cloud, to which is given a vague semblance of the beatified Beatrice. As if just fallen back in sleep, the beautiful lady lies in death, her hands folded across her breast, and a glory of golden hair flowing over her shoulders. With measured tread Dante approaches the couch led by the winged and scarlet Love, but, as though fearful of so near and unaccustomed an approach, draws slowly backward on his half-raised foot, while the mystical emblem of his earthly passion stands droopingly between him the living, and his lady the dead, and takes the kiss that he himself might never have. In life they must needs be apart, but thus in death they are united, for the hand of the pilgrim, who is the embodiment of his love, holds his hand even as the master's lips touch her lips. Two ladies of the chamber are covering her with a pall, and on the dreamer they fix sympathetic eyes. The floor is strewn with poppies--emblems equally of the sleep in which the lover walks, and of the sleep that is the sleep of death. The may-bloom in the pall, the apple-blossom in the hand of Love, the violets and roses in the frieze of the alcove, symbolise purity and virginity, the life that is cut off in its spring, the love that is consummated in death before the coming of fruit. Suspended from the roof is a scroll, bearing the first words of the wail from the Lamentations of Jeremiah, quoted by Dante himself:--"How doth the city sit solitary, that was full of people! How is she become as a widow, she that was great among the nations!" In the ascending and descending staircase on either iand fly doves of the same glowing colour as Love, and these are emblems of his presence in the house. Over all flickers the last beam of a lamp which has burnt through the long night, and which the dawn of a new day sees die away--fit symbol of the life that has now taken flight with the heavenly host, leaving behind it only the burnt-out socket where the live flame lived.

Full of symbol as this picture is, it is furthermore permeated by a significance that is not occult. It bears witness to the possible strength of a passion that is so spiritual as to be without taint of sense; and to a confident belief in an immortality wherein the utmost limits of a blessedness not of this world may be compassed. Such are in this picture the simpler, yet deeper, symbols, that all who look may read. Sir Noel Paton has written of this work:

I was so dumbfounded by the beauty of that great picture of Rosetti's, called ***Dante's Dream***, that I was usable to give any expression to the emotions it excited--emotions such as I do not think any other picture, except the ***Madonna di San Sisto*** at Dresden, ever stirred within me. The memory of such a picture is like the memory of sublime and perfect music; it makes any one who ***fully*** feels it--silent. Fifty years hence it will be named among the half-dozen supreme pictures of the world.

Rossetti had buried the only complete copy of his poems with his wife at High-gate, and for a time he had been able to put by the thought of them; but as one by one his friends, Mr. Morris, Mr. Swinburne, and others, attained to distinction as

poets, he began to hanker after poetic reputation, and to reflect with pain and regret upon the hidden fruits of his best effort. Rossetti--in all love of his memory be
it spoken--was after all a frail mortal; of unstable character: of variable purpose: a
creature of impulse and whim, and with a plentiful lack of the backbone of volition. With less affection he would not have buried his book; with more strength of
will he had not done so; or, having done so, he had never wished to undo what he
had done; or having undone it, he would never have tormented himself with the
memory of it as of a deed of sacrilege. But Rossetti had both affection enough to do
it and weakness enough to have it undone. After an infinity of self-communions
he determined to have the grave opened, and the book extracted. Endless were the
preparations necessary before such a work could be begun. Mr. Home Secretary
Bruce had to be consulted. At length preliminaries were complete, and one night,
seven and a half years after the burial, a fire was built by the side of the grave, and
then the coffin was raised and opened. The body is described as perfect upon coming to light.

Whilst this painful work was being done the unhappy author of it was sitting
alone and anxious, and full of self-reproaches at the house of the friend who had
charge of it. He was relieved and thankful when told that all was over. The volume
was not much the worse for the years it had lain in the grave. Deficiencies were
filled in from memory, the manuscript was put in the press, and in 1870 the reclaimed work was issued under the simple title of ***Poems***.

The success of the book was almost without precedent; seven editions were
called for in rapid succession. It was reviewed with enthusiasm in many quarters.
Yet that was a period in which fresh poetry and new poets arose, even as they now
arise, with all the abundance and timeliness of poppies in autumn. It is probable
enough that of the circumstances attending the unexampled early success of this
first volume only the remarkable fact is still remembered that, from a bookseller's
standpoint, it ran a neck-and-neck race with Disraeli's ***Lothair*** at a time when political romance was found universally appetising, and poetry, as of old, a drug. But
it will not be forgotten that certain subsidiary circumstances were thought to have
contributed to the former success. Of these the most material was the reputation
Rossetti had already achieved as a painter by methods which awakened curiosity as
much as they aroused enthusiasm. The public mind became sensibly affected by the

idea that the poems of the new poet were not to be regarded as the emanations of a single individual, but as the result of a movement in which Rossetti had played one of the most prominent parts. Mr. F. Hueffer, in prefacing the Tauchnitz edition of the poems with a pleasant memoir, has comprehensively denominated that movement the ***renaissance of mediaeval feeling***, but at the outset it acquired popularly, for good or ill, the more rememberable name of pre-Raphaelitism. What the shibboleth was of the originators of the school that grew out of it concerned men but little to ascertain; and this was a condition of indifference as to the logic of the movement which was occasioned partly by the known fact that the most popular of its leaders, Mr. Millais, had long been shifting ground. It was enough that the new sect had comprised dissenters from the creed once established, that the catholic spirit of art which lived with the lives of Elmore, Goodall, and Stone was long dead, and that none of the coteries for love of which the old faith, exemplified in the works of men such as these, had been put aside, possessed such an appeal for the imagination as this, now that twenty years of fairly consistent endeavour had cleared away the cloud of obloquy that gathered about it when it began. And so it came to be thought that the poems of Rossetti were to exhibit a new phase of this movement, involving kindred issues, and opening up afresh in the poetic domain the controversies which had been waged and won in the pictorial. Much to this purpose was said at the time to account for the success of a book whose popular qualities were I manifestly inconsiderable; and much to similar purpose will doubtless long be said by those who affect to believe that a concatenation of circumstances did for Rossetti's earlier work a service which could not attend his subsequent one. But the explanation was inadequate, and had for its immediate outcome a charge of narrowed range of poetic sympathy with which Rossetti's admirers had not laid their account.

A renaissance of mediaeval feeling the movement in art assuredly involved, but the essential part of it was another thing, of which mediaevalism was palpably independent. How it came to be considered the fundamental element is not difficult to show. In an eminent degree the originators of the new school in painting were colourists, having, perhaps, in their effects, a certain affinity to the early Florentine masters, and this accident of native gift had probably more to do in determining the precise direction of the ***intellectual*** sympathy than any external agency. The art feeling which formed the foundation of the movement existed apart from it, or bore no closer relation to it than kinship of powers induced. When Rossetti's poetry came it was seen to be animated by a choice of subject-matter akin to that which gave individual character to his painting, but this was because coeval efforts in two totally distinct arts must needs bear the family resemblance, each to each, which belong to all the offspring of a thoroughly harmonised mind. The poems and the pictures, however, had not more in common than can be found in the early poems and early dramas of Shakspeare. Nay, not so much; for whereas in his poems Shakspeare was constantly evolving certain shades of feeling and begetting certain movements of thought which were soon to find concrete and final collocation in the dramatic creations, in his pictures Rossetti was first of all a dissenter from all prescribed canons of taste, whilst in his poems he was in harmony with the catholic spirit which was as old as Shakspeare himself, and found revival, after temporary eclipse, in Coleridge, Shelley, Keats, and Tennyson. Choice of mediaeval theme would not in itself have been enough to secure a reversal of popular feeling against work that contained no germs of the sensational; and hence we must conclude that Mr. Swinburne accounted more satisfactorily for the instant popularity of Rossetti's poetry when he claimed for it those innate utmost qualities of beauty and strength which are always the first and last constituents of poetry that abides. Indeed those qualities and none other, wholly independent of auxiliary aids, must now as then go farthest to determine Rossetti's final place among poets.

Such as is here described was the first reception given to Rossetti's volume of poetry; but at the close of 1871, there arose out of it a long and acrimonious controversy. It seems necessary to allude to this painful matter, because it involved serious issues; but an effort alike after brevity and impartiality of comment shall be observed in what is said of it. In October of the year mentioned, an article entitled *The Fleshly School of Poetry*, and signed "Thomas Maitland," appeared in *The Contemporary Review*.[2] It consisted in the main of an impeachment of Rossetti's poetry on the ground of sensuality, though it embraced a broad denunciation of the sensual tendencies of the age in art, music, poetry, the drama, and social life generally. Sensuality was regarded as the phenomenon of the age. "It lies," said the writer, "on the drawing-room table, shamelessly naked and dangerously fair. It is part of the

2 In this summary, the pamphlet reprint has been followed in preference to the original article as it appeared in the Review.

pretty poem which the belle of the season reads, and it breathes away the pureness of her soul like the poisoned breath of the girl in Hawthorne's tale. It covers the shelves of the great Oxford-Street librarian, lurking in the covers of three-volume novels. It is on the French booksellers' counters, authenticated by the signature of the author of the ***Visite de Noces***. It is here, there, and everywhere, in art, literature, life, just as surely as it is in the ***Fleurs de Mal***, the Marquis de Sade's ***Justine***, or the ***Monk*** of Lewis. It appeals to all tastes, to all dispositions, to all ages. If the querulous man of letters has his Baudelaire, the pimpled clerk has his ***Day's Doings***, and the dissipated artisan his ***Day and Night.***" When the writer set himself to inquire into the source of this social cancer, he refused to believe that English society was honeycombed and rotten. He accounted for the portentous symptoms that appalled him by attributing the evil to a fringe of real English society, chiefly, if not altogether, resident in London: "a sort of demi-monde, not composed, like that other in France, of simple courtesans, but of men and women of indolent habits and aesthetic tastes, artists, literary persons, novel writers, actors, men of genius and men of talent, butterflies and gadflies of the human kind, leading a lazy existence from hand to mouth." It was to this Bohemian fringe of society that the writer attributed the "gross and vulgar conceptions of life which are formulated into certain products of art, literature, and criticism." Dealing with only one form of the social phenomenon, with sensualism so far as it appeared to affect contemporary poetry, the writer proceeded with a literary retrospect intended to show that the fair dawn of our English poetry in Chaucer and the Elizabethan dramatists had been over-clouded by a portentous darkness, a darkness "vaporous," "miasmic," coming from a "fever-cloud generated first in Italy and then blown westward," sucking up on its way "all that was most unwholesome from the soil of France."

Just previously to and contemporaneously with the rise of Dante, there had flourished a legion of poets of greater or less ability, but all more or less characterised by affectation, foolishness, and moral blindness: singers of the falsetto school, with ballads to their mistress's eyebrow, sonnets to their lady's lute, and general songs of a fiddlestick; peevish men for the most part, as is the way of all fleshly and affected beings; men so ignorant of human subjects and materials as to be driven in their sheer bankruptcy of mind to raise Hope, Love, Fear, Rage (everything but Charity) into human entities, and to treat the body and upholstery of a dollish woman as if, in itself, it constituted a whole universe.

After tracing the effect of the "moral poison" here seen in its inception through English poetry from Surrey and Wyat to Cowley, the writer recognised a "tranquil gleam of honest English light" in Cowper, who "spread the seeds of new life" soon to re-appear in Wordsworth, Coleridge, Southey, Lamb, and Scott. In his opinion the "Italian disease would now have died out altogether," but for a "fresh importation of the obnoxious matter from France."

At this stage came a denunciation of the representation of "abnormal types of diseased lust and lustful disease" as seen in Charles Baudelaire's ***Fleurs de Mal***, with the conclusion that out of "the hideousness of ***Femmes Damnees***" came certain English poems. "This," said the writer, "is our double misfortune--to have a nuisance, and to have it at second-hand. We might have been more tolerant to an unclean thing if it had been in some sense a product of the soil" All that is here summarised, however, was but preparatory to the real object of the article, which was to assail Rossetti's new volume.

The poems were traversed in detail, with but little (and that the most grudging) admission of their power and beauty, and the very sharpest accentuation of their less spiritual qualities. Since the publication of the article in question, events have taken such a turn that it is no longer either necessary or wise to quote the strictures contained in it, however they might be fenced by juster views. The gravamen of the charge against Rossetti, Mr. Swinburne, and Mr. Morris alike--setting aside all particular accusations, however serious--was that they had "bound themselves into a solemn league and covenant to extol fleshliness as the distinct and supreme end of poetic and pictorial art; to aver that poetic expression is greater than poetic thought, and by inference that the body is greater than the soul, and sound superior to sense."

Such, then, is a synopsis of the hostile article of which the nucleus appeared in *The Contemporary Review*, and it were little less than childish to say that events so important as the publication of the article and subsequent pamphlet, and the controversy that arose out of them, should, from their unpleasantness and futility, from the bad passions provoked by them, or yet from the regret that followed after them, be passed over in sorrow and silence. For good or ill, what was written on both sides will remain. It has stood and will stand. Sooner or later the story of this literary quarrel will be told in detail and in cold blood, and perhaps with less than sufficient knowledge of either of the parties concerned in it, or sympathy with their aims. No better fate, one might think, could befall it than to be dealt with, however briefly, by a writer whose affections were warmly engaged on one side, while his convictions and bias of nature forced him to recognise the justice of the other--stripped, of course, of the cruelties with which literary error but too obviously enshrouded it.

Whatever the effect produced upon the public mind by the article in question (and there seems little reason to think it was at all material), the effect upon two of the writers attacked was certainly more than commensurate with the assault. Mr. Morris wisely attempted no reply to the few words of adverse criticism in which his name was specifically involved; but Mr. Swinburne retorted upon his adversary with the torrents of invective of which he has a measureless command. Rossetti's course was different. Greatly concerned at the bitterness, as well as startled by the unexpectedness of the attack, he wrote in the first moments of indignation a full and point-for-point rejoinder, and this he printed in the form of a pamphlet, and had a great number struck off; but with constitutional irresolution (wisely restraining him in this case), he destroyed every copy, and contented himself with writing a temperate letter on the subject to *The Athenaeum*, December 16, 1871. He said:

A sonnet, entitled *Nuptial Sleep*, is quoted and abused at page 338 of the Review, and is there dwelt upon as a "whole poem," describing "merely animal sensations." It is no more a whole poem in reality than is any single stanza of any poem throughout the book. The poem, written chiefly in sonnets, and of which this is one sonnet-stanza, is entitled *The House of Life*; and even in my first published instalment of the whole work (as contained in the volume under notice), ample evidence is included that no such passing phase of description as the one headed *Nuptial Sleep* could possibly be put forward by the author of *The House of Life* as his own representative view of the subject of love. In proof of this I will direct attention (among the love-sonnets of this poem), to Nos. 2, 8, 11, 17, 28, and more especially 13. [Here *Love Sweetness* is printed.] Any reader may bring any artistic charge he pleases against the above sonnet; but one charge it would be impossible to maintain against the writer of the series in which it occurs, and that is, the wish on his part to assert that the body is greater than the soul. For here all the passionate and just delights of the body are declared--somewhat figuratively, it is true, but unmistakeably--to be as naught if not ennobled by the concurrence of the soul at all times. Moreover, nearly one half of this series of sonnets has nothing to do with love, but treats of quite other life-influences. I would defy any one to couple with fair quotation of sonnets 29, 30, 31, 39, 40, 43, or others, the slander that their author was not impressed, like all other thinking men, with the responsibilities and higher mysteries of life; while sonnets 35, 36, and 37, entitled *The Choice*, sum up the general view taken in a manner only to be evaded by conscious insincerity. Thus much for *The House of Life*, of which the sonnet *Nuptial Sleep* is one stanza, embodying, for its small constituent share, a beauty of natural universal function, only to be reprobated in art if dwelt on (as I have shown that it is not here), to the exclusion of those other highest things of which it is the harmonious concomitant.

It had become known that the article in the *Review* was not the work of the unknown Thomas Maitland, whose name it bore, and on this head Rossetti wrote:

Here a critical organ, professedly adopting the principle of open signature, would seem, in reality, to assert (by silent practice, however, not by annunciation) that if the anonymous in criticism was--as itself originally indicated--but an early caterpillar stage, the nominate too is found to be no better than a homely transitional chrysalis, and that the ultimate butterfly form for a critic who likes to sport in sunlight, and yet elude the grasp, is after all the pseudonymous.

It transpired, in subsequent correspondence (of which there was more than enough), that the actual writer was Mr. Robert Buchanan, then a young author who had risen into distinction as a poet, and who was consequently suspected, by the writers and disciples of the Rossetti school, of being actuated much more by feelings of rivalry than by desire for the public good. Mr. Buchanan's reply to the serious accusation of having assailed a brother-poet pseudonymously was that the false signature was affixed to the article without his knowledge, "in order that the criticism might rest upon its own merits, and gain nothing from the name of the real writer."

It was an unpleasant controversy, and what remains as an impartial synopsis of it appears to be this: that there was actually manifest in the poetry of certain writers a tendency to deviate from wholesome reticence, and that this dangerous tendency came to us from France, where deep-seated unhealthy passion so gave shape to the glorification of gross forms of animalism as to excite alarm that what had begun with the hideousness of **Femmes Damnees** would not even end there; finally, that the unpleasant truth demanded to be spoken--by whomsoever had courage enough to utter it--that to deify mere lust was an offence and an outrage. So much for the justice on Mr. Buchanan's side; with the mistaken criticism linking the writers of Dante's time with French writers of the time of Baudelaire it is hardly necessary to deal. On the other hand, it must be said that the sum-total of all the English poetry written in imitation of the worst forms of this French excess was probably less than one hundred lines; that what was really reprehensible in the English imitation of the poetry of the French School was, therefore, too inconsiderable to justify a wholesale charge against it of an endeavour to raise the banner of a black ambition whose only aim was to ruin society; that Rossetti, who was made to bear the brunt of attack, was a man who never by direct avowal, or yet by inference, displayed the faintest conceivable sympathy with the French excesses in question, and who never wrote a line inspired by unwholesome passion. As the pith of Mr. Buchanan's accusation of 1871 lay here, and as Mr. Buchanan has, since then, very manfully withdrawn it,[3] we need hardly go further; but, as more recent articles in prominent places, **The**

---

3   Writing to me on this subject since Rossetti's death, Mr.
      Buchanan says:--"In perfect frankness, let me say a few
      words concerning our old quarrel. While admitting freely
      that my article in the C. R. was unjust to Rossetti's claims
      as a poet, I have ever held, and still hold, that it
      contained nothing to warrant the manner in which it was
      received by the poet and his circle. At the time it was
      written, the newspapers were full of panegyric; mine was a
      mere drop of gall in an ocean of **eau sucree**. That it could
      have had on any man the effect you describe, I can scarcely
      believe; indeed, I think that no living man had so little to
      complain of as Rossetti, on the score of criticism. Well, my
      protest was received in a way which turned irritation into
      wrath, wrath into violence; and then ensued the paper war
      which lasted for years. If you compare what I have written
      of Rossetti with what his admirers have written of myself, I
      think you will admit that there has been some cause for me
      to complain, to shun society, to feel bitter against the
      world; but happily, I have a thick epidermis, and the

Edinburgh Review, The British Quarterly Review, and again The Contemporary Review, have repeated what was first said by him on the alleged unwholesomeness of Rossetti's poetic impulses, it may be as well to admit frankly, and at once (for the subject will arise in the future as frequently as this poetry is under discussion) that love of bodily beauty did underlie much of the poet's work. But has not the same passion made the back-bone of nine-tenths of the noblest English poetry since Chaucer? If it is objected that Rossetti's love of physical beauty took new forms, the rejoinder is that it would have been equally childish and futile to attempt to prescribe limits for it. All this we grant to those unfriendly critics who refuse to see that spiritual beauty and not sensuality was Rossetti's actual goal.

courage of an approving conscience. I was unjust, as I have said; most unjust when I impugned the purity and misconceived the passion of writings too hurriedly read and reviewed currente calamo; but I was at least honest and fearless, and wrote with no personal malignity. Save for the action of the literary defence, if I may so term it, my article would have been as ephemeral as the mood which induced its composition. I make full admission of Rossetti's claims to the purest kind of literary renown, and if I were to criticise his poems now, I should write very differently. But nothing will shake my conviction that the cruelty, the unfairness, the pusillanimity has been on the other side, not on mine. The amende of my Dedication in God and the Man was a sacred thing; between his spirit and mine; not between my character and the cowards who have attacked it. I thought he would understand,--which would have been, and indeed is, sufficient. I cried, and cry, no truce with the horde of slanderers who hid themselves within his shadow. That is all. But when all is said, there still remains the pity that our quarrel should ever have been. Our little lives are too short for such animosities. Your friend is at peace with God,--that God who will justify and cherish him, who has dried his tears, and who will turn the shadow of his sad life-dream into full sunshine. My only regret now is that we did not meet,--that I did not take him by the hand; but I am old-fashioned enough to believe that this world is only a prelude, and that our meeting may take place--even yet."

To Rossetti, the poet, the accusation of extolling fleshliness as the distinct and supreme end of art was, after all, only an error of critical judgment; but to Rossetti, the man, the charge was something far more serious. It was a cruel and irremediable wound inflicted upon a fine spirit, sensitive to attack beyond all sensitiveness hitherto known among poets. He who had withheld his pictures from exhibition from dread of the distracting influences of popular opinion, he who for fifteen years had withheld his poems from print in obedience first to an extreme modesty of personal estimate and afterwards to the commands of a mastering affection was likely enough at forty-two years of age (after being loaded by the disciples that idolised him with only too much of the "frankincense of praise and myrrh of flattery") to feel deeply the slander that he had unpacked his bosom of unhealthy passions. But to say that Rossetti felt the slander does not express his sense of it. He had replied to his reviewer and had acted unwisely in so doing; but when one after one--in the ***Quarterly Review, the North American Review***, and elsewhere, in articles more or less ignorant, uncritical, and stupid--the accusations he had rebutted were repeated with increased bitterness, he lost all hope of stemming the torrent of hostile criticism. He had, as we have seen, for years lived in partial retirement, enjoying at intervals a garden party behind the house, or going about occasionally to visit relatives and acquaintances, but now he became entirely reclusive, refusing to see any friends except the three or four intimate ones who were constantly with him. Nor did the mischief end there. We have spoken of his habitual use of chloral, which was taken at first in small doses as a remedy for insomnia and afterwards indulged in to excess at moments of physical prostration or nervous excitement. To that false friend he came at this time with only too great assiduity, and the chloral, added to the seclusive habit of life, induced a series of terrible though intermittent illnesses and a morbid condition of mind in which for a little while he was the victim of many painful delusions. It was at this time that the soothing friendship of Dr. Gordon Hake, and his son Mr. George Hake, was of such inestimable service to Rossetti. Having appeared myself on the scene much later I never had the privilege of knowing either of these two gentlemen, for Mr. George Hake was already gone away to Cyprus and Dr. Hake had retired very much into the bosom of his own family where, as is rumoured, he has been engaged upon a literary work which will establish his fame. But I have often heard Mr. Theodore Watts speak with deep emotion and eloquent enthusiasm of the tender kindness and loyal zeal shown to Rossetti during this crisis by Mr. Bell Scott, and by Dr. Hake and his son. As to Mr. Theodore Watts, whose brotherly devotion to him, and beneficial influence over him from that time forward are so well known, this must be considered by those who witnessed it to be almost without precedent or parallel even in the beautiful story of literary friendships, and it does as much honour to the one as to the other. No light matter it must have been to lay aside one's own long-cherished life-work and literary ambitions to be Rossetti's closest friend and brother, at a moment like the present, when he imagined the world to be conspiring against him; but through these evil days, and long after them down to his death, the friend that clung closer than a brother was with him, as he himself said, to protect, to soothe, to comfort, to divert, to interest, and inspire him--asking, meantime, no better reward than the knowledge that a noble mind and nature was by such sacrifice lifted out of sorrow. Among the world's great men the greatest are sometimes those whose names are least on our lips, and this is because selfish aims have been so subordinate in their lives to the welfare of others as to leave no time for the personal achievements that win personal distinction; but when the world comes to the knowledge of the price that has been paid for the devotion that enables others to enjoy their renown, shall it not reward with a double meed of gratitude the fine spirits to whom ambition has been as nothing against fidelity of friendship? Among the latest words I heard from Rossetti was this: "Watts is a hero of friendship;" and indeed he has displayed his capacity for participation in the noblest part of comradeship, that part, namely, which is far above the mere traffic that too often goes by the name, and wherein self-love always counts upon being the gainer. If in the end it should appear that he has in his own person done less than might have been hoped for from one possessed of his splendid gifts, let it not be overlooked that he has influenced in a quite incalculable degree, and influenced for good, several of the foremost among those who in their turn have influenced the age. As Rossetti's faithful friend, and gifted medical adviser, Mr. John Marshall has often declared, there were periods when Rossetti's very life may be said to have hung upon Mr. Watts's power to cheer and soothe.

Efforts were afoot about the year 1872 to induce Rossetti to visit Italy--a journey which, strangely enough, he had never made--but this he could not be prevailed upon to do. In the hope of diverting his mind from the unwholesome matters that too largely engaged it, his brother and friends, prominent among whom at this time were Mr. Bell Scott, Mr. Ford Madox Brown, Mr. W. Graham, and Dr. Gordon Hake, as well as his assistant and friend, Mr. H. T. Dunn, and Mr. George Hake, induced him to seek a change in Scotland, and there he speedily recovered tone.

Immediately upon the publication of his first volume, and incited thereto by the early success of it, he had written the poem **Rose Mary**, as well as two lyrics published at the time in *The Fortnightly Review*; but he suffered so seriously from the subsequent assaults of criticism, that he seemed definitely to lay aside all hope of producing further poetry, and, indeed, to become possessed of the delusion that he had for ever lost all power of doing so. It is an interesting fact, well known in his own literary circle, that his taking up poetry afresh was the result of a fortuitous occurrence. After one of his most serious illnesses, and in the hope of drawing off his attention from himself, and from the gloomy forebodings which in an invalid's mind usually gather about his own too absorbing personality, a friend prevailed upon him, with infinite solicitation, to try his hand afresh at a sonnet. The outcome was an effort so feeble as to be all but unrecognisable as the work of the author of the sonnets of *The House of Life*, but with more shrewdness and friendliness (on this occasion) than frankness, the critic lavished measureless praise upon it, and urged the poet to renewed exertion. One by one, at longer or shorter intervals, sonnets were written, and this exercise did more towards his recovery than any other medicine, with the result besides that Rossetti eventually regained all his old dexterity and mastery of hand. The artifice had succeeded beyond every expectation formed of it, serving, indeed, the twofold end of improving the invalid's health by preventing his brooding over unhealthy matters, and increasing the number of his accomplished works. Encouraged by such results, the friend went on to induce Rossetti to write a ballad, and this purpose he finally achieved by challenging the poet's ability to compose in the simple, direct, and emphatic style, which is the style of the ballad proper, as distinguished from the elaborate, ornate, and condensed diction which he had hitherto worked in. Put upon his mettle, the outcome of this second artifice practised upon him, was that he wrote *The White Ship*, and afterwards *The King's Tragedy*.

Thus was Rossetti already immersed in this revived occupation of poetic composition, and had recovered a healthy* tone of body, before he became conscious of what was being done with him. It is a further amusing fact that one day he requested to be shown the first sonnet which, in view of the praise lavished upon it by the friend on whose judgment he reposed, had encouraged him to renewed effort. The sonnet was bad: the critic knew it was bad, and had from the first hour of its production kept it carefully out of sight, and was now more than ever unwilling to show it. Eventually, however, by reason of ceaseless importunity, he returned it to its author, who, upon reading it, cried: "You fraud! you said this sonnet was good, and it's the worst I *ever* wrote." "The worst ever written would perhaps be a truer criticism," was the reply, as the studio resounded with a hearty laugh, and the poem was committed to the flames. It would appear that to this occurrence we probably owe a large portion of the contents of the volume of 1881.

As we say, **Rose Mary** was the first to be written of the leading poems that found places in his final volume. This ballad (or ballad romance, for ballad it can hardly be called) is akin to **Sister Helen** in **motif**. The superstition involved owes something in this case as in the other to the invention and poetic bias of the poet. It has, however, less of what has been called the Catholic element, and is more purely Pagan. It is, therefore, as entirely undisturbed by animosity against heresy, and is concerned only with an ultimate demoniacal justice visiting the wrongdoer. The main point of divergency lies in the circumstance that Rose Mary, unlike Helen, is the undesigning instrument of evil powers, and that her blind deed is the means by which her own and her lover's sin and his treachery become revealed. A further material point of divergency lies in the fact that unlike Helen, who loses her soul (as the price of revenge, directed against her betrayer), Rose Mary loses her life (as the price of vengeance directed against the evil race), whilst her soul gains rest. The superstition is that associated with the beryl stone, wherein the pure only may read the future, and from which sinful eyes must chase the spirits of grace and leave their realm to be usurped by the spirits of fire, who seal up the truth or reveal it by contraries. Rose Mary, who has sinned with her lover, is bidden to look in the beryl and learn where lurks the ambush that waits to take his life as he rides at break of day. Hiding, but remembering her transgression, she at first shrinks, but at length submits, and the blessed spirits by whom the stone has been tenanted give place to the fiery train. The stone is not sealed to her; and the long spell being ministered, she is satisfied. But she has read the stone by contraries, and her lover falls into the hand of his enemy. By his death is their secret sin made known. And then a newer shame is revealed, not to her eyes, but to her mother's: even the treachery of the murdered man. Ignorant of this to the end, Eose Mary seeks to work a twofold ransoming by banishing from the beryl the evil powers. With the sword of her father (by whom the accursed gift had been brought from Palestine), she cleaves the heart of the stone, and with the broken spell her own life breaks.

It will readily be seen that the scheme of the ballad does not afford opportunity for a memorable incursion in the domain of character. Rose Mary herself as a creation is not comparable with Helen. But the ballad throughout is nevertheless a triumph of the higher imagination. Nowhere else (to take the lowest ground) has Rossetti displayed so great a gift of flashing images upon the mind at once by a single expression.

> Closely locked, they clung without speech,
> And the mirrored souls shook each to each,
> As the cloud-moon and the water-moon
> Shake face to face when the dim stars swoon
> In stormy bowers of the night's mid-noon.
>
> Deep the flood and heavy the shock
> When sea meets sea in the riven rock:
> But calm is the pulse that shakes the sea
> To the prisoned tide of doom set free
> In the breaking heart of Rose Mary.
>
> She knew she had waded bosom-deep
> Along death's bank in the sedge of sleep.
> And now in Eose Mary's lifted eye
> 'Twas shadow alone that made reply
> To the set face of the soul's dark shy.

Nor has Rossetti anywhere displayed a more sustained picturesqueness. One episode stands forth vividly even among so many that are conspicuous. The mother has left her daughter in a swoon to seek help of the priest who has knelt unweariedly by the dead body of her daughter's lover, now lying on the ingle-bench in the hall. When the priest has gone and the castle folk have left her alone, the lady sinks to her knees beside the corpse. Great wrong the dead man has done to her and hers, and perhaps God has wrought this doom of his for a sign; but well she knows, or thinks she knows, that if life had remained with him his love would have been security for their honour. She stoops with a sob to kiss the dead, but before her lips touch the cold brow she sees a packet half-hidden in the dead man's breast. It is a folded paper about which the blood from a spear-thrust has grown clotted, and inside is a tress of golden hair. Some pledge of her child's she thinks it, and proceeds to undo the paper's folds, and then learns the treachery of the fallen knight and suffers a bitterer pang than came of the knowledge of her daughter's dishonour. It is a love-missive from the sister of his foe and murderer.

> She rose upright with a long low moan,
> And stared in the dead man's face new-known.
> Had it lived indeed? she scarce could tell:
> 'Twas a cloud where fiends had come to dwell,--
> A mask that hung on the gate of Hell.
>
> She lifted the lock of gleaming hair,
> And smote the lips and left it there.
> "Here's gold that Hell shall take for thy toll!
> Full well hath thy treason found its goal,
> O thou dead body and damned soul!"

Anything finer than this it would be hard to discover in English narrative poetry. Every word goes to build up the story: every line is quintessential: every flash of thought helps to heighten the emotion. Indeed the closing lines rise entirely above the limits of ballad poetry into the realm of dramatic diction. But perhaps the crowning glory and epic grandeur of the poem comes at the close. Awakened from her swoon, Rose Mary makes her way to the altar-cell and there she sees the beryl-stone lying between the wings of some sculptured beast. Within the fated glass she beholds Death, Sorrow, Sin and Shame marshalled past in the glare of a writhing flame, and thereupon follows a scene scarcely less terrible than Juliet's vision of the tomb of the Capulets. But she has been told within this hour that her weak hand shall send hence the evil race by whom the stone is possessed, and with a stern purpose she reaches her father's dinted sword. Then when the beryl is cleft to the core, and Rose Mary lies in her last gracious sleep--

> With a cold brow like the snows ere May,
> With a cold breast like the earth till spring,
> With such a smile as the June days bring--
> A clear voice pronounces her beatitude:

> Already thy heart remembereth
> No more his name thou sought'st in death:
> For under all deeps, all heights above,--
> So wide the gulf in the midst thereof,--
> Are Hell of Treason and Heaven of Love.

> Thee, true soul, shall thy truth prefer
> To blessed Mary's rose-bower:
> Warmed and lit is thy place afar
> With guerdon-fires of the sweet love-star,
> Where hearts of steadfast lovers are.

The White Ship was written in 1880; *The King's Tragedy* in the spring of 1881. These historical ballads we must briefly consider together. The memorable events of which Rossetti has made poetic record are, in *The White Ship*, those associated with the wreck of the ship in which the son and daughter of Henry I. of England set sail from France, and in *The King's Tragedy*, with the death of James the First of Scots. The story of the one is told by the sole survivor, Herold, the butcher of Rouen; and of the other by Catherine Douglas, the maid of honour who received popularly the name of Kate Barlass, in recognition of her heroic act when she barred the door with her arm against the murderers of the King. It is scarcely possible to conceive in either case a diction more perfectly adapted to the person by whom it is employed. If we compare the language of these ballads with that of the sonnets or other poems spoken in the author's own person, we find it is not first of all gorgeous, condensed, emphatic. It is direct, simple, pure and musical; heightened, it is true, by imagery acquired in its passage through the medium of the poet's mind, but in other respects essentially the language of the historical personages who are made to speak. The diction belongs in each case to the period of the ballad in which it is employed, and yet there is no wanton use of archaisms, or any disposition manifested to resort to meretricious artifices by which to impart an appearance of probability to the story other than that which comes legitimately of sheer narrative excellence. The characterisation is that of history with the features softened that constituted the prose of real life, and with the salient, moral, and intellectual lineaments brought into relief. Herein the ballad may do that final justice which history itself withholds. Thus the King Henry of *The White Ship* is governed by lust of dominion more than by parental affection; and the Prince, his son, is a lawless, shameless youth; intolerant, tyrannical, luxurious, voluptuous, yet capable of self-sacrifice even amidst peril of death.

> When he should be King, he oft would vow,
> He 'd yoke the peasant to his own plough.
> O'er him the ships score their furrows now.
> God only knows where his soul did wake,
> But I saw him die for his sister's sake.

The King James of *The King's Tragedy* is of a righteous and fearless nature, strong yet sensitive, unbending before the pride and hate of powerful men, resolute, and ready even where fate itself declares that death lurks where his road must lie; his beautiful Queen Jane is sweet, tender, loving, devoted--meet spouse for a poet and king. The incidents too are those of history: the choice and final collocation of them, and the closing scene in which the queen mourns her husband, being the sum of the author's contribution. And those incidents are in the highest degree varied and picturesque. The author has not achieved a more vivid pictorial presentment than is displayed in these latest ballads from his pen. It would be hard to find in his earlier work anything bearing more clearly the stamp of reality than the descriptions of the wreck in *The White Ship*, of the two drowning men together on the mainyard, of the morning dawning over the dim sea-sky--

> At last the morning rose on the sea
> Like an angel's wing that beat towards me--

and of the little golden-haired boy in black whose foot patters down the court of the king. Certainly Rossetti has never attained a higher pictorial level than he reaches in the descriptions of the summoned Parliament in *The King's Tragedy*, of the journey to the Charterhouse of Perth, of the woman on the rock of the black beach of the Scottish sea, of the king singing to the queen the song he made while immured by Bolingbroke at Windsor, of the knock of the woman at the outer gate, of her voice at night beneath the window, of the death in *The Pit of Fortune's Wheel*. But all lesser excellencies must make way in our regard before a distinguishing spiritualising element which exists in these ballads only, or mainly amongst the author's works. Natural portents are here first employed as factors of poetic creation. Presentiment, foreboding, omen become the essential tissue of works that are lifted by them into the higher realm of imagination. These supernatural constituents penetrate and pervade *The White Ship*; and *The King's Tragedy* is saturated in the spirit of them. We do not speak of the incidents associated with the wraith that haunts the isles, but of the less palpable touches which convey the scarce explicable sense of a change of voice when the king sings of the pit that is under fortune's wheel:

> And under the wheel, beheld I there
> An ugly Pit as deep as hell,
> That to behold I quaked for fear:
> And this I heard, that who therein fell
> Came no more up, tidings to tell:
> Whereat, astound of the fearful sight,
> I wot not what to do for fright.
> (The King's Quair.)

It is the shadow of the supernatural that hangs over the king, and very soon it must enshroud him. One of the most subtle and impressive of the natural portents is that which presents itself to the eyes of Catherine when the leaguers have first left the chamber, and the moon goes out and leaves black the royal armorial shield on the painted window-pane:

> And the rain had ceased, and the moonbeams lit
> The window high in the wall,--
> Bright beams that on the plank that I knew
> Through the painted pane did fall
> And gleamed with the splendour of Scotland's crown
> And shield armorial.
>
> But then a great wind swept up the skies,
> And the climbing moon fell back;
> And the royal blazon fled from the floor,
> And nought remained on its track;
> And high in the darkened window-pane
> The shield and the crown were black.

It has been said that **Sister Helen** strikes the keynote of Rossetti's creative gift; it ought to be added that **The King's Tragedy** touches his highest reach of imagination.

Having in the early part of 1881 brought together a sufficient quantity of fresh poetry to fill a volume, Rossetti began negotiations for publishing it. Anticipatory announcements were at that time constantly appearing in many quarters, not rarely accompanied by an outspoken disbelief in the poet's ability to achieve a second success equal to his first. In this way it often happens to an author, that, having achieved a single conspicuous triumph, the public mind, which has spontaneously offered him the tribute of a generous recognition, forthwith gravitates towards a disposition to become silently but unmistakeably sceptical of his power to repeat it. Subsequent effort in such a case is rarely regarded with that confidence which might be looked for as the reward of achievement, and which goes far to prepare the mind for the ready acceptance of any genuine triumph. Indeed, a jealous attitude is often unconsciously adopted, involving a demand for special qualities, for which, perchance, the peculiar character of the past success has created an appetite, or obedience to certain arbitrary tests, which, though passively present in the recognised work, have grown mainly out of critical analysis of it, and are neither radical nor essential. Where, moreover, such conspicuous success has been followed by an interval of years distinguished by no signal effort, the sceptical bias of the public mind sometimes complacently settles into a conviction (grateful alike to its pride and envy, whilst consciously hurtful to its more generous impulses), that the man who made it lived once indeed upon the mountains, but has at length come down to dwell finally upon the plain. Literary biography furnishes abundant examples of this imperfection of character, a foible, indeed, which in its multiform manifestations, probably goes as far as anything else to interfere with the formation of a just and final judgment of an author's merit within his own lifetime. When it goes the length of affirming that even a great writer's creative activity usually finds not merely central realisation, but absolute exhaustion within the limits of some single work, to reason against it is futile, and length of time affords it the only satisfying refutation. One would think that it could scarcely require to be urged that creative impulse, once existent within a mind, can never wholly depart from it, but must remain to the end, dependent, perhaps, for its expression in some measure on external promptings, variable with the variations of physical environments, but always gathering innate strength for the hour (silent perchance, or audible only within other spheres), when the inventive faculty shall be harmonised, animated, and lubricated to its utmost height. Nevertheless, Coleridge encountered the implied doubtfulness of his contemporaries, that the gift remained with him to carry to its completion the execution of that most subtle mid-day witchery, which, as begun in *Christabel*, is probably the most difficult and elusive thing ever attempted in the field of romance. Goethe, too, found himself face to face with outspoken distrust of his continuation of *Faust*; and even Cervantes had perforce to challenge the popular judgment which long refused to allow that the second part of *Don Quixote*, with all its added significance, was adequate to his original simple conception. Indeed that author must be considered fortunate who effects a reversal of the public judgment against the completion of a fragment, and the repetition of a complete and conspicuous success.

When Rossetti published his first volume of poems in 1870, he left only his *House of Life* incomplete; but amongst the readers who then offered spontaneous tribute to that series of sonnets, and still treasured it as a work of all but faultless symmetry, built up by aid of a blended inspiration caught equally from Shakspeare and from Dante, with a superadded psychical quality peculiar to its author, there were many, even amongst the friendliest in sympathy, who heard of the completed sequence with a sense of doubt. Such is the silent and unreasoning and all but irrevocable edict of all popular criticism against continuations of works which have in fragmentary form once made conquest of the popular imagination. Moreover, Rossetti's first volume achieved a success so signal and unexpected as to subject this second and maturer book to the preliminary ordeal of such a questioning attitude of mind as we speak of, as the unfailing and ungracious reward of a conspicuous triumph. In the interval of eleven years, Rossetti had essayed no notable achievement, and his name had been found attached only to such fugitive efforts as may have lived from time to time a brief life in the pages of the *Athenaeum* and *Fortnightly*. Of the works in question two only come now within our province to mention. The first and most memorable was the poem *Cloud Confines*. Inadequate as the critical attention necessarily was which this remarkable lyric obtained, indications were not wanting that it had laid unconquerable siege to the sympathies of that section of the public in whose enthusiasm the life of every creative work is seen chiefly to abide. There was in it a lyrical sweetness scarcely ever previously compassed by its author, a cadent undertoned symphony that first gave testimony that the poet held the power of conveying by words a sensible eflfect of great music, even as former works of his had given testimony to his power of conveying a sensible eflfect by great painting. But to these metrical excellencies was added an element new to Rossetti's poetry, or seen here for the first time conspicuously. Insight and imagination of a high order, together with a poetic instinct whose promptings were sure, had already found expression in more than one creation moulded into an innate chasteness of perfected parts and wedded to nature with an unerring fidelity. But the range of nature was circumscribed, save only in the one exception of a work throbbing with the sufferings and sorrows of a shadowed side of modern life. To this lyric, however, there came as basis a fundamental conception that made aim to grapple with the pro-foundest problems compassed by the mysteries of life and death, and a temper to yield only where human perception fails. Abstract indeed in theme the lyric is, but few are the products of thought out of which imagination has delved a more concrete and varied picturesqueness:

> What of the heart of hate
> That beats in thy breast, O Time?--
> Bed strife from the furthest prime,
> And anguish of fierce debate; that shatters her slain,
> And peace that grinds them as grain,
> And eyes fixed ever in vain
> On the pitiless eyes of Fate.

The second of the fugitive efforts alluded to was a prose work entitled **Hand and Soul**. More poem than story, this beautiful idyl may be briefly described as mainly illustrative of the struggles of the transition period through which, as through a slough, all true artists must pass who have been led to reflect deeply upon the aims and ends of their calling before they attain that goal of settled purpose in which they see it to be best to work from their own heart simply, without regard for the spectres that would draw them apart into quagmires of moral aspiration. These two works and an occasional sonnet, such as that on the greatly gifted and untimely lost Oliver Madox Brown, made the sum of all[4] that was done, in the interval of eleven years between the dates of the first volume and of that which was now to be published, to keep before the public a name which rose at once into distinction, and had since, without feverish periodical bolstering, grown not less but more in the ardent upholding of sincere men who, in number and influence, comprised a following as considerable perhaps as owned allegiance to any contemporary.

Having brought these biographical and critical notes to the point at which they overlap the personal recollections that form the body of this volume, it only remains to say that during the years in which the poems just reviewed were being written Rossetti was living at his house in Chelsea a life of unbroken retirement.

---

4   A ballad appeared in The Dark Blue.

At this time, however (1877-81), his seclusion was not so complete as it had been when he used to see scarcely any one but Mr. Watts and his own family, with an occasional visit from Lord and Lady Mount Temple, Mrs. Sumner, etc. Once weekly he was now visited by his brother William, twice weekly by his attached and gifted friend Frederick J. Shields, occasionally by his old friends William Bell Scott and Ford Madox Brown. For the rest, he rarely if ever left the precincts of his home. It was a placid and undisturbed existence such as he loved. Health too (except for one serious attack in 1877), was good with him, and his energies were, as we have seen, at their best. His personal amiability was, perhaps, never more conspicuous than in these tranquil years; yet this was the very time when paragraphs injurious to his character found their way into certain journals. Among the numerous stories illustrative of his alleged barbarity of manners was the one which has often been repeated both in conversation and in print to the effect that H.E.H. the Princess Louise was rudely repulsed from his door. Rossetti was certainly not easy to approach, but the geniality of his personal bearing towards those who had commands upon his esteem was always unfailing, and knowledge of this fact must have been enough to give the lie to the injurious calumny just named. Nevertheless, Rossetti, who was deeply moved by the imputation, thought it necessary to contradict it emphatically, and as the letter in which he did this is a thoroughly outspoken and manly one, and touches an important point in his character, I reprint it in this place:

16 Cheyne Walk, Chelsea, S.W., December 28, 1878.

My attention has been directed to the following paragraph which has appeared in the newspapers:--"A very disagreeable story is told about a neighbour of Mr. Whistler's, whose works are not exhibited to the vulgar herd; the Princess Louise in her zeal, therefore, graciously sought them at the artist's studio, but was rebuffed by a 'Not at home' and an intimation that he was not at the beck and call of princesses. I trust it is not true," continues the writer of the paragraph, "that so medievally minded a gentleman is really a stranger to that generous loyalty to rank and sex, that dignified obedience," etc.

The story is certainly "disagreeable" enough; but if I am pointed at as the "near neighbour of Mr. Whistler's" who rebuffed, in this rude fashion, the Princess Louise, I can only say that it is a **canard** devoid of the smallest nucleus of truth. Her Royal Highness has never called upon me; and I know of only two occasions when she has expressed a wish to do so. Some years ago Mr. Theodore Martin spoke to me upon the subject; but I was at that time engaged upon an important work, and the delays thence arising caused the matter to slip through. And I heard no more upon the subject till last summer, when Mr. Theodore Watts told me that the Princess, in conversation, had mentioned my name to him, and that he had then assured her that I should "feel honoured and charmed to see her," and suggested her making an appointment. Her Royal Highness knew that Mr. Watts, as one of my most intimate friends, would not have thus expressed himself without feeling fully warranted in so doing; and had she called she would not, I trust, have found me wanting in that "generous loyalty" which is due not more to her exalted position than to her well-known charm of character and artistic gifts. It is true enough that I do not run after great people on account of their mere social position, but I am, I hope, never rude to them; and the man who could rebuff the Princess Louise must be a curmudgeon indeed.

D. G. Rossetti.

At the very juncture in question Lord Lome was suddenly and unexpectedly appointed Governor-General of Canada, and, leaving England, Her Royal Highness did not return until Rossetti's health had somewhat suddenly broken down, and it was impossible for him to see any but his most intimate friends.

CHAPTER III.

My intercourse with Rossetti, epistolary and personal, extended over a period of between three and four years. During the first two of these years I was, as this volume must show, his constant correspondent, during the third year his attached friend, and during the portion of the fourth year of our acquaintance terminating with his life, his daily companion and housemate. It is a part of my purpose to help towards the elucidation of Rossetti's personal character by a simple, and I trust, unaffected statement of my relations to him, and so I begin by explaining that my knowledge of the man was the sequel to my admiration of the poet. Not accident (the agency that usually operates in such cases), but his genius and my love of it, began the friendship between us. Of Rossetti's pictorial art I knew little, until very recent years, beyond what could be gathered from a few illustrations to books. My acquaintance with his poetry must have been made at the time of the publication of the first volume in 1870, but as I did not then possess a copy of the book, and do not remember to have seen one, my knowledge of the work must have been merely such as could be gleaned from the reading of reviews. The unlucky controversy, that subsequently arose out of it, directed afresh my attention, in common with that of others, to Rossetti and his school of poetry, with the result of impressing my mind with qualities of the work that were certainly quite outside the issues involved in the discussion. Some two or three years after that acrimonious controversy had subsided, an accident, sufficiently curious to warrant my describing it, produced the effect of converting me from a temperate believer in the charm of music and colour in Rossetti's lyric verse, to an ardent admirer of his imaginative genius as displayed in the higher walks of his art.

I had set out with a knapsack to make one of my many periodical walking tours of the beautiful lake country of Westmoreland and Cumberland. Beginning the journey at Bowness--as tourists, if they will accept the advice of one who knows perhaps the whole of the country, ought always to do--I walked through Dungeon Ghyll, climbed the Stake Pass, descended into Borrowdale, and traced the course of the winding Derwent to that point at which it meets the estuary of the lake, and where stands the Derwentwater Hotel. A rain and thunder storm was gathering over the Black Sail and Great Gable as I reached the summit of the Pass, and travelling slowly northwards it had overtaken me. Before I reached the hotel, my resting-place for the night, I was certainly as thoroughly saturated as any one in reasonable moments could wish to be. I remember that as I passed into the shelter of the porch an elderly gentleman, who was standing there, remarked upon the severity of the storm, inquired what distance I had travelled, and expressed amazement that on such a day, when mists were floating, any one could have ventured to cover so much dangerous mountain-country,--which he estimated as nearly thirty miles in extent. Beyond observing that my interlocutor was friendly in manner and knew the country intimately, I do not remember to have reflected either then or afterwards upon his personality except perhaps that he might have answered to Wordsworth's scarcely definite description of his illustrious friend as "a noticeable man," with the further parallel, I think, of possessing "large grey eyes." After attending to the obvious necessity of dry garments in exchange for wet ones, and otherwise comforting myself after a fatiguing day's march, I descended to the drawing-room of the hotel, where a company of persons were trying, with that too formal cordiality peculiar to English people, who are accidentally thrown together in the course of a holiday, to get rid of the depression which results upon dishearteningly unpropitious weather. Music, as usual, was the gracious angel employed to banish the fiend of ennui, but among those who took no part either in the singing or playing, other than that of an enforced auditor, was the elderly gentleman, my quondam acquaintance of the porch, who stood apart in an alcove looking through a window. I stepped up to him and renewed our talk. The storm had rather increased than abated since my arrival; the thunder which before had rumbled over the distant Langdale Pikes was breaking in sharp peals over our heads, and flashes of sheeted lightning lit up the gathering darkness that lay between us and Castle Crag. A playful allusion to "poor Tom" and to King Lear's undisputed sole enjoyment of such a scene (except as viewed from the ambush of a comfortable hotel) led to the discovery, very welcome to both at a moment when we were at bay for an evening's occupation, that besides knowledge and love of the country round about us, we had in common some knowledge and much love of the far wider realm of books. Thereupon ensued a talk chiefly on authors and their works which lasted until long after the music had ceased, until the elemental as well as instrumental storm had passed, and the guests had slipped away one after one, and the last remaining servant of the house had, by the introduction of a couple of candles, given us a palpable hint that in the opinion of that guardian of a country inn the hour was come and gone when well-regulated persons should betake themselves to bed. To my delight my friend knew nearly every prominent living author, could give me personal descriptions of them, as well as scholarly and well-digested criticisms of their works. He was certainly no ordinary man, but who he was I have never learned with certainty, though I cherish the agreeable impression that I could give a shrewd guess. At one moment the talk turned on *Festus*, and then I heard the most lucid and philosophical account of that work I have ever listened to or read. I was told that the author of *Festus* had never (in all the years that had elapsed since its publication, when he was in his earliest manhood, though now he is grown elderly) ceased to emend it, notwithstanding the protestations of critics; and that an improved and enlarged edition of the poem might probably appear after his death. Struck with the especial knowledge displayed of the author in question, I asked if he happened to be a friend. Then, with a scarcely perceptible smile playing about the corners of the mouth (a circumstance without significance for me at the time and only remembered afterwards), my new acquaintance answered: "He is my oldest and dearest friend." Next morning I saw my night-long conversationalist in company with a clergyman get on to the Buttermere coach and wave his hand to me as they vanished under the trees that overhung the Buttermere road, but in answer to many inquiries the utmost I could learn of my interesting acquaintance was that he was somehow understood to be a great author, and a friend of Charles Kingsley, who, I think they said, was or had been with him there or elsewhere that year. Whether besides being the "oldest and dearest friend" of the author of *Festus*, my delightful companion was Philip James Bailey himself I have never learned to this day, and can only cherish a pleasant trust; but what remains as really important in this connexion is that whosoever he was he originated my first real love of Rossetti's poetry, and gave me my first realisable idea of the man. Taking up from the table some popular **Garland, Casket, Treasury**, or other anthology of English poetry, he pointed out a sonnet entitled **Lost Days** (to which, indeed, a friend at home had directed my attention), and dwelt upon its marvellous strength of spiritual insight, and power of symbolic phrase. Of course the sonnet was Rossetti's. It is impossible for me to describe the effect produced upon me by sonnet and exposition. I resolved not to live many days longer without acquiring a knowledge of the body of Rossetti's work. Perceiving that the gentleman knew something of the poet, I put questions to him which elicited the fact that he had met him many years earlier at, I think he said, Mrs. Gaskell's, when Rossetti was a rather young man, known only as a painter and the leader of an eccentric school in art. He described him as a little dark man, with fine eyes under a broad brow, with a deep voice, and Bohemian habits--"a little Italian, in short." [Little, by the way, Rossetti could not properly be said to be, but opinions as to physical proportions being so liable to vary, I may at once mention that he was exactly five feet eight inches in height, and except in early manhood, when he was somewhat attenuated, well built in proportion.] He further described Rossetti's manners as those of a man in deliberate revolt against society; delighting in an opportunity to startle well-ordered persons out of their propriety, and to silence by sheer vehemence of denunciation the seemly protests of very good and very gentle folk. The portraiture seems to me now to bear the impress of truth, unlike as it is in some particulars to the man as I knew him. When once, however, years after the event recorded, I bantered Rossetti on the amiable picture of him I had received from a stranger, he admitted that it was in the main true to his character early in life, and recounted an instance in which, from sheer perversity, or at best for amusement, he had made the late Dean Stanley aghast with horror at the spectacle of a young man, born in a Christian country, and in the nineteenth century, defending (in sport) the vices of Neronian Home.

The outcome of this first serious and sufficient introduction to Rossetti's poetry was that I forthwith devoted time to reading and meditating upon it. Ultimately I lectured twice or thrice on the subject in Liverpool, first at the Royal Institution, and afterwards at the Free Library. The text of that lecture I still preserve, and as in all probability it did more than anything else to originate the friendship I afterwards enjoyed with the poet, I shall try to convey very briefly an idea of its purpose.

Against both friendly and unfriendly critics of Rossetti I held that to place him among the "aesthetic" poets was an error of classification. It seemed to me that, unlike the poets properly so described, he had nothing in common with the Caliban of Mr. Browning, who worked "for work's sole sake;" and, unlike them yet further, the topmost thing in him was indeed love of beauty, but the deepest thing was love of uncomely right. The fusion of these elements in Rossetti softened the mythological Italian Catholicism that I recognised as a leading thing in him, and subjugated his sensuous passion. I thought it wrong to say that Rossetti had part or lot with those false artists, or no artists, who assert, without fear or shame, that the manner of doing a thing should be abrogated or superseded by the moral purpose of its being done. On the other hand, Rossetti appeared to make no conscious compromise with the Puritan principle of doing good; and to demand first of his work the lesson or message it had for us were wilfully to miss of pleasure while we vainly strove for profit. He was too true an artist to follow art into its byeways of moral significance, and thereby cripple its broader arms; but at the same time all this absorption of the artist in his art seemed to me to live and work together with the personal instincts of the man. An artist's nature cannot escape the colouring it gets from the human side of his nature, because it is of the essence of art to appeal to its own highest faculties largely through the channel of moral instincts: that music is exquisite and colour splendid, first, because they have an indescribable significance, and next because they respond to mere sense. But it appeared to me to be one thing to work for "work's sole sake," with an overruling moral instinct that gravitates, as Mr. Arnold would say, towards conduct, and quite another thing to absorb art in moral purposes. I thought that Rossetti's poetry showed how possible it is, without making conscious compromise with that puritan principle of doing good of which Keats at one period became enamoured, to be unconsciously making for moral ends. There was for me a passive puritanism in *Jenny* which lived and worked together with the poet's purely artistic passion for doing his work supremely well. Every thought in **Dante at Verona** and **The Last Confession** seemed mixed with and coloured by a personal moral instinct that was safe and right.

This was perhaps the only noticeable feature of my lecture, and knowing Rossetti's nature, as since the lecture I have learned to know it, I feel no great surprise that such pleading for the moral impulses animating his work should have been of all things the most likely to engage his affections. Just as Coleridge always resented the imputation that he had ever been concerned with Wordsworth and Southey in the establishment of a school of poetry, and contended that, in common with his colleagues, he had been inspired by no desire save that of imitating the best examples of Greece and Home, so Rossetti (at least throughout the period of my acquaintance with him) invariably shrank from classification with the poetry of aestheticism, and aspired to the fame of a poet who had been prompted primarily by the highest of spiritual emotions, and to whom the sensations of the body were as naught, unless they were sanctified by the concurrence of the soul. My lecture was printed, but quite a year elapsed after its preparation before it occurred to me that Rossetti himself might derive a moment's gratification from knowledge of the fact that he had one ardent upholder and sincere well-wisher hitherto unknown to him. At length I sent him a copy of the magazine containing my lecture on his poetry. A post or two later brought me the following reply:

Dear Mr. Caine,--

I am much struck by the generous enthusiasm displayed in your Lecture, and by the ability with which it is written. Your estimate of the impulses influencing my poetry is such as I should wish it to suggest, and this suggestion, I believe, it will have always for a true-hearted nature. You say that you are grateful to me: my response is, that I am grateful to you: for you have spoken up heartily and unfalteringly for the work you love.

I daresay you sometimes come to London. I should be very glad to know you, and would ask you, if you thought of calling, to give me a day's notice when to expect you, as I am not always able to see visitors without appointment. The afternoon, about 5, might suit me, or else the evening about 9.30. With all best wishes, yours sincerely,

D. G. Rossetti.

This was the first of nearly two hundred letters in all received from Rossetti in the course of our acquaintance. A day or two later the following supplementary note reached me:

> I return your article. In reading it, I feel it a
> distinction that my minute plot in the poetic field should
> have attracted the gaze of one who is able to traverse its
> widest ranges with so much command. I shall be much pleased
> if the plan of calling on me is carried out soon--at any
> rate I trust it will be so eventually.... Have you got, or
> do you know, my book of translations called Dante and his
> Circle? If not, I 'll send you one....
>
> I have been reading again your article on The Supernatural
> in Poetry. It is truly admirable--such work must soon make
> you a place. The dramatic paper I thought suffered from some
> immaturity.

It is hardly necessary to say that I was equally delighted with the warmth of the reception accorded to my essay, and with the revelation the letters appeared to contain of a sincere and unselfish nature. My purpose, however, which was a modest one, had been served, and I made no further attempt to continue the correspondence, least of all did I expect or desire to originate anything of the nature of a friendship. In my reply to his note, however, I had asked him to accept the dedication of a little work of mine, and when, with abundant courtesy, he had declined to do so on very sufficient grounds, I felt satisfied that matters between us should rest where they were. It is a pleasing recollection, nevertheless, that Rossetti himself had taken a different view of the relation that had grown up between us, and by many generous appeals induced me to put by all further thoughts of abandoning the correspondence out of regard for him. There had ensued an interval in which I did not write to him, whereupon he addressed to me a hurried note, saying:

Let me have a line from you. I am haunted by the idea, that
in declining the dedication, I may have hurt you. I assure
you I should be proud to be associated in any way with your
work, but gave you my very reasons.

I shall be pleased if you do not think them sufficient, and
still carry out your original intention.... At least write
to me.

I replied to this letter (containing, as it did, the expression of so much more
than the necessary solicitude), by saying that I too had been haunted, but it had
been by the fear that I had been asking too much of his attention. As to the dedication, so far from feeling hurt, by Rossetti's declining it, I had grown to see that
such was the only course that remained to him to take. The terms in which he had
replied to my offer of it (so far from being of a kind to annoy or hurt me), had, to my
thinking, been only generous, sympathetic, and beautiful. Again he wrote:

My dear Caine,--

Let me assure you at once that correspondence with yourself
is one of my best pleasures, and that you cannot write too
much or too often for *me*; though after what you have told
me as to the apportioning of your time, I should be
unwilling to encroach unduly upon it. Neither should I on my
side prove very tardy in reply, as you are one to whom I
find there *is* something to say when I sit down with a pen
and paper. I have a good deal of enforced evening leisure,
as it is seldom I can paint or draw by gaslight. It would
not be right in me to refrain from saying that to meet with
one so "leal and true" to myself as you are has been a
consolation amid much discouragement.... I perceive you have
had a complete poetic career which you have left behind to
strike out into wider waters.... The passage on Night, which

you say was written under the planet Shelley, seems to me (and to my brother, to whom I read it) to savour more of the "mortal moon"--that is, of a weird and sombre Elizabethanism, of which Beddoes may be considered the modern representative. But we both think it has an unmistakeable force and value; and if you can write better poetry than this, let your angel say unto you, **Write**.

I take it that it would be wholly unwise of me in selecting excerpts from Rossetti's letters entirely to withhold the passages that concern exclusively (so far as their substance goes) my own early doings or try-ings-to-do; for it ought to be a part of my purpose to lay bare the beginnings of that friendship by virtue of which such letters exist. I can only ask the readers of these pages to accept my assurance, that whatever the number and extent of the passages which I publish that are necessarily in themselves of more interest to myself personally than to the public generally, they are altogether disproportionate to the number and extent of those I withhold. I cannot, however, resist the conclusion that such picture as they afford of a man beyond the period of middle life capable of bending to a new and young friend, and of thinking with and for him, is not without an exceptional literary interest as being so contrary to every-day experience. Hence, I am not without hope that the occasional references to myself which in the course of these extracts I shall feel it necessary to introduce, may be understood to be employed by me as much for their illustrative value (being indicative of Rossetti's character), as for any purpose less purely impersonal.

The passage of verse referred to was copied out for Rossetti in reply to an inquiry as to whether I had written poetry. Prompted no doubt by the encouragement derived in this instance, I submitted from time to time other verses to Rossetti, as subsequent letters show, but it says something for the value of his praise that whatever the measure of it when his sympathies were fairly aroused, and whatever his natural tendency to look for the characteristic merits rather than defects of compositions referred to his judgment, his candour was always prominent among his good qualities when censure alone required to be forthcoming. Among many frank utterances of an opinion early formed, that whatever my potentialities as a writer of prose, I had but small vocation as a writer of poetry, I preserve one such utterance, which will, I trust, be found not less interesting to other readers from affording a glimpse of the writer's attitude towards the old controversy touching the several and distinguishing elements that contribute to make good prose on the one hand and good verse on the other.

On one occasion he had sent me his fine sonnet on Keats, then just written, and, in acknowledging the receipt of it with many expressions of admiration, I remarked that for some days I had been struggling desperately, in all senses, to in-cubate a sonnet on the same somewhat hackneyed subject. I had not written a line or put pen to paper for the purpose, but I could tell him, in general terms, what my unaccomplished marvel of sonnet-craft was to be about.

Rossetti replied saying that the scheme for a sonnet was "extremely beautiful," and urging me to "do it at once." Alas for my intrepidity, "do it" I did, with the re-sult of awakening my correspondent to the certainty that, whatever embowerings I had in my mind, that shy bird the sonnet would seek in vain for a nest to hide in there. It asked so much special courage to send a first attempt at sonneteering to the greatest living master of the sonnet that moral daring alone ought to have got me off lightly, but here is Rossetti's reply, valuable now, as well for the view it affords of the poet's attitude towards the sonnet as a medium of expression, as for other reasons already assigned. The opening passage alludes to a lyric of humble life.

You may be sure I do not mean essential discouragement when I say that, full as *Nell* is of reality and pathos, your swing of arm seems to me firmer and freer in prose than in verse. I do think I see your field to lie chiefly in the achievements of fervid and impassioned prose.... I am sure that, when sending me your first sonnet, you wished me to say quite frankly what I think of it. Well, I do not think it shows a special vocation for this condensed and emphatic form. The prose version you sent me seems to say much more distinctly what this says with some want of force. The octave does not seem to me very clearly put, and the sestet does not emphasize in a sufficiently striking way the idea which the prose sketch conveyed to me,--that of Keats's special privilege in early death: viz., the lovely monumentalized image he bequeathed to us of the young poet. Also I must say that more special original-ity and even *newness* (though this might be called a vulgarizing word), of thought and picture in individual lines--more of this than I find here--seems to me the very first qualification of a sonnet--otherwise it puts forward no right to be so short, but might seem a severed passage from a longer poem depending on development. I would almost counsel you to try the same theme again--or else some other theme in sonnet-form. I thought the passage on Night you sent showed an aptitude for choice imagery. I should much like to see something which you view as your best poetic effort hitherto. After all, there is no need that every gifted writer should take the path of poetry--still less of sonneteering. I am confident in your preference for frankness on my part.

I tried the theme again before I abandoned it, and was so fortunate as to get him to admit a degree of improvement such as led to his desiring to recall his conjectural judgment on my possibilities as a sonnet-writer, but as the letters in which he characterises the advance are neither so terse in criticism, nor so interesting from the exposition of principles, as the one quoted, I pass them by. With more confidence in my ultimate comparative success than I had ever entertained, Rossetti was only anxious that I should engage in that work to which I. could address myself with a sense of command; and I think it will be agreed that, where temperate confidence in what the future may legitimately hold for one is united to earnest and rightly directed endeavour in the present, it is often a good thing for the man who stands on the threshold of life (to whom, nevertheless, the path passed seems ever to stretch out of sight backwards) to be told the extent to which, little enough at the most, his clasp (to use a phrase of Mr. Browning) may be equal to his grasp.

My residing, as I did, at a distance from London, was at once the difficulty which for a time prevented our coming together and the necessity for correspondence by virtue of which these letters exist. As I failed, however, from hampering circumstance, to meet at once with himself, Rossetti invariably displayed a good deal of friendly anxiety to bring me into contact with his friends as frequently as occasion rendered it feasible to do so. In this way I met with Mr. Madox Brown, who was at the moment engaged on his admirable frescoes in the Manchester Town Hall, and in this way also I met with other friends of his resident in my neighbourhood. When I came to know him more intimately I perceived that besides the kindliness of intention which had prompted him to bring me into what he believed to be agreeable associations, he had adopted this course from the other motive of desiring to be reassured as to the comparative harmlessness of my personality, for he usually followed the introduction to a friend by a private letter of thanks for the reception accorded me, and a number of dexterously manipulated allusions, which always, I found, produced the desired result of eliciting the required information (to be gleaned only from personal intercourse) as to my manner and habits. Later in our acquaintance, I found that he, like all meditative men, had the greatest conceivable dread of being taken unawares, and that there was no safer way for any fresh acquaintance to insure his taking violently against him, than to take the step of coming down upon him suddenly, and without appointment, or before a sufficient time had elapsed between the beginning of the friendship and the actual personal encounter, to admit of his forming preconceived ideas of the manner of man to expect. The agony he suffered upon the unexpected visit of even the most ardent of well-wishers could scarcely be realised at the moment, from the apparent ease, and assumed indifference of his outward bearing, and could only be known to those who were with him after the trying ordeal had been passed, or immediately before the threatened intrusion had been consummated.

Early in our correspondence a friend of his, an art critic of distinction, visited Liverpool with the purpose of lecturing on the valuable examples of Byzantine art in the Eoyal Institution of that city. The lecture was, I fear, almost too good and quite too technical for some of the hearers, many of whom claim (and with reason) to be lovers of art, and cover the walls of their houses with beautiful representations of lovely landscape, but at the same time erect huge furnaces which emit vast volumes of black smoke such as prevent the sky of any Liverpool landscape being for an instant lovely. I doubt if the lecture could have been treated more popularly, but there was manifestly a lack of merited appreciation. The archaisms of some of the pictures chosen for illustration (early Byzantine examples exclusively) appeared to cause certain of the audience to smile at much of the lecturer's enthusiasm. Fortunately the man chiefly concerned seemed unconscious of all this. And indeed, however he fared in public, in private he was only too "dreadfully attended." After the lecture a good many folks gave him the benefit of their invaluable opinions on various art questions, and some, as was natural, made pitiful slips. I observed with secret and scarcely concealed satisfaction his courageous loyalty in defence of his friends, and his hitting out in their defence when he believed them to be assailed. One superlative intelligence, eager to do honour to the guest, yet ignorant of his claim to such honour, gave him a wonderfully facile and racy comment on the pre-Raphaelite painters, and, in particular, made the ridiculous blunder of a deliberate attack upon Rossetti, and then paused for breath and for the lecturer's appreciative response; of course, Rossetti's friend was not to be drawn into such disloyalty for an instant, even to avoid the risk of ruffling the plumage of the mightiest of the corporate cacklers. Rossetti had permitted me in his name to meet his friend, and in writing subsequently I alluded to the affection with which he had been mentioned, also to something that had been said of his immediate surroundings, and to that frank championing of his claims which I have just described. Rossetti's reply to this is interesting as affording a pathetic view of his isolation of life and of the natural affectionateness of his nature:

I am very glad you were welcomed by dear staunch S------, as I felt sure you would be. He holds the honourable position of being almost the only living art-critic who has really himself worked through the art-schools practically, and learnt to draw and paint. He is one of my oldest and best friends, of whom few can be numbered at my age, from causes only too varying.

Go from me, summer friends, and tarry not,-- I am no summer friend, but wintry cold, etc.

So be it, as needs must be,--not for all, let us hope, and not with all, as good S------ shews. I have not seen him since his return. I wrote him a line to thank him for his friendly reception of you, and he wrote in return to thank me for your acquaintance, and spoke very pleasantly of you. Your youth seems to have surprised him. I sent a letter of his to your address. I hope you may see more of him. . . . You mention something he said to you of me and my surroundings. They are certainly *quiet* enough as fax as retirement goes, and I have often thought I should enjoy the

presence of a congenial and intellectual housefellow and
boardfellow in this big barn of mine, which is actually
going to rack and ruin for want of use. But where to find
the welcome, the willing, and the able combined in one? . . .
I was truly concerned to hear of the attack of ill-health
you have suffered from, though you do not tell me its exact
nature. I hope it was not accompanied by any such symptoms
as you mentioned before. . . . I myself have had similar
symptoms (though not so fully as you describe), and have
spat blood at intervals for years, but now think nothing of
it--nor indeed ever did,--waiting for further alarm signals
which never came.

. . . By-the-bye, I have since remembered that Burne Jones,
many years ago, had such an experience as you spoke of
before--quite as bad certainly. He was weak for some time
after, and has frequently been reminded in minor ways of it,
but seems now (at about forty-six or forty-seven) to be more
settled in health and stronger, perhaps, than ever
before.... Your letter holds out the welcome probability of
meeting you here ere long.

This friendly solicitude regarding my health was excited by the revelation of
what seemed to me at the time a startling occurrence, but has doubtless frequently
happened to others, and has certainly since happened to myself without provoking
quite so much outcry. The blood-spitting to which Rossetti here alleges he was liable was of a comparatively innocent nature. In later years he was assuredly not altogether a hero as to personal suffering, and I afterwards found that, upon the periodical recurrence of the symptom, he never failed to become convinced that he spat
arterial blood, and that on each occasion he had received his death-warrant. Proof
enough was adduced that the blood came from the minor vessels of the throat, and
this was undoubtedly the case in the majority of instances, but whether the same
explanation applied to one alarming occurrence which I shall now recount, seems

to me uncertain.

During the two or three weeks preceding our departure for Cumberland, in the autumn of 1881, during the time of our residence there and during the first few weeks after our return to London, Rossetti was afflicted by a violent cough. I noticed that it troubled him almost exclusively in the night-time, and after the taking of chloral; that it was sometimes attended by vomiting; and that it invariably shook his whole system so terribly as to leave him for a while entirely prostrate from sheer physical exhaustion. The spectacle was a painful one, and I watched closely its phenomena, with the result of convincing myself that whatever radical mischief lay at the root of it, the damage done was seriously augmented by a conscious giving way to it, induced, I thought, by hope of the relief it sometimes afforded the stomach to get rid of the nauseous drug at a moment of reduced digestive vitality. Then it became my fear that in these violent and prolonged retchings internal injury might be sustained, and so I begged him to try to restrain the tendency to cough so much and often. He took the remonstrance with great goodnature (observing that he perceived I thought he was putting it on), but I was not conscious that at any moment he acted upon my suggestion. At the time in question I was under the necessity of leaving him for a day or two every week in order to fulfil, a course of lecturing engagements at a distance; and upon my return in each instance I was told much of all that had happened to him in the interval. On one occasion, however, I was conscious that something had occurred of which he desired to make a disclosure, for amongst the gifts that Rossetti had not got was that of concealing from his intimate friends any event, however trifling, or however important, which weighed upon his mind. At length I begged him to say what had happened, whereupon, with great reluctance and many protestations of his intention to observe silence, and constant injunctions as to secrecy, he told me that during the night of my absence, in the midst of one of his bouts of coughing, he had discharged an enormous quantity of blood. "I know this is the final signal," he said, "and I shall die." I did my utmost to compose him by recounting afresh the personal incident hinted at, with many added features of (I trust) justifiable exaggeration, but it is hardly necessary to say that I did not hold the promise I gave him as to secrecy sufficiently sacred, or so exclusive, as to forbid my revealing the whole circumstance to his medical attendant. I may add that from that moment the cough entirely disappeared.

To return from this reminiscence of a later period to the beginnings, three years earlier, of our correspondence, I will bring the present chapter to a close by quoting short passages from three letters written on the eve of my first visit to Rossetti, in 1880:

> I will be truly glad to meet you when you come to town. You
> will recognise the hole-and-cornerest of all existences; but
> I'll read you a ballad or two, and have Brown's report to
> back my certainty of liking you.... I would propose that you
> should dine with me at 8.30 on the Monday of your visit, and
> spend the evening.... Better come at 5.30 to 6 (if feasible
> to you), that I may try to show you a picture by daylight...
> Of course, when I speak of your dining with me, I mean tete-
> a-tete, and without ceremony of any kind. I usually dine in
> my studio, and in my painting coat. I judge this will reach
> you in time for a note to reach *me*. Telegrams I hate. In
> hope of the pleasure of a meeting, yours ever.

How that "hole-and-cornerest of all existences" struck an ardent admirer of the poet-painter's genius, and a devoted lover of his personal character, as then revealed to me, I hope to describe in a later section of this book. Meantime I must proceed to cull from the epistolary treasures I possess a number of interesting passages on literary subjects, called forth in the course of an intercourse which, at that stage, had few topics of a private nature to divert it from a channel of impersonal discussion. It is a fact that the letters written to me by Rossetti in the year 1880 deal so largely with literary affairs (chiefly of the past) as to be almost capable of ***verbatim*** reproduction, even at the present short interval after his death. If they were to be reproduced, they would be found to cover two hundred pages of the present volume, and to be so easy, fluent, varied, and wholly felicitous as to style, and full of research and reflection as to substance, as probably to earn for the writer a foremost place for epistolary power. Indeed, I am not without hope that this accession of a fresh reputation may result even upon the excerpts I have decided to introduce.

CHAPTER IV.

It was very natural that our earliest correspondence should deal chiefly with Rossetti's own works, for those works gave rise to it. He sent me a copy of his translations from early Italian poets (Dante and his Circle), and a copy of his story, entitled **Hand and Soul**. In posting the latter, he said:

I don't know if you ever saw a sort of story of mine called Hand and Soul. I send you one with this, as printed to go in my poems (though afterwards omitted, being, nevertheless, more poem than story). I printed it since in the Fortnightly--and, I believe, abolished one or two extra sentimentalities. You may have seen it there. In case it's stale, I enclose with this a sonnet which *must* be new, for I only wrote it the other day.

I have already, in the proper place in this volume, said how the story first struck me. Perhaps I had never before reading it seen quite so clearly the complete mission as well as enforced limitations of true art. All the many subtle gradations in the development of purpose were there beautifully pictured in a little creation that was charming in the full sense of a word that has wellnigh lost its charm. For all such as cried out against pursuits originating in what Keats had christened "the infant chamber of sensation," and for all such as demanded that everything we do should be done to "strengthen God among men," the story provided this answer: "When at any time hath He cried unto thee, saying, 'My son, lend me thy shoulder, for I fall'?"

The sonnet sent, and spoken of as having just been written (the letter bears post-mark February 1880), was the sonnet on the sonnet. It is throughout beautiful and in two of its lines (those depicting the dark wharf and the black Styx) truly magnificent. It appears most to be valued, however, as affording a clue to the attitude of mind adopted towards this form of verse by the greatest master of it in modern poetry. I think it is Mr. Pater who says that a fine poem in manuscript carries an aroma with it, and a sensation of music. I must have enjoyed the pleasure of such a presence somewhat frequently about this period, for many of the poems that afterwards found places in the second volume of ballads and sonnets were sent to me from time to time.

I should like to know what were the three or four vols. on Italian poetry which you mentioned in a former letter, and which my book somewhat recalled to your mind. I was not aware of any such extensive **English** work on the subject. Or do you perhaps mean Trucchi's Italian Dugento Poesie inedite? I am sincerely delighted at your rare interest in what I have sent you--both the translations, story, etc.--I enclose three printed pieces meant for my volume but omitted:--the ballad, because it deals trivially with a base amour (it was written **very** early) and is therefore really reprehensible to some extent; the Shakspeare sonnet, because of its incongruity with the rest of the poems, and also because of the insult (however jocose) to the worshipful body of tailors; and the political sonnet for reasons which are plain enough, though the date at which I wrote it (not

without feeling) involves now a prophetic value. In a MS.
vol. I have a sonnet (1871) After the German Subjugation of
France, which enforces the prophecy by its fulfilment. In
this MS. vol. are a few pieces which were the only ones I
copied in doubt as to their admission when I printed the
poems, but none of which did I admit. One day I 'll send it
for you to look at. It contains a few sonnets bearing on
public matters, but only a few. Tell me what you think on
reading my things. All you said in your letter of this
morning was very grateful to me. I have a fair amount by me
in the way of later MS. which I may shew you some day when
we meet. Meanwhile I feel that your energies are already in
full swing--work coming on the heels of work--and that your
time cannot long be deferred as regards your place as a
writer.

The ballad of which Rossetti here speaks as dealing trivially with a base amour
is entitled **Dennis Shand**. Though an early work, it affords perhaps the best evidence extant of the poet's grasp of the old ballad style: it runs easiest of all his ballads, and is in some respects his best. Mr. J. A. Symonds has, in my judgment, made
the error of speaking of Rossetti as incapable of reproducing the real note of such
ballads as **Chevy Chase** and **Sir Patrick Spens**. Mr. Symonds was right in his eloquent comments (Macmillan's Magazine, February 1882), so far as they concern the
absence from **Rose Mary, The King's Tragedy, and The White Ship** of the sinewy
simplicity of the old singers. But in those poems Rossetti attempted quite another
thing. There is a development of the English ballad that is entirely of modern product, being far more complex than the primitive form, and getting rid to some extent
of the out-worn notion of the ballad being actually sung to set music, but retaining
enough of the sweep of a free rhythm to carry a sensible effect as of being chanted
when read. This is a sort of ballad-romance, such as **Christabel** and **The Lay of the
Last Minstrel**; and this, and this only, was what Rossetti aimed after, and entirely
compassed in his fine works just mentioned. But (as Rossetti himself remarked to
me in conversation when I repeated Mr. Symonds's criticism, and urged my own

grounds of objection to it), that the poet was capable of the directness and simplicity which characterise the early ballad-writers, he had given proof in ***The Staff and Scrip and Stratton Water. Dennis Shand*** is valuable as evidence going in the same direction, but the author's objection to it, on ethical grounds, must here prevail to withhold it from publication.

The Shakspeare sonnet, spoken of in the letter as being withheld on account of its incongruity with the rest of the poems, was published in an early ***Academy***, notwithstanding its jocose allusion to the worshipful body of tailors. As it is little known, and really very powerful in itself, and interesting as showing the author's power over words in a new direction, I print it in this place.

ON THE SITE OF A MULBERRY TREE.

Planted by Wm. Shakspeare; felled by the Rev. F. Gastrell.
This tree, here fall'n, no common birth or death
Shared with its kind. The world's enfranchised son,
Who found the trees of Life and Knowledge one,
Here set it, frailer than his laurel-wreath.

Shall not the wretch whose hand it fell beneath
Rank also singly--the supreme unhung?
Lo! Sheppard, Turpin, pleading with black tongue
This viler thief's unsuffocated breath!

We 'U search thy glossary, Shakspeare! whence almost,
And whence alone, some name shall be reveal'd
For this deaf drudge, to whom no length of ears
Sufficed to catch the music of the spheres;
Whose soul is carrion now,--too mean to yield
Some tailor's ninth allotment of a ghost.

Stratford-on-Avon.

The other sonnets referred to, those, namely, on the *French Liberation of Italy*, and the *German Subjugation of France*, display all Rossetti's mastery of craftsmanship. In strength of vision, in fertility of rhythmic resource, in pliant handling, these sonnets are, in my judgment, among the best written by the author; and if I do not quote them here, or altogether regret that they do not appear in the author's works, it is not because I have any sense of their possibly offending against the delicate sensibilities of an age in which it seems necessary to hide out of sight whatever appears to impinge upon the domain of what is called our lower nature.

The circumstance has hardly obtained even so much as a passing mention that Rossetti made certain very important additions to the ballad of *Sister Helen*, just before passing the old volume through the press afresh for publication, contemporaneously with the new book. The letters I am now to quote show the origin of those additions, and are interesting, as affording a view of the author's estimate of the gain in respect of completeness of conception, and sterner tragic spirit which resulted upon their adoption.

I was very glad to have the three articles together, including the one in which you have written on myself. Looking at this again, it seems to me you must possess the *best* edition (the Tauchnitz, which has my last emendations). Otherwise I have been meaning all along to offer you a copy of this edition, as I have some. Who was your informant as to dates of the poems, etc.? They are not correct, yet show some inkling. *Jenny* (in a first form) was written almost as early as *The Blessed Damozel*, which I wrote (and have altered little since), when I was eighteen. It was first printed when I was twenty-one. Of the first *Jenny*, perhaps fifty lines survive here and there, but I felt it was quite beyond me then (a world I was then happy enough to be a stranger to), and later I re-wrote it completely. I will give you correct particulars at some time. *Sister Helen*, I may mention, was written either in 1851 or beginning of 1852, and was printed in something called *The Duesseldorf Annual* [5] (published in Germany) in 1853; though since much revised in detail--not in the

---

5   In The Duesseldorf Annual the poem was signed H. H. H., and
      in explanation of this signature Rossetti wrote on his own
      copy the following characteristic note:--"The initials as
      above were taken from the lead-pencil."

main. You will be horror-struck to hear that the first main addition to this poem was made by me only a few days ago!--eight stanzas (six together, and two scattered ones) involving a new incident!! Your hair is on end, I know, but if you heard the stanzas, they would smooth if not curl it. The gain is immense.

In reply to this I told Rossetti that, as a "jealous honourer" of his, I confessed to some uneasiness when I read that he had been making important additions to *Sister Helen*. That I could not think of a stage of the story that would bear so to be severed from what goes before or comes after it as to admit of interpolation might not of itself go for much; but the entire ballad was so rounded into unity, one incident so naturally begetting the next, and the combined incidents so properly building up a fabric of interest of which the meaning was all inwoven, that I could not but fear that whatever the gain in certain directions, the additions of any stanzas involving a new incident might, in some measure, cripple the rest. Even though the new stanzas were as beautiful, or yet more beautiful than the old ones, and the incident as impressive as any that goes before it, or comes after it, the gain to the poem as an individual creation was not, I thought, assured because people used to say my style was hard.

Rossetti was mistaken in supposing that I possessed the latest and best edition of his *Poems*, but I had seen the latest of all English editions, and had noted in it several valuable emendations which, in subsequent quotation, I had been careful to employ. One of these seemed to me to involve an immeasurable gain. A stanza of *Sister Helen*, in its first form, ran:

> Oh, the wind is sad in the iron chill,
> Sister Helen,
> And weary sad they look by the hill;
> But Keith of Ewern 's sadder still,
> Little brother.--etc. etc.
> In the later edition the fourth line of this stanza ran:

> But he and I are sadder still.

The change adds enormously to one's estimate of the characterisation. All through the ballad one wants to feel that, despite the bitterness of her speech, the heart of the relentless witch is breaking. Like *The Broken Heart* of Ford, the ballad with the amended line was a masterly picture of suppressed emotion. I hoped the new incident touched the same chord. Rossetti replied:

> Thanks for your present letter, which I will answer with pleasurable care. At present I send you the Tauchnitz edition of my things. The bound copy is hideous, but more convenient--the other pretty. You will find a good many things bettered (I believe) even on the *latest* English edition. I did not remember that the line you quote from Sister Helen appeared in the new form at all in an English issue. I am greatly pleased at your thinking it, as I do, quite a transfiguring change... The next point I have marked in your letter is that about the additions to Sister Helen. Of course I knew that your hair must arise from your scalp in protest. But what should you say if Keith of Ewern were a three days' bridegroom--if the spell had begun on the wedding-morning--and if the bride herself became the last pleader for mercy? I fancy you will see your way now. The culminating, irresistible provocation helps, I think, to humanize Helen, besides lifting the tragedy to a yet sterner height.

If I had felt (as Rossetti predicted I should) an uneasy sensation about the roots of the hair upon hearing that he was making important additions to the ballad which seemed to me to be the finest of his works, the sensation in that quarter was not less, but more, upon learning the nature of those additions. But I mistook the character of the new incidents. That Sister Helen should be herself the aban-doned *bride* of Ewern (for so I understood the poet's explanation), and, as such, the last pleader for mercy, pointed, I thought, in the direction of the humanizing emendation ("But he and I are sadder still ") which had given me so much pleasure. That Keith of Ewern should be a three-days' bridegroom, and that the spell should begin on the wedding morning, were incidents that seemed to intensify every line of the poem. In this view of Rossetti's account of the additions, there were certainly difficulties out of which I could see no way, but I seemed to realise that Helen's hate, like Macbeth's ambition, had overleaped itself, and fallen on the other side, and that she would undo her work, if to return were not harder than to go on; her initiate sensibility had gained hard use, but even as hate recoils on love, so out of the ashes of hate love had arisen. In this view of the characterisation of Helen, the parallel with Macbeth struck me more and more as I thought of it. When Macbeth kills Duncan, and hears the grooms of the chamber cry in their sleep--"God bless us," he cannot say "Amen,"

> I had most need of blessing, and Amen
> Stuck in my throat.

Helen pleading too late for mercy against the potency of the spell she herself had raised, seemed to me an incident that raised her to the utmost height of tragic creation. But Rossetti's purpose was at once less ambitious and more satisfying.

> Your passage as to the changes in **Sister Helen** could not
> well (with all its fine suggestiveness) be likely to meet
> exactly a reality which had not been submitted to your eye
> in the verses themselves. It is the **bride of Keith** who is
> the last pleader--as vainly as the others, and with a yet
> more exulting development of vengeance in the forsaken
> witch. The only acknowledgment by her of a mutual misery is
> still found in the line you spotted as so great a gain
> before, and in the last line she speaks. I ought to have
> sent the stanzas to explain them properly, but have some
> reluctance to ventilate them at present, much as I should
> like the opportunity of reading them to you. They will meet
> your eye in due course, and I am sure of your approval also
> as regards their value to the ballad.... Don't let the
> changes in **Helen** get wind overmuch. I want them to be new

when published. Answer this when you can. I like getting
your epistles.

The fresh stanzas in question, which had already obtained the suffrages of his
brother, of Mr. Bell Scott, and other qualified critics, were subsequently sent to
me. They are as follows. After Keith of Keith, the father of Sister Helen's sometime
lover, has pleaded for his son in vain, the last suppliant to arrive is his son's bride:

A lady here, by a dark steed brought,
Sister Helen,
So darkly clad I saw her not.
"See her now or never see aught,
Little brother!"
(O Mother, Mary Mother,
Whit more to see, between Hell and Heaven?)

"Her hood falls back, and the moon shines fair,
Sister Helen,
On the Lady of Ewern's golden hair."
"Blest hour of my power and her despair,
Little brother!"
(O Mother, Mary Mother,
Hour blest and bann'd, between Hell and Heaven!)

"Pale, pale her cheeks, that in pride did glow,
Sister Helen,
'Neath the bridal-wreath three days ago."
"One morn for pride and three days for woe,
Little brother!"
(O Mother, Mary Mother,
Three days, three nights, between Hell and Heaven!)

"Her clasp'd hands stretch from her bending head,

Sister Helen;
With the loud wind's wail her sobs are wed."
"What wedding-strains hath her bridal bed,
Little brother?"
(O Mother, Mary Mother,
What strain but death's, between Hell and Heaven?)

"She may not speak, she sinks in a swoon,
Sister Helen,--
She lifts her lips and gasps on the moon."
"Oh! might I but hear her soul's blithe tune,
Little brother!"
(O Mother, Mary Mother,
Her woe's dumb cry, between Hell and Heaven!)

"They've caught her to Westholm's saddle-bow,
Sister Helen,
And her moonlit hair gleams white in its flow."
"Let it turn whiter than winter snow,
Little brother!"
(O Mother, Mary Mother,
Woe-withered gold, between Hell and Heaven!)

Besides these there are two new stanzas, one going before, and the other following after, the six stanzas quoted, but as the scattered passages involve no farther
incident, and are rather of interest as explaining and perfecting the idea here expressed, than valuable in themselves, I do not reprint them.

I think it must be allowed, by fit judges, that nothing more subtly conceived
than this incident can be met with in English poetry, though something akin to
it was projected by Coleridge in an episode of his contemplated *Michael Scott*. It
is--in the full sense of an abused epithet--too weird to be called picturesque. But
the crowning merit of the poem still lies, as I have said, in the domain of character.
Through all the outbursts of her ignescent hate Sister Helen can never lose the in-

eradicable relics of her human love:

But he and I are sadder still.

As Rossetti from time to time made changes in his poems, he transcribed the amended verses in a copy of the Tauchnitz edition which he kept constantly by him. Upon reference to this little volume some days after his death, I discovered that he had prefaced **Sister Helen** with a note written in pencil, of which he had given me the substance in conversation about the time of the publication of the altered version, but which he abandoned while passing the book through the press. The note (evidently designed to precede the ballad) runs:

It is not unlikely that some may be offended at seeing the additions made thus late to the ballad of **S. H.** My best excuse is that I believe some will wonder with myself that such a climax did not enter into the first conception.
At the foot of the poem this further note is written:

I wrote this ballad either in 1851 or early in 1852. It was printed in a thing called **The Duesseldorf Annual** in (I think) 1853--published in Germany.[6]

6   In the same private copy of the Poems the following explanatory passage was written over the much-discussed sonnet, entitled, The Monochord:--"That sublimated mood of the soul in which a separate essence of itself seems as it were to oversoar and survey it." Neither the style nor the substance is characteristic of Rossetti, and though I do not at the moment remember to have met with the passage elsewhere, I doubt not it is a quotation. That quotation marks are employed is not in itself evidence of much moment, for Rossetti had Coleridge's enjoyment of a literary practical joke, and on one occasion prefixed to a story in manuscript a long passage on noses purporting to be from Tristram Shandy, but which is certainly not discoverable in Sterne's story.
The next letter I shall quote appears to explain itself:

It seemed certain that **Hand and Soul** ought not to continue to lie in the back numbers, of a magazine. The story, being more poem than aught else, might properly lay claim to a place in any fresh collection of the author's works. I could see no natural objection on the score of its being written in prose. As Coleridge and Wordsworth both aptly said, prose is not the antithesis of poetry; science and poetry may stand over-against each other, as Keats implied by his famous toast: "Confusion to the man who took the poetry out of the moon," but prose and poetry surely are or may be practically one. We know that in rhythmic flow they sometimes come very close together, and nowhere closer than in the heightened prose and the poetry of Rossetti. Poetic prose may not be the best prose, just as (to use a false antithesis) dull poetry is called prosaic; but there is no natural antagonism between prose and <u>verse as literary mediums, provided always that the spir</u>it that animates them be

There is a last point in your long letter which I have not noticed, though it interested me much: viz., what you say of your lecture on my poetry; your idea of possibly returning to and enlarging it would, if carried out, be welcome to me. I suppose ere long I must get together such additional work as I have to show--probably a good deal added to the old vol. (which has been for some time out of print) and one longer poem by itself. *The House of Life*, when next issued, will I trust be doubled in number of sonnets; it is nearly so already. Your writing that essay in one day, and the information as to subsequent additions, I noted, and should like to see the passage on *Jenny* which you have not yet used, if extant. The time taken in composition reminds me of the fact (so long ago!) that I wrote the tale of Hand and Soul (with the exception of an opening page or two) all in one night in December 1849, beginning I suppose about 2 A.M. and ending about 7. In such a case a landscape and sky all unsurmised open gradually in the mind--a sort of spiritual *Turner*, among whose hills one ranges and in whose waters one strikes out at unknown liberty; but I have found this only in nightlong work, which I have seldom attempted, for it leaves one entirely broken, and this state was mine when I described the like of it at the close of the story, ah! once again, how long ago! I have thought of including this story in next issue of poems, but am uncertain. What think you?

akin. Rossetti himself constantly urged that in prose the first necessity was that it should be direct, and he knew no reproach of poetry more damning than to say it was written in proseman's diction. This was the key to his depreciation of Wordsworth, and doubtless it was this that ultimately operated with him to exclude the story from his published works. I took another view, and did not see that an accidental difference of outward form ought to prevent his uniting within single bookcovers productions that had so much of their essential spirit in common. Unlike the Chinese, we do not read by sight only, and there is in the story such richness, freshness, and variety of cadence, as appeal to the ear also. Prose may be the lowest order of rhythmic composition, but we know it is capable of such purity, sweetness, strength, and elasticity, as entitle it to a place as a sister art with poetry. Milton, however, although he wrote the noblest of English prose, seemed more than half ashamed of it, as of a kind of left-handed performance. Goethe and Wordsworth, on the other hand, not to speak of Coleridge and Shelley (or yet of Keats, whose letters are among the very best examples extant of the English epistolary style), wrote prose of wonderful beauty and were not ashamed of it. In Milton's case the subjects, I imagine, were to blame for his indifference to his achievements in prose, for not even the Westminster Convention, or the divorce topics of *Tetrachordon*, or yet the liberty of the press, albeit raised to a level of philosophic first principles, were quite up to those fixed stars of sublimity about which it was Milton's pleasure to revolve. *Hand and Soul* is in faultless harmony with Rossetti's work in verse, because distinguished by the same strength of imagination. That it was written in a single night seems extraordinary when viewed in relation to its sustained beauty; but it is done in a breath, and has all the excellencies of fervour and force that result upon that method of composition only.

A year or two later than the date of the correspondence with which I am now dealing, Rossetti read aloud a fragment of a story written about the period of *Hand and Soul*. It was to be entitled *St. Agnes of Intercession*, and it dealt in a mystic way with the doctrine of the transmigration of souls. He constantly expressed his intention of finishing the story, and said that, although in its existing condition it was fully as long as the companion story, it would require twice as much more to complete it. During the time of our stay at Birchington, at the beginning of 1882, he seemed anxious to get to work upon it, and had the manuscript sent down from

London for that purpose; but the packet lay unopened until after his death, when I glanced at it again to refresh my memory as to its contents. The fragment is much too inconclusive as to design to admit of any satisfying account of its plot, of which there is more, than in **Hand and Soul**. As far as it goes, it is the story of a young English painter who becomes the victim of a conviction that his soul has had a prior existence in this world. The hallucination takes entire possession of him, and so unsettles his life that he leaves England in search of relic or evidence of his spiritual "double." Finally, in a picture-gallery abroad, he comes face to face with a portrait which' he instantly recognises as the portrait of himself, both as he is now and as he was in the time of his antecedent existence. Upon inquiry, the portrait proves to be that of a distinguished painter centuries dead, whose work had long been the young Englishman's guiding beacon in methods of art. Startled beyond measure at the singular discovery of a coincidence which, superstition apart, might well astonish the most unsentimental, he sickens to a fever. Here the fragment ends. Late one evening, in August 1881, Rossetti gave me a full account of the remaining incidents, but I find myself without memoranda of what was said (it was never my habit to keep record of his or of any man's conversation), and my recollection of what passed is too indefinite in some salient particulars to make it safe to attempt to complete the outlines of the story. I consider the fragment in all respects finer than **Hand and Soul**, and the passage descriptive of the artist's identification of his own personality in the portrait on the walls of the gallery among the very finest pieces of picturesque, impassioned, and dramatic writing that Rossetti ever achieved. On one occasion I remarked incidentally upon something he had said of his enjoyment of rivers of morning air[7] in the spring of the year, that it would be an inquiry fraught with a curious interest to find out how many of those who have the greatest love of the Spring were born in it.

One felt that one could name a goodly number among the English poets living and dead. It would be an inquiry, as Hamlet might say, such as would become a woman. To this Rossetti answered that he was born on old May-day (May 12), 1828;

7   Within the period of my personal knowledge of Rossetti's
     habits, he certainly never enjoyed any "rivers of morning
     air" at all, unless they were such as visited him in a
     darkened bedchamber.

and thereupon he asked the date of my own birth.

> The comparative dates of our births are curious.... I myself
> was born on old May-Day (12th), in the year (1828) after
> that in which Blake died.... You were born, in fact, just as
> I was giving up poetry at about 25, on finding that it
> impeded attention to what constituted another aim and a
> livelihood into the bargain, *i.e.* painting. From that date
> up to the year when I published my poems, I wrote extremely
> little,--I might almost say nothing, except the renovated
> Jenny in 1858 or '59. To this again I added a passage or
> two when publishing in 1870.

Often since Rossetti's death I have reflected upon the fact that in that lengthy correspondence between us which preceded personal intimacy, he never made more than a single passing allusion to those adverse criticisms which did so much at one period to sadden and alter his life. Barely, indeed, in conversation did he touch upon that sore subject, but it was obvious enough to the closer observer, as well from his silence as from his speech, that though the wounds no longer rankled, they did not wholly heal. I take it as evidence of his desire to put by unpleasant reflections (at least whilst health was whole with him, for he too often nourished melancholy retrospects when health was broken or uncertain), that in his correspondence with me, as a young friend who knew nothing at first hand of his gloomier side, he constantly dwelt with radiant satisfaction and hopefulness on the friendly words that had been said of him. And as frequently as he called my attention to such favourable comment, he did so without a particle of vanity, and with only such joy as he may feel who knows in his secret heart he has depreciators, to find that he has ardent upholders too. In one letter he says:

I should say that between the appearance of the poems and your lecture, there was one article on the subject, of a very masterly kind indeed, by some very scholarly hand (unknown to me), in the **New York Catholic World** (I think in 1874). I retain this article, and will some day send it you to read.

He sent me the article, and I found it, as he had found it, among the best things written on the subject. Naturally, the criticism was best where the subject dealt with impinged most upon the spirit of mediaeval Catholicism. Perhaps Catholicism is itself essentially mediaeval, and perhaps a man cannot possibly be, what the ***Catholic World*** article called Rossetti, a "mediaeval artist heart and soul," without partaking of a strong religious feeling that is primarily Catholic--so much were the religion and art of the middle ages knit each to each. Yet, upon reading the article, I doubted one of the writer's inferences, namely, that Rossetti had inherited a Catholic devotion to the Madonna. Not his ***Ave*** only seemed to me to live in an atmosphere of tender and sensitive devotion, but I missed altogether in it, as in other poems of Rossetti, that old, continual, and indispensable Catholic note of mystic Divine love lost in love of humanity which, I suppose, Mr. Arnold would call anthropomorphism. Years later, when I came to know Rossetti personally, I perceived that the writer of the article in question had not made a bad shot for the truth. True it was, that he had inherited a strong religious spirit--such as could only be called Catholic--inherited I say, for, though from his immediate parents, he assuredly did not inherit any devotion to the Madonna, his own submission to religious influences was too unreasoning and unquestioning to be anything but intuitive. Despite some worldly-mindedness, and a certain shrewdness in the management of the more important affairs of daily life, Rossetti's attitude towards spiritual things was exactly the reverse of what we call Protestant. During the last months of his life, when the prospect of leaving the world soon, and perhaps suddenly, impressed upon his mind a deep sense of his religious position, he yielded himself up unhesitatingly to the intuitive influences I speak of; and so far from being touched by the interminable controversies which have for ages been upsetting and uprearing creeds, he seemed both naturally incapable of comprehending differences of belief, and unwilling to dwell upon them for an instant. Indeed, he constantly impressed me during the last days of his life with the conviction, that he was by religious bias of nature a monk of the middle ages.

As to the article in ***The Catholic Magazine*** I thought I perceived from a curious habit of biblical quotation that it must have been written by an Ecclesiastic. A remark in it to the effect that old age is usually more indulgent than middle life to the work of first manhood, and that, consequently, Rossetti would be a less censorious judge of his early efforts at a later period of life, seemed to show that the writer himself was no longer a young man. Further, I seemed to see that the reviewer was not a professional critic, for his work displayed few of the well-recognised trademarks with which the articles of the literary market are invariably branded. As a small matter one noticed the somewhat slovenly use of the editorial *we*, which at the fag-end of passages sometimes dropped into *I*. [Upon my remarking upon this to Rossetti he remembered incidentally that a similar confounding of the singular and plural number of the pronoun produces marvellously suggestive effects in a very different work, *Macbeth*, where the kingly *we* is tripped up by the guilty *I* in many places.] Rossetti wrote:

I am glad you liked the *Catholic World* article, which I certainly view as one of rare literary quality. I have not the least idea who is the writer, but am sorry now I never wrote to him under cover of the editor when I received it. I did send the *Dante and Circle*, but don't know if it was ever received or reviewed. As you have the vols, of *Fortnightly*, look up a little poem of mine called the *Cloud Confines*, a few months later, I suppose, than the tale. It is one of my favourites, among my own doings.

I noticed at this early period, as well as later, that in Rossetti's eyes a favourable review was always enhanced in value if the writer happened to be a stranger to him; and I constantly protested that a friend's knowledge of one's work and sympathy with it ought not to be less delightful, as such, than a stranger's, however less surprising, though at the same time the tribute that is true to one's art without auxiliary aids being brought to bear in its formation must be at once the most satisfying assurance of the purity, strength, and completeness of the art itself, and of the safe and enduring quality of the appreciation. It is true that friends who are accustomed to our habit of thought and manner of expression sometimes catch our meaning before we have expressed it Not rarely, before our thought has reached that stage at which it becomes intelligible to a stranger, a word, a look, or a gesture will convey it perfectly and fully to a friend. And what goes on between minds that exist in more or less intimate communion, goes on to a greater degree within the individual mind where the metaphysical equivalents to a word or a look answer to, and are answered by, the half-realised conception. Hence it often happens that even where our touch seems to ourselves delicate and precise, a mind not initiated in our self-chosen method of abbreviation finds only impenetrable obscurity. It is then in the tentative condition of mind just indicated that the spirit of art comes in, and enables a man so to clothe his thought in lucid words and fitting imagery that strangers may know, when they see it, all that it is, and how he came by it. Although, therefore, the praise of friends should not be less delightful, as praise, than that tendered by strangers, there is an added element of surprise and satisfaction in the latter which the former cannot bring. Rossetti certainly never over-valued the applause of his own immediate circle, but still no man was more sensible of the value of the good opinion of one or two of his immediate friends. Returning to the correspondence, he says:

> In what I wrote as to critiques on my poems, I meant to express *special* gratification from those written by strangers to myself and yet showing full knowledge of the subject and full sympathy with it. Such were Formans at the time, the American one since (and far from alone in America, but this the best) and more lately your own. Other known and unknown critics of course wrote on the book when it appeared, some very favourably and others *quite* sufficiently abusive.

As to *Cloud Confines*, I told Rossetti that I considered it in philosophic grasp the most powerful of his productions, and interesting as being (unlike the body of his works) more nearly akin to the spirit of music than that of painting.

> By the bye, you are right about *Cloud Confines*, which *is* my very best thing--only, having been foolishly sent to a magazine, no notice whatever resulted.

Rossetti was not always open to suggestions as to the need of clarifying obscure phrases in his verses, but on one or two occasions, when I was so bold as to hint at changes, I found him in highly tractable moods. I called his attention to what I imagined might prove to be merely a printer's slip in his poem (a great favourite of mine) entitled *The Portrait*. The second stanza ran:

Yet this, of all love's perfect prize,
Remains; save what in mournful guise
Takes counsel with my soul alone,--
Save what is secret and unknown,
Below the earth, above the sky.

The words "yet" and "save" seemed to me (and to another friend) somewhat puzzling, and I asked if "but" in the sense of *only* had been meant. He wrote:

That is a very just remark of yours about the passage in
Portrait beginning *yet*. I meant to infer *yet only*, but
it certainly is truncated. I shall change the line to

Yet only this, of love's whole prize,
Remains, etc.

But would again be dubious though explicable. Thanks for the
hint.... I shall be much obliged to you for any such hints
of a verbal nature.

CHAPTER V.

The letters printed in the foregoing chapter are valuable as settling at first-hand all question of the chronology of the poems of Rossetti's volume of 1870. The poems of the volume of 1881 (Rose Mary and certain of the sonnets excepted) grew under his hand during the period of my acquaintance with him, and their origin I shall in due course record. The two preceding chapters have been for the most part devoted to such letters (and such explanatory matter as must needs accompany them) as concern principally, perhaps, the poet and his correspondent; but I have thrown into two further chapters a great body of highly interesting letters on subjects of general literary interest (embracing the fullest statement yet published of Rossetti's critical opinions), and have reserved for a more advanced section of the work a body of further letters on sonnet literature which arose out of the discussion of an anthology that I was at the time engaged in compiling.

It was very natural that Coleridge should prove to be one of the first subjects discussed by Rossetti, who admired him greatly, and when it transpired that Coleridge was, perhaps, my own chief idol, and that whilst even yet a child I had perused and reperused not only his poetry but even his mystical philosophy (impalpable or obscure even to his maturer and more enlightened, if no more zealous, admirers), the disposition to write upon him became great upon both sides. "You can never say too much about Coleridge for me," Rossetti would write, "for I worship him on the right side of idolatry, and I perceive you know him well." Upon this one of my first remarks was that there was much in Coleridge's higher descriptive verse equivalent to the landscape art of Turner. The critical parallel Rossetti warmly approved of, adding, however, that Coleridge, at his best as a pictorial artist, was a spiritualised Turner. He instanced his,

We listened and looked sideways up,
The moving moon went up the sky
And no where did abide,
Softly she was going up,
And a star or two beside--
The charmed water burnt alway
A still and awful red.

I remarked that Shelley possessed the same power of impregnating landscape with spiritual feeling, and this Rossetti readily allowed; but when I proceeded to say that Wordsworth sometimes, though rarely, displayed a power akin to it, I found him less warmly responsive. "I grudge Wordsworth every vote he gets,"[8] Rossetti frequently said to me, both in writing, and afterwards in conversation. "The three greatest English imaginations," he would sometimes add, "are Shakspeare, Coleridge, and Shelley." I have heard him give a fourth name, Blake.

He thought Wordsworth was too much the High Priest of Nature to be her lover: too much concerned to transfigure into poetry his pantheo-Christian philosophy regarding Nature, to drop to his knees in simple love of her to thank God that she was beautiful. It was hard to side with Rossetti in his view of Wordsworth, partly because one feared he did not practise the patience necessary to a full appreciation of that poet, and was consequently apt to judge of him by fugitive lines read at random. In the connection in question, I instanced the lines (much admired by Coleridge) beginning

Suck, little babe, O suck again!
It cools my blood, it cools my brain,
and ending--

---

8   There is a story frequently told of how, seeing two camels
      walking together in the Zoological Gardens, keeping step in
      a shambling way, and conversing with one another, Rossetti
      exclaimed: "There's Wordsworth and Ruskin virtuously taking
      a walk!"

The breeze I see is in the tree,
It comes to cool my babe and me.

But Rossetti would not see that this last couplet denoted the point of artistic vision at which the poet of nature identified himself with her, in setting aside or superseding all proprieties of mere speech. To him Wordsworth's Idealism (which certainly had the German trick of keeping close to the ground) only meant us to understand that the forsaken woman through whose mouth the words are spoken (in *The Affliction of Margaret* ------ of ------) saw *the breeze shake the tree* afar off. And this attitude towards Wordsworth Rossetti maintained down to the end. I remember that sometime in March of the year in which he died, Mr. Theodore Watts, who was paying one of his many visits to see him in his last illness at the sea-side, touched, in conversation, upon the power of Wordsworth's style in its higher vein, and instanced a noble passage in the *Ode to Duty*, which runs:

Stern Lawgiver! yet thou dost wear
The Godhead's most benignant grace;
Nor know we anything so fair
As is the smile upon thy face;
Flowers laugh before thee on their beds;
And fragrance in thy footing treads;
Thou dost preserve the stars from wrong;
And the most ancient heavens, through Thee, are
fresh and strong.

Mr. Watts spoke with enthusiasm of the strength and simplicity, the sonorousness and stately march of these lines; and numbered them, I think, among the noblest verses yet written, for every highest quality of style.

But Rossetti was unyielding, and though he admitted the beauty of the passage, and was ungrudging in his tribute to another passage which I had instanced--

O joy that in our embers--

he would not allow that Wordsworth ever possessed a grasp of the great style, or that (despite the Ode on Immortality and the sonnet on *Toussaint L'Ouverture*, which he placed at the head of the poet's work) vital lyric impulse was ever fully developed in his muse. He said:

> As to Wordsworth, no one regards the great Ode with more
> special and unique homage than I do, as a thing absolutely
> alone of its kind among all greatest things. I cannot say
> that anything else of his with which I have ever been
> familiar (and I suffer from long disuse of all familiarity
> with him) seems at all on a level with this.

In all humility I regard his depreciatory opinion, not at all as a valuable example of literary judgment, but as indicative of a clear radical difference of poetic bias between the two poets, such as must in the same way have made Wordsworth resist Rossetti if he had appeared before him. I am the more confirmed in this view from the circumstance that Rossetti, throughout the period of my acquaintance with him, seemed to me always peculiarly and, if I may be permitted to say so without offence, strangely liable to Mr. Watts's influence in his critical estimates, and that the case instanced was perhaps the only one in which I knew him to resist Mr. Watts's opinion upon a matter of poetical criticism, which he considered to be almost final, as his letters to me, printed in Chapter VIII. of this volume, will show. I had a striking instance of this, and of the real modesty of the man whom I had heard and still hear spoken of as the most arrogant man of genius of his day, on one of the first occasions of my seeing him. He read out to me an additional stanza to the beautiful poem *Cloud Confines*: As he read it, I thought it very fine, and he evidently was very fond of it himself. But he surprised me by saying that he should not print it. On my asking him why, he said:

"Watts, though he admits its beauty, thinks the poem would be better without it."

"Well, but you like it yourself," said I.

"Yes," he replied; "but in a question of gain or loss to a poem, I feel that Watts must be right."

And the poem appeared in *Ballads and Sonnets* without the stanza in question. The same thing occurred with regard to the omission of the sonnet *Nuptial*

Sleep from the new edition of the Poems in 1881. Mr. Watts took the view (to Rossetti's great vexation at first) that this sonnet, howsoever perfect in structure and beautiful from the artistic point of view, was "out of place and altogether incongruous in a group of sonnets so entirely spiritual as *The House of Life*," and Rossetti gave way: but upon the subject of Wordsworth in his relations to Coleridge, Keats, and Shelley, he was quite inflexible to the last.

In a letter treating of other matters, Rossetti asked me if I thought "Christabel" really existed as a mediaeval name, or existed at all earlier than Coleridge. I replied that I had not met with it earlier than the date of the poem. I thought Coleridge's granddaughter must have been the first person to bear the name. The other names in the poem appear to belong to another family of names,--names with a different origin and range of expression,--Leoline, Geraldine, Roland, and most of all Bracy. It seemed to me very possible that Coleridge invented the name, but it was highly probable that he brought it to England from Germany, where, with Wordsworth, he visited Klopstock in 1798, about the period of the first part of the poem. The Germans have names of a kindred etymology and, even if my guess proved wide of the truth, it might still be a fact that the name had German relations. Another conjecture that seemed to me a reasonable one was that Coleridge evolved the name out of the incidents of the opening passages of the poem. The beautiful thing, not more from its beauty than its suggestiveness, suited his purpose exactly. Rossetti replied:

> Resuming the thread of my letter, I come to the question of the name Christabel, viz.:--as to whether it is to be found earlier than Coleridge. I have now realized afresh what I knew long ago, viz.:--that in the grossly garbled ballad of Syr Cauline, in Percy's *Reliques*, there is a Ladye Chrystabelle, but as every stanza in which her name appears would seem certainly to be Percy's own work, I suspect him to be the inventor of the name, which is assuredly a much better invention than any of the stanzas; and from this wretched source Coleridge probably enriched the sphere of symbolic nomenclature. However, a genuine source may turn up, but the name does not sound to me like a real one. As to

a German origin, I do not know that language, but would not the second syllable be there the one accented? This seems to render the name shapeless and improbable.

I mentioned an idea that once possessed me despotically. It was that where Coleridge says

Her silken robe and inner vest
Dropt to her feet, and full in view
Behold! her bosom and half her side--
A sight to dream of and not to tell,. . .
Shield the Lady Christabel!

he meant ultimately to show *eyes* in the *bosom* of the witch. I fancied that if the poet had worked out this idea in the second part, or in his never-compassed continuation, he must have electrified his readers. The first part of the poem is of course immeasurably superior in witchery to the second, despite two grand things in the latter--the passage on the severance of early friendships, and the conclusion; although the dexterity of hand (not to speak of the essential spirit of enchantment) which is everywhere present in the first part, and nowhere dominant in the second, exhibits itself not a little in the marvellous passage in which Geraldine bewitches Christabel. Touching some jocose allusion by Rossetti to the necessity which lay upon me to startle the world with a continuation of the poem based upon the lines of my conjectural scheme, I asked him if he knew that a continuation was actually published in Coleridge's own paper, *The Morning Post*. It appeared about 1820, and was satirical of course--hitting off many peculiarities of versification, if no more. With Coleridge's playful love of satirising himself anonymously, the continuation might even be his own. Rossetti said:

I do not understand your early idea of *eyes* in the bosom
of Geraldine. It is described as "that bosom old," "that
bosom cold," which seems to show that its withered character
as combined with Geraldine's youth, was what shocked and

warned Christabel. The first edition says--

A sight to dream of, not to tell:--
And she is to sleep with Christabel!

I dare say Coleridge altered this, because an idea arose,
which I actually heard to have been reported as Coleridge's
real intention by a member of contemporary circles (P. G.
Patmore, father of Coventry P. who conveyed the report to
me)--viz., that Geraldine was to turn out to be a man!! I
believe myself that the conclusion as given by Gillman from
Coleridge's account to him is correct enough, only not
picturesquely worded. It does not seem a bad conclusion by
any means, though it would require fine treatment to make it
seem a really good one. Of course the first part is so
immeasurably beyond the second, that one feels Chas. Lamb's
view was right, and it should have been abandoned at that
point. The passage on sundered friendship is one of the
masterpieces of the language, but no doubt was written quite
separately and then fitted into **Christabel**. The two lines
about Roland and Sir Leoline are simply an intrusion and an
outrage. I cannot say that I like the conclusion nearly so
well as this. It hints at infinite beauty, but somehow
remains a sort of cobweb. The conception, and partly the
execution, of the passage in which Christabel repeats by
fascination the serpent-glance of Geraldine, is magnificent;
but that is the only good narrative passage in part two. The
rest seems to have reached a fatal facility of jingling, at
the heels whereof followed Scott.

There are, I believe, many continuations of **Christabel**. Tupper did one! I myself saw a continuation in childhood, long before I saw the original, and was all agog
to see it for years. Our household was all of Italian, not English environment, and it

was only when I went to school later that I began to ransack bookstalls. The continuation in question was by one Eliza Stewart, and appeared in a shortlived monthly thing called ***Smallwood's Magazine***, to which my father contributed some Italian poetry, and so it came into the house. I thought the continuation spirited then, and perhaps it may have been so. This must have been before 1840 I think.

The other day I saw in a bookseller's catalogue--Christabess, by S. T. Colebritche, translated from the Doggrel by Sir Vinegar Sponge (1816). This seems a parody, not a continuation, in the very year of the poem's first appearance! I did not think it worth two shillings,--which was the price.... Have you seen the continuation of ***Christabel*** in ***European Magazine?*** of course it *might* have been Coleridge's, so far as the date of the composition of the original was concerned; but of course it was not his.

I imagine the "Sir Vinegar Sponge" who translated "Christabess from the ***Doggerel***" must belong to the family of Sponges described by Coleridge himself, who give out the liquid they take in much dirtier than they imbibe it. I thought it very possible that Coleridge's epigram to this effect might have been provoked by the lampoon referred to, and Rossetti also thought this probable. Immediately after meeting with the continuation of ***Christabel*** already referred to, I came across great numbers of such continuations, as well as satires, parodies, reviews, etc., in old issues of ***Blackwood, The Quarterly, and The Examiner***. They seemed to me, for the most part, poor in quality--the highest reach of comicality to which they attained being concerned with side slaps at ***Kubla Khan***:

> Better poetry I make
> When asleep than when awake.
> Am I sure, or am I guessing?
> Are my eyes like those of Lessing?

This latter elegant couplet was expected to serve as a scorching satire on a letter in the ***Biographia Literaria*** in which Coleridge says he saw a portrait of Lessing at Klopstock's, in which the eyes seemed singularly like his own. The time has gone by when that flight of egotism on Coleridge's part seemed an unpardonable offence, and to our more modern judgment it scarcely seems necessary that the author of **Christabel** should be charged with a desire to look radiant in the glory reflected by an accidental personal resemblance to the author of **Laokoon**. Curiously enough I found evidence of the Patmore version of Coleridge's intentions as to the ultimate disclosure of the sex of Geraldine in a review in the **Examiner**. The author was perhaps Hazlitt, but more probably the editor himself, but whether Hazlitt or Hunt, he must have been within the circle that found its rallying point at Highgate, and consequently acquainted with the earliest forms of the poem. The review is an unfavourable one, and Coleridge is told in it that he is the dog-in-the-manger of literature, and that his poem is proof of the fact that he can write better nonsense poetry than any man in England. The writer is particularly wroth with what he considers the wilful indefiniteness of the author, and in proof of a charge of a desire not to let the public into the secret of the poem, and of a conscious endeavour to mystify the reader, he deliberately accuses Coleridge of omitting one line of the poem as it was written, which, if printed, would have proved conclusively that Geraldine had seduced Christabel after getting drunk with her,--for such sequel is implied if not openly stated. I told Rossetti of this brutality of criticism, and he replied:

> As for the passage in **Christabel**, I am not sure we quite
> understand each other. What I heard through the Patmores (a
> complete mistake I am sure), was that Coleridge meant
> Geraldine to prove to be a man bent on the seduction of
> Christabel, and presumably effecting it. What I inferred (if
> so) was that Coleridge had intended the line as in first
> ed.: "And she is to sleep with Christabel!" as leading up
> too nearly to what he meant to keep back for the present.
> But the whole thing was a figment.

What is assuredly not a figment is, that an idea, such as the elder Patmore referred to, really did exist in the minds of Coleridge's so-called friends, who after praising the poem beyond measure whilst it was in manuscript, abused it beyond reason or decency when it was printed. My settled conviction is that the **Examiner** criticism, and **not** the sudden advent of the idea after the first part was written, was the cause of Coleridge's adopting the correction which Rossetti mentions.

Rossetti called my attention to a letter by Lamb, about which he gathered a good deal of interesting conjecture:

> There is (given in **Cottle**) an inconceivably sarcastic, galling, and admirable letter from Lamb to Coleridge, regarding which I never could learn how the deuce their friendship recovered from it. Cottle says the only reason he could ever trace for its being written lay in the three parodied sonnets (one being **The House that Jack Built**) which Coleridge published as a skit on the joint volume brought out by himself, Lamb, and Lloyd. The whole thing was always a mystery to me. But I have thought that the passage on division between friends was not improbably written by Coleridge on this occasion. Curiously enough (if so) Lamb, who is said to have objected greatly to the idea of a second part of **Christabel**, thought (on seeing it) that the mistake was redeemed by this very passage. He **may** have traced its meaning, though, of course, its beauty alone was enough to make him say so.

The three satirical sonnets which Rossetti refers to appear not only in **Cottle** but in a note to the **Biographia Literaria** They were published first under a fictitious name in **he Monthly Magazine** They must be understood as almost wholly satirical of three distinct facets of Coleridge's own manner, for even the sonnet in which occur the words

Eve saddens into night,[9]
has its counterpart in **The Songs of the Pixies**--

---

9   So in the Biographia Literaria; in Cottle, "Eve darkens into night."

Hence! thou lingerer, light!
Eve saddens into night,

and nearly all the phrases satirised are borrowed from Coleridge's own poetry, not from that of Lamb or Lloyd. Nevertheless, Cottle was doubtless right as to the fact that Lamb took offence at Coleridge's conduct on this account, and Rossetti almost certainly made a good shot at the truth when he attributed to the rupture thereupon ensuing the passage on severed friendship. The sonnet on ***The House that Jack Built*** is the finest of the three as a satire.

Indeed, the figure used therein as an equipoise to "the hindward charms" satirises perfectly the style of writing characterised by inflated thought and imagery. It may be doubted if there exists anything more comical; but each of the companion sonnets is good in its way. The egotism, which was a constant reproach urged by ***The Edinburgh*** critics and by the "Cockney Poets" against the poets of the Lake School, is splendidly hit off in the first sonnet; the low and creeping meanness, or say, simpleness, as contrasted with simplicity, of thought and expression, which was stealing into Wordsworth's work at that period, is equally cleverly ridiculed in the second sonnet. In reproducing the sonnets, Coleridge claims only to have satirised types. As to Lamb's letter, it is, indeed, hard to realise the fact that the "gentle-hearted Charles," as Coleridge himself named him, could write a galling letter to the "inspired charity-boy," for whom at an early period, and again at the end, he had so profound a reverence. Every word is an outrage, and every syllable must have hit Coleridge terribly. I called Rossetti's attention to the surprising circumstance that in a letter written immediately after the date of the one in question, Loyd tells Cottle that he has never known Lamb (who is at the moment staying with him) so happy before as ***just then!*** There can hardly be a doubt, however, that Rossetti's conjecture is a just one as to the origin of the great passage in the second part of ***Christabel***. Touching that passage I called his attention to an imperfection that I must have perceived, or thought I perceived long before,--an imperfection of craftsmanship that had taken away something of my absolute enjoyment of its many beauties. The passage ends--

They parted, ne'er to meet again!
But never either found another
To free the hollow heart from paining--
They stood aloof, the scars remaining,
Like cliffs which had been rent asunder;
A dreary sea now flows between,
But neither heat, nor frost, nor thunder,
Shall wholly do away, I ween,
The marks of that which once hath been.

This is, it is needless to say, in almost every respect, finely felt, but the words italicised appeared to display some insufficiency of poetic vision. First, nothing but an earthquake would (speaking within limits of human experience) unite the two sides of a ravine; and though ***frost*** might bring them together temporarily, ***heat and thunder*** must be powerless to make or to unmake the ***marks*** that showed the cliffs to have once been one, and to have been violently torn apart. Next, ***heat*** (supposing ***frost*** to be the root-conception) was obviously used merely as a balancing phrase, and ***thunder*** simply as the inevitable rhyme to ***asunder***. I have not seen this matter alluded to, though it may have been mentioned, and it is certainly not important enough to make any serious deduction from the pleasure afforded by a passage that is in other respects so rich in beauty as to be able to endure such modest discounting. Rossetti replied:

Your geological strictures on Coleridge's "friendship"
passage are but too just, and I believe quite new. But I
would fain think that this is "to consider too nicely." I am
certainly willing to bear the obloquy of never having been

struck by what is nevertheless obvious enough.[10].... Lamb's letter *is* a teazer. The three sonnets in The Monthly Magazine were signed "Nehemiah Higginbotham," and were meant to banter good-humouredly the joint vol. issued by Coleridge, Lamb, and Lloyd,--C. himself being, of course, the most obviously ridiculed. I fancy you have really hit the mark as regards Coleridge's epigram and Sir Vinegar Sponge. He might have been worth two shillings after all.... I also remember noting Lloyd's assertion of Lamb's exceptional happiness just after that letter. It is a puzzling affair. However C. and Lamb got over it (for I certainly believe they were friends later in life) no one seems to have recorded. The second vol. of Cottle, after the raciness of the first, is very disappointing.

On one occasion Rossetti wrote, saying he had written a sonnet on Coleridge, and I was curious to learn what note he struck in dealing with so complex a subject. The keynote of a man's genius or character should be struck in a poetic address to him, just as the expressional individuality of a man's features (freed of the modifying or emphasising effects of passing fashions of dress), should be reproduced in his portrait; but Coleridge's mind had so many sides to it, and his character had such varied aspects--from keen and beautiful sensibility to every form of suffering, to almost utter disregard of the calls of domestic duty--that it seemed difficult to think what kind of idea, consistent with the unity of the sonnet and its simplicity of scheme, would call up a picture of the entire man. It goes against the grain to hint, adoring the man as we must, that Coleridge's personal character was anything less than one of untarnished purity, and certainly the persons chiefly concerned in the alleged

---

10   In a note on this passage, Canon Dixon writes: What is meant is that in cliffs, actual cliffs, the action of these agents, heat, cold, thunder even, might have an obliterating power; but in the severance of friendship, there is nothing (heat of nature, frost of time, thunder of accident or surprise) that can wholly have the like effect.

neglect, Southey and his own family, have never joined in the strictures commonly levelled against him: but whatever Coleridge's personal ego may have been, his creative ego was assuredly not single in kind or aim. He did some noble things late in life (instance the passage on "Youth and Age," and that on "Work without Hope"), but his poetic genius seemed to desert him when Kant took possession of him as a gigantic windmill to do battle with, and it is now hard to say which was the deeper thing in him: the poetry to which he devoted the sunniest years of his young life, or the philosophy which he firmly believed it to be the main business of his later life to expound. In any discussion of the relative claims of these two to the gratitude of the ages that follow, I found Rossetti frankly took one side, and constantly said that the few unequal poems Coleridge had left us, were a legacy more stimulating, solacing, and enduring, than his philosophy could have been, even if he had perfected that attempt of his to reconcile all learning and revelation, and if, when perfected, the whole effort had not proved to be a work of supererogation. I doubt if Rossetti quite knew what was meant by Coleridge's "system," as it was so frequently called, and I know that he could not be induced by any eulogiums to do so much as look at the *Biographia Literaria*, though once he listened whilst I read a chapter from it. He had certainly little love of the German elements in Coleridge's later intellectual life, and hence it is small matter for surprise that in his sonnet he chose for treatment the more poetic side of Coleridge's genius. Nevertheless, I think it remains an open question whether the philosophy of the author of *The Ancient Mariner* was more influenced by his poetry, or his poetry by his philosophy; for the philosophy is always tinged by the mysticism of his poetry, and his poetry is always adumbrated by the disposition, which afterwards become paramount, to dig beneath the surface for problems of life and character, and for "suggestions of the final mystery of existence." I have heard Rossetti say that what came most of all uppermost in Coleridge, was his wonderful intuitive knowledge and love of the sea, whose billowy roll, and break, and sibilation, seemed echoed in the very mechanism of his verse. Sleep, too, Rossetti thought, had given up to Coleridge her utmost secrets; and perhaps it was partly due to his own sad experience of the dread curse of insomnia, as well as to keen susceptibility to poetic beauty, that tears so frequently filled his eyes, and sobs rose to his throat when he recited the lines beginning

O sleep! it is a gentle thing--

affirming, meantime, that nothing so simple and touching had ever been written on the subject. As to the sonnet, he wrote:

About Coleridge (whom I only view as a poet, his other
aspects being to my apprehension mere bogies) I conceive the
leading point about his work is its human love, and the
leading point about his career, the sad fact of how little
of it was devoted to that work. These are the points made in
my sonnet, and the last is such as I (alas!) can sympathise
with, though what has excluded more poetry with me
(mountains of it I don't want to heap) has chiefly been
livelihood necessity. I 'll copy the sonnet on opposite
page, only I 'd rather you kept it to yourself. **Five** years
of **good** poetry is too long a tether to give his Muse, I
know.

His Soul fared forth (as from the deep home-grove
The father Songster plies the hour-long quest)
To feed his soul-brood hungering in the nest;
But his warm Heart, the mother-bird above
Their callow fledgling progeny still hove
With tented roof of wings and fostering breast
Till the Soul fed the soul-brood. Richly blest
From Heaven their growth, whose food was Human Love.

Tet ah! Like desert pools that shew the stars
Once in long leagues--even such the scarce-snatched hours
Which deepening pain left to his lordliest powers:--
Heaven lost through spider-trammelled prison-bars!
Five years, from seventy saved! yet kindling skies
Own them, a beacon to our centuries.

As a minor point I called Rossetti's attention to the fact that Coleridge lived to be scarcely more than sixty, and that his poetic career really extended over six good years; and hence the thirteenth line was amended to

Six years from sixty saved.

I doubted if "deepening pain" could be charged with the whole burden of Coleridge's constitutional procrastination, and to this objection Rossetti replied:

Line eleven in my first reading was "deepening *sloth*;" but
it seemed harsh--and--damn it all! much too like the spirit
of Banquo!

Before Coleridge, however, as to warmth of admiration, and before him also as to date of influence, Keats was Rossetti's favourite among modern English poets. Our friend never tired of writing or talking about Keats, and never wearied of the society of any one who could generate a fresh thought concerning him. But his was a robust and masculine admiration, having nothing in common with the effeminate extra-affectionateness that has of late been so much ridiculed. His letters now to be quoted shall speak for themselves as to the qualities in Keats whereon Rossetti's appreciation of him was founded: but I may say in general terms that it was not so much the wealth of expression in the author of *Endymion* which attracted the author of *Rose Mary* as the perfect hold of the supernatural which is seen in *La Belle Dame Sans Merci* and in the fragment of the *Eve of St. Mark*. At the time of our correspondence, I was engaged upon an essay on Keats, and *a propos* of this Rossetti wrote:

I shall take pleasure in reading your Keats article when
ready. He was, among all his contemporaries who established
their names, the one true heir of Shakspeare. Another
(unestablished then, but partly revived since) was Charles
Wells. Did you ever read his splendid dramatic poem Joseph
and his Brethren?

In this connexion, as a better opportunity may not arise, I take occasion to tell briefly the story of the revival of Wells. The facts to be related were communicated to me by Rossetti in conversation years after the date of the letter in which this first allusion to the subject was made. As a boy, Rossetti's chief pleasure was to ransack old book-stalls, and the catalogues of the British Museum, for forgotten works in the bye-ways of English poetry. In this pursuit he became acquainted with nearly every curiosity of modern poetic literature, and many were the amusing stories he used to tell at that time, and in after life, of the titles and contents of the literary oddities he unearthed. If you chanced at any moment to alight upon any obscure book particularly curious from its pretentiousness and pomposity, from the audacity of its claim, or the obscurity and absurdity of its writing, you might be sure that Rossetti would prove familiar with it, and be able to recapitulate with infinite zest its salient features; but if you happened to drop upon ever so interesting an edition of a book (not of verse) which you supposed to be known to many a reader, the chances were at least equal that Rossetti would prove to know nothing of it but its name. In poring over the forgotten pages of the poetry of the beginning of the century, Rossetti, whilst still a boy, met with the scriptural drama of *Joseph and his Brethren*. He told me the title did not much attract him, but he resolved to glance at the contents, and with that swiftness of insight which throughout life distinguished him, he instantly perceived its great qualities. I think he said he then wrote a letter on the subject to one of the current literary journals, probably *The Literary Gazette*, and by this means came into correspondence with Charles Wells himself. Rather later a relative of Wells's sought out the young enthusiast in London, intending to solicit his aid in an attempt to induce a publisher to undertake a reprint, but in any endeavours to this end he must have failed. For many years a copy of the poem, left by the author's request at Rossetti's lodgings, lay there untouched, and meantime the growing reputation of the young painter brought about certain removals from Blackfriars Bridge to other chambers, and afterwards to the house in Cheyne Walk. In the course of these changes the copy got hidden away, and it was not until numerous applications for it had been made that it was at length ferreted forth from the chaos of some similar volumes huddled together in a corner of the studio. Full of remorse for having so long abandoned a laudable project, Rossetti then took up afresh the cause of the neglected poem, and enlisted Mr. Swinburne's interest so warmly as to prevail with him to use his influence to secure its publication. This failed however; but in *The Athenaeum* of April 8, 1876, appeared Mr. Watts's elaborate account of Wells and the poem and its vicissitudes, whereupon Messrs. Chatto and Windus offered to take the risk of publishing it, and the poem went forth with the noble commendatory essay of the young author of *Atalanta*, whose reputation was already almost at its height, though it lacked (doubtless from a touch of his constitutional procrastination) the appreciative comment of the discerning critic who first discovered it. To return to the Keats correspondence:

> I am truly delighted to hear how young you are. In original
> work, a man does some of his best things by your time of
> life, though he only finds it out in a rage much later, at
> some date when he expected to know no longer that he had
> ever done them. Keats hardly died so much too early--not at
> all if there had been any danger of his taking to the modern
> habit eventually--treating material as product, and shooting
> it all out as it comes. Of course, however, he wouldn't; he
> was getting always choicer and simpler, and my favourite
> piece in his works is *La Belle Dame Sans Merci*--I suppose
> about his last. As to Shelley, it is really a mercy that he
> has not been hatching yearly universes till now. He might, I
> suppose; for his friend Trelawny still walks the earth
> without great-coat, stockings, or underclothing, this
> Christmas (1879). In criticism, matters are different, as to
> seasons of production.... I am writing hurriedly and
> horribly in every sense. Write on the subject again and I'll
> try to answer better. All greetings to you.
>
> P.S.--I think your reference to Keats new, and on a high
> level It calls back to my mind an adaptation of his self-
> chosen epitaph which I made in my very earliest days of
> boyish rhyming, when I was rather proud to be as cockney as
> Keats *could* be. Here it is,--

Through one, years since damned and forgot
Who stabbed backs by the Quarter,
Here lieth one who, while Time's stream
Still runs, as God hath taught her,
Bearing man's fame to men, hath writ
His name upon that water.

Well, the rhyme is not so bad as Keats's

Ear
Of Goddess of Theraea!--

nor (tell it not in Gath!) as---

I wove a crown before her
For her I love so dearly,
A garland for Lenora!

Is it possible the laurel crown should now hide a venerated
and impeccable ear which was once the ear of a cockney?

This letter was written in 1879, and the opening clauses of it were no doubt penned under the impression, then strong on Rossetti's mind, that his first volume of poems would prove to be his only one; but when, within two years afterwards he completed *Rose Mary*, and wrote *The King's Tragedy* and *The White Ship*, this accession of material dissipated the notion that a man does much his best work before twenty-five. It can hardly escape the reader that though Rossetti's earlier volume displayed a surprising maturity, the subsequent one exhibited as a whole infinitely more power and feeling, range of sympathy, and knowledge of life. The poet's dramatic instinct developed enormously in the interval between the periods of the two books, and, being conscious of this, Rossetti used to say in his later years that he would never again write poems as from his own person.

You say an excellent thing [he writes] when you ask, "Where can we look for more poetry per page than Keats furnishes?" It is strange that there is not yet one complete edition of him.[11] No doubt the desideratum (so far as care and exhaustiveness go), will be supplied when

Forman's edition appears. He is a good appreciator too, as I have reason to say. You will think it strange that I have not seen the Keats love-letters, but I mean to do so. However, I am told they add nothing to one's idea of his epistolary powers.... I hear sometimes from Buxton Forman, and was sending him the other day an extract (from a book called *The Unseen World*) which doubtless bears on the superstition which Keats intended to develope in his lovely Eve of St. Mark--a fragment which seems to me to rank with La Belle Dame Sans Merci, as a clear advance in direct simplicity.... You ought to have my recent Keats sonnet, so I send it. Your own plan, for one on the same subject, seems to me most beautiful. Do it at once. You will see that mine is again concerned with the epitaph, and perhaps my reviving the latter in writing you was the cause of the sonnet.

Rossetti formed a very different opinion of Keats's love-letters, when, a year later, he came to read them. At first he shared the general view that letters so *intimes* should never have been made public. Afterwards the book had irresistible charms for him, from the first page whereon his old friend, Mr. Bell Scott, has vigorously etched Severn's drawing of the once redundant locks of rich hair, dank and matted over the forehead cold with the death-dew, down to the last line of the

11 Rossetti afterwards admitted in conversation that the
     Aldine Edition seemed complete, though I think he did not
     approve of the chronological arrangement therein adopted; at
     least he thought that arrangement had many serious
     disadvantages.

letterpress. He thought Mr. Forman's work admirably done, and as for the letters themselves, he believed they placed Keats indisputably among the highest masters of English epistolary style. He considered that all Keats's letters proved him to be no weakling, and that whatever walk he had chosen he must have been a master. He seemed particularly struck with the apparently intuitive perception of Shakspeare's subtlest meanings, which certain of the letters display. In a note he said:

> Forman gave me a copy of Keats's letters to Fanny Brawne.
> The silhouette given of the lady is sadly disenchanting, and
> may be the strongest proof existing of how much a man may
> know about abstract Beauty without having an artist's eye
> for the outside of it.
> The Keats sonnet, as first shown to me, ran as follows:

> The weltering London ways where children weep,--
> Where girls whom none call maidens laugh, where gain,
> Hurrying men's steps, is yet by loss o'erta'en:--
> The bright Castalian brink and Latinos' steep:--
> Such were his paths, till deeper and more deep,
> He trod the sands of Lethe; and long pain,
> Weary with labour spurned and love found vain,
> In dead Rome's sheltering shadow wrapped his sleep.

> O pang-dowered Poet, whose reverberant lips
> And heart-strung lyre awoke the moon's eclipse,--
> Thou whom the daisies glory in growing o'er,--
> Their fragrance clings around thy name, not writ,
> But rumour'd in water, while the fame of it
> Along Time's flood goes echoing evermore.

I need hardly say that this sonnet seemed to me extremely noble in sentiment, and in music a glorious volume of sound. I felt, however, that it would be urged against it that it did not strike the keynote of the genius of Keats; that it would be said that in all the particulars in which Rossetti had truthfully and pathetically described London, Keats was in rather than of it; and that it would be affirmed that Keats lived in a fairy world of his own inventing, caring little for the storm and stress of London life. On the other hand, I knew it could be replied that Keats was not indifferent to the misery of city life; that it bore heavily upon him; that it came out powerfully and very sadly in his **Ode to the Nightingale**, and that it may have been from sheer torture in the contemplation of it that he fled away to a poetic world of his own creating. Moreover, Rossetti's sonnet touched the life, rather than the genius, of Keats, and of this it struck the keynote in the opening lines. I ventured to think that the second and third lines wanted a little clarifying in the relation in which they stood. They seemed to be a sudden focussing of the laughter and weeping previously mentioned, rather than, what they were meant to be, a natural and necessary equipoise showing the inner life of Keats as contrasted with his outer life. To such an objection as this, Rossetti said:

> I am rather aghast for my own lucidity when I read what you
> say as to the first quatrain of my Keats sonnet. However, I
> always take these misconceptions as warnings to the Muse,
> and may probably alter the opening as below:
>
> The weltering London ways where children weep
> And girls whom none call maidens laugh,--strange road,
> Miring his outward steps who inly trode
> The bright Castalian brink and Latinos' steep:--
> Even such his life's cross-paths: till deathly deep
> He toiled through sands of Lethe, etc.
> I 'll say more anent Keats anon.

About the period of this portion of the correspondence (1880) I was engaged reading up old periodicals dating from 1816 to 1822. My purpose was to get at first-hand all available data relative to the life of Keats. I thought I met with a good deal of fresh material, and as the result of my reading I believed myself able to correct a few errors as to facts into which previous writers on the subject had fallen. Two things at least I realised--first, that Keats's poetic gift developed very rapidly, more rapidly perhaps than that of Shelley; and, next, that Keats received vastly more attention and appreciation in his day than is commonly supposed. I found it was quite a blunder to say that the first volume of miscellaneous poems fell flat. Lord Houghton says in error that the book did not so much as seem to signal the advent of a new Cockney poet! It is a fact, however, that this very book, in conjunction with one of Shelley's and one of Hunt's, all published 1816-17, gave rise to the name "The Cockney School of Poets," which was invented by the writer signing "Z." in *Blackwood* in the early part of 1818. Nor had Keats to wait for the publication of the volume before attaining to some poetic distinction. At the close of 1816, an article, under the head of "Young Poets," appeared in *The Examiner*, and in this both Shelley and Keats were dealt with. Then *The Quarterly* contained allusions to him, though not by name, in reviews of Leigh Hunt's work, and *Blackwood* mentioned him very frequently in all sorts of places as "Johnny Keats"--all this (or much of it) before he published anything except occasional sonnets and other fugitive poems in *The Examiner* and elsewhere. And then when *Endymion* appeared it was abundantly reviewed. *The Edinburgh* reviewers had nothing on it (the book cannot have been sent to them, for in 1820 they say they have only just met with it), and I could not find anything in the way of *original* criticism in *The Examiner*; but many provincial papers (in Manchester, Exeter, and elsewhere) and some metropolitan papers retorted on *The Quarterly*. All this, however, does not disturb the impression which (Lord Houghton and Mr. W. M. Rossetti notwithstanding) I have been from the first compelled to entertain, namely, that "labour spurned" did more than all else to kill Keats *in 1821*.

Most men who rightly know the workings of their own minds will agree that an adverse criticism rankles longer than a flattering notice soothes; and though it be shown that Keats in 1820 was comparatively indifferent to the praise of *The Edinburgh*, it cannot follow that in 1818 he must have been superior to the blame of *The Quarterly*. It is difficult to see why a man may not be keenly sensitive to what the world says about him, and yet retain all proper manliness as a part of his literary character. Surely it was from the mistaken impression that this could not be, and that an admission of extreme sensitiveness to criticism exposed Keats to a charge of effeminacy that Lord Houghton attempted to prove, against the evidence of all immediate friends, against the publisher's note to **Hyperion**, against the | poet's self-chosen epitaph, and against all but one or two of the most self-contained of his letters, that the soul of Keats was so far from being "snuffed out by an article," that it was more than ordinarily impervious to hostile comment, even when it came in the shape of rancorous abuse. In all discussion of the effects produced upon Keats by the reviews in **Blackwood and The Quarterly**, let it be remembered, first, that having wellnigh exhausted his small patrimony, Keats was to be dependent upon literature for his future subsistence; next, that Leigh Hunt attempted no defence of Keats when the bread was being taken out of his mouth, and that Keats felt this neglect and remarked upon it in a letter in which he further cast some doubt upon the purity of Hunt's friendship. Hunt, after Keats's death, said in reference to this: "Had he but given me the hint!" The **hint**, forsooth! Moreover, I can find no sort of allusion in *The Examiner* for 1821, to the death of Keats. I told Rossetti that by the reading of the periodicals of the time, I formed a poor opinion of Hunt. Previously I was willing to believe in his unswerving loyalty to the much greater men who were his friends, but even that poor confidence in him must perforce be shaken when one finds him silent at a moment when Keats most needs his voice, and abusive when Coleridge is a common subject of ridicule. It was all very well for Hunt to glorify himself in the borrowed splendour of Keats's established fame when the poet was twenty years dead, and to make much of his intimacy with Coleridge after the homage of two generations had been offered him, but I know of no instance (unless in the case of Shelley) in which Hunt stood by his friends in the winter of their lives, and gave them that journalistic support which was, poor man, the only thing he ever had to give, whatever he might take. I have, however, heard Mr. H. A. Bright (one of Hawthorne's intimate friends in England) say that no man here impressed the American romancer so much as Hunt for good qualities, both of heart and head. But what I have stated above, I believe to be facts; and I have gathered them at first-hand, and by the light of them I do not hesitate to say that there is no reason to believe that it was Keats's illness alone that caused him to regard Hunt's friendship with suspicion. It is true, however, that when one reads Hunt's letter to Severn at Borne, one feels that he must be forgiven. On this pregnant subject Rossetti wrote:

Thanks for yours received to-day, and for all you say with
so much more kind solicitousness than the matter deserved,
about the opening of the Keats sonnet. I have now realized
that the new form is a gain in every way; and am therefore
glad that, though arising in accident, I was led to make the
change.... All you say of Keats shows that you have been
reading up the subject with good results. I fancy it would
hardly be desirable to add the sonnets you speak of (as
being worthless) at this date, though they might be valuable
for quotation as to the course of his mental and physical
state. I do not myself think that any poems now included
should be removed, but the reckless and tasteless plan of
the gatherings hitherto (in which the **Nightingale** and other
such masterpieces are jostled indiscriminately, with such
wretched juvenile trash as Lines to some Ladies on
receiving a Shelly etc), should of course be amended, and
the rubbish (of which there is a fair quantity), removed to
a "Juvenile" or other such section. It is a curious fact
that among a poet's early writings, some will really be
juvenile in this sense, while others, written at the same
time, will perhaps take rank at last with his best efforts.
This, however, was not substantially the case with Keats.

As to Leigh Hunt's friendship for Keats, I think the points
you mention look equivocal; but Hunt was a many-laboured and
much belaboured man, and as much allowance as may be made on
this score is perhaps due to him--no more than that much.
His own powers stand high in various ways--poetically higher
perhaps than is I at present admitted, despite his
detestable flutter and airiness for the most part. But
assuredly by no means could he have stood so high in the
long-run, as by a loud and earnest defence of Keats. Perhaps

the best excuse for him is the remaining possibility of an idea on his part, that any defence coming from one who had himself so many powerful enemies might seem to Keats rather to! damage than improve his position.

I have this minute (at last) read the first instalment of your Keats paper, and return it.... One of the most marked points in the early recognition of Keats's claims, as compared with the recognition given to other poets, is the fact that he was the only one who secured almost at once a great poet as a close and obvious imitator--viz., Hood, whose first volume is more identical with Keats's work than could be said of any other similar parallel. You quote some of Keats's sayings. One of the most characteristic I think is in a letter to Haydon:--

"I value more the privilege of seeing great things in loneliness, than the fame of a prophet." I had not in mind the quotations you give from Keats as bearing on the poetic (or prophetic) mission of "doing good." I must say that I should not have thought a longer career thrown away upon him (as you intimate) if he had continued to the age of anything only to give joy. Nor would he ever have done any "good" at all. Shelley did good, and perhaps some harm with it. Keats's joy was after all a flawless gift.

Keats wrote to Shelley:--"You, I am sure, will forgive me for sincerely remarking that you might curb your magnanimity and be more of an artist, and load every rift of your subject with ore." Cheeky!--but not so much amiss. Poetry, and no prophecy however, must come of that mood,--and no pulpit would have held Keats's wings,--the body and mind together were not heavy enough for a counterweight.... Did you ever meet with

ENDIMION
AN EXCELLENT FANCY FIRST COMPOSED IN FRENCH
By Monsieur GOMBAULD
AND NOW ELEGANTLY INTERPRETED
By RICHARD HURST, Gentleman
1639.

It has very finely engraved plates of the late Flemish type.
There is a poem of Vaughan's on Gombauld's ***Endimion***, which
might make one think it more fascinating than it really is.
Though rather prolix, however, it has attractions as a
somewhat devious romantic treatment of the subject. The
little book is one of the first I remember in this world,
and I used to dip into it again and again as a child, but
never yet read it through. I still possess it. I dare say it
is not easily met with, and should suppose Keats had
probably never seen it. If he had, he might really have
taken a hint or two for his scheme, which is hardly so clear
even as Gombauld's, though its endless digressions teem with
beauty.... I do not think you would benefit at all by seeing
Gombauld's ***Endimion***. Vaughan's poem on it might be worth
quoting as showing what attention the subject had received
before Keats. I have the poem in Gilfillan's Less-Known
Poets.

Rossetti took a great interest in the fund started for the relief of Mme. de Llanos, Keats's sister, whose circumstances were seriously reduced. He wrote:

By the bye, I don't know whether the subscription for
Keats's old and only surviving sister (Madme de Llanos) has

been at all ventilated in Liverpool. It flags sorely. Do you
think there would be any chance in your neighbourhood? If
so, prospectuses, etc., could be sent.

I did not view the prospect of subscriptions as very hopeful, and so conceived
the idea of a lecture in the interests of the fund. On this project, Rossetti wrote:

I enclose prospectuses as to the Keats subscription. I may
say that I did not know the list would accompany them--still
less that contributions would be so low generally as to
leave me near the head of the list--an unenviable sort of
parade.... My own opinion about the lecture question is
this. You know best whether such a lecture could be turned
to the purposes of your Keats article (now in progress), or
rather be so much deduction from the freshness of its
resources: and this should be the ***absolute*** test of its
being done or not done.... I think, if it can be done
without impoverishing your materials, the method of getting
Lord Houghton to preside and so raising as much from it as
possible is doubtless the right one. Of course I view it as
far more hopeful than mere distribution of any number of
prospectuses.... Even L25 would be a great contribution to
the fund.

The lecture project was not found feasible, and hence it was abandoned. Meantime the kindness of friends enabled me to add to the list a good number of subscriptions, but feeling scarcely satisfied with any such success as I might be likely
to have in that direction, I opened, by the help of a friend, a correspondence with
Lord Houghton with a view to inducing him to apply for a pension for the lady. It
then transpired that Lord Houghton had already applied to Lord Beaconsfield for
a pension for Mme. Llanos, and would doubtless have got it, had not Mr. Buxton
Forman applied for a grant from the Royal Bounty, which was easier to give. I told
Rossetti of this fact and he said:

I am not surprised about Lord H., and feel sure it is a pity
he was not left to try Beaconsfield, but I judge the
projectors on the other side knew nothing of his intentions.
However, *I* was in no way a projector.

In the end Lord Houghton repeated to Mr. Gladstone the application he had made to Lord Beaconsfield, and succeeded.

Rossetti must have been among the earliest admirers of Keats. I remarked on one occasion that it was very natural that Lord Houghton should consider himself in a sense the first among men now living to champion the poet and establish his name, and Rossetti admitted that this was so, and was ungrudging in his tribute to Lord Houghton's services towards the better appreciation of Keats; but he contended, nevertheless, that he had himself been one of the first writers of the generation succeeding the poet's own to admire and uphold him, and that this was at a time when it made demand of some courage to class him among the immortals, when an original edition of any of his books could be bought for sixpence on a bookstall, and when only Leigh Hunt, Cowden Clarke, Hood, Benjamin Haydon, and perhaps a few others, were still living of those who recognised his great gifts.

CHAPTER VI.

Rossetti's primary interest in Chatterton dates back to an early period, as I find by the date, 1848, in the copy he possessed of the poet's works. But throughout a long interval he neglected Chatterton, and it was not until his friend Theodore Watts, who had made Chatterton a special study, had undertaken to select from and write upon him in Ward's ***English Poets***, that he revived his old acquaintance. Whatever Rossetti did he did thoroughly, and hence he became as intimate perhaps with the Rowley antiques as any other man had ever been. His letters written during the course of his Chatterton researches must, I think, prove extremely interesting. He says:

> Glancing at your Keats MS., I notice (in a series of
> parallels) the names of Marlowe and Savage; but not the less
> "marvellous" than absolutely miraculous Chatterton. Are you
> up in his work? He is in the very first rank! Theod. Watts
> is "doing him" for the new selection of poets by Arnold and
> Ward, and I have contributed a sonnet to Watts's article....
> I assure you Chatterton's name ***must*** come in somewhere in
> the parallel passage. He was as great as any English poet
> whatever, and might absolutely, had he lived, have proved
> the only man in England's theatre of imagination who could
> have bandied parts with Shakspeare. The best way of getting
> at him is in Skeat's Aldine edition (G. Bell and Co., 1875).
> Read him carefully, and you will find his acknowledged work
> essentially as powerful as his antiques, though less evenly
> successful--the Rowley work having been produced in Bristol

leisure, however indigent, and the modern poetry in the very fangs of London struggle. Strong derivative points are to be found in Keats and Coleridge from the study of Chatterton. I feel much inclined to send the sonnet (on Chatterton) as you wish, but really think it is better not to ventilate these things till in print. I have since written one on Blake. Not to know Chatterton is to be ignorant of the **true** day-spring of modern romantic poetry.... I believe the 3d vol. of Ward's **Selections of English Poetry**, for which Watts is selecting from Chatterton, will soon be out,--but these excerpts are very brief, as are the notices. The rendering from the Rowley antique will be much better than anything formerly done. Skeat is a thorough philologist, but no hand at all when substitution becomes unavoidable in the text.... Read the Ballad of Charity, the Eclogues, the songs in AElla, as a first taste. Among the modern poems Narva and Mared, and the other **African Eclogues**. These are alone in that section **poetry absolute**, and though they are very unequal, it has been most truly said by Malone that to throw the **African Eclogues** into the Rowley dialect would be at once a satisfactory key to the question whether Chatterton showed in his own person the same powers as in the person of Rowley. Among the satirical and light modern pieces there are many of a first-. rate order, though generally unequal. Perfect specimens, however, are The Revenge, a Burletta, Skeat, vol i; Verses to a Lady, p. 84; Journal Sixth, p. 33; The Prophecy, p. 193; and opening of Fragment, p. 132. I would advise you to consult the original text.

Mr. Watts, it seems, with all his admiration of Chatterton, finding that he could not go to Rossetti's length in comparing him with Shakspeare, did not in the result consider the sonnet on Chatterton referred to in the foregoing letter, and given below, suitable to be embodied in his essay:

With Shakspeare's manhood at a boy's wild heart,--
Through Hamlet's doubt to Shakspeare near allied,
And kin to Milton through his Satan's pride,--
At Death's sole door he stooped, and craved a dart;
And to the dear new bower of England's art,--
Even to that shrine Time else had deified,
The unuttered heart that soared against his side,--
Drove the fell point, and smote life's seals apart.

Thy nested home-loves, noble Chatterton,
The angel-trodden stair thy soul could trace
Up Redcliffe's spire; and in the world's armed space
Thy gallant sword-play:--these to many an one
Are sweet for ever; as thy grave unknown,
And love-dream of thine unrecorded face.

Some mention was made in this connection of Rossetti's young connection, Oliver Madox Brown, who wrote **Gabriel Denver** (otherwise **The Black Swan**) at seventeen years of age. I mentioned the indiscreet remark of a friend who said that Oliver had enough genius to stock a good few Chattertons, and thereupon Rossetti sent me the following outburst:

You must take care to be on the right tack about Chatterton.
I am very glad to find the gifted Oliver M. B. already an
embryo classic, as I always said he would be; but those who
compare net results in such cases as his and Chatterton's
cannot know what criticism means. The nett results of
advancing epochs, however permanent on accumulated
foundation-work, are the poorest of all tests as to relative
values. Oliver was the product of the most teeming hot-beds
of art and literature, and even of compulsory addiction to
the art of painting, in which nevertheless he was rapidly
becoming as much a proficient as in literature. What he

would have been if, like the ardent and heroic Chatterton, he had had to fight a single-handed battle for art and bread together against merciless mediocrity in high places,--what he would **_then_** have become, I cannot in the least calculate; but we know what Chatterton became. Moreover, C. at his death, was two years younger than Oliver--a whole lifetime of advancement at that age frequently--indeed always I believe in leading cases. There are few indeed whom the facile enthusiasm for contemporary models does not deaden to the truly balanced claims of successful efforts in art. However, look at Watts's remodelled extracts when the vol comes out, and also at what he says in detail as to Chatterton, Coleridge, and Keats.

Of course Rossetti was right in what he said of comparative criticism when brought to bear in such cases as those of Chatterton and Oliver Madox Brown. Net results are certainly the poorest tests of relative values where the work done belongs to periods of development. We cannot, however, see or know any man except through and in his work, and net results must usually be accepted as the only concrete foundation for judging of the quality of his genius. Such judgment will always be influenced, nevertheless, by considerations such as Rossetti mentions. Touching Chatterton's development, it were hardly rash to say that it appears incredible that the **_African Eclogues_** should have been written by a boy of seventeen, and, in judging of their place in poetry, one is apt to be influenced by one's first feeling of amazement. Is it possible that the Rowley poems may owe much of their present distinction to the early astonishment that a boy should have written them, albeit they have great intrinsic excellencies such as may insure them a high place when the romance, intertwined with their history, has been long forgotten? But Chatterton is more talked of than read, and this has been so from the first. The antiques are all but unknown; certain of the acknowledged poems are remembered, and regarded as fervid and vigorous, and many of the lesser pieces are thought slight, weak, and valueless. People do not measure the poorer things in Chatterton with his time and opportunities, or they would see only amazing strength and knowledge of the world in all he did. Those lesser pieces were many of them dashed off to answer the calls of necessity, to flatter the egotism of a troublesome friend, or to wile away a moment of vacancy. Certainly they must not be set against his best efforts. As for Chatterton's life, the tragedy of it is perhaps the most moving example of what Coleridge might have termed the material pathetic. Pathetic, however, as his life was, and marvellous as was his genius, I miss in him the note of personal purity and majesty of character. I told Rossetti that, in my view, Chatterton lacked sincerity, and on this point he wrote:

> I must protest finally about Chatterton, that he lacks
> nothing because lacking the gradual growth of the emotional
> in literature which becomes evident in Keats--still less its
> excess, which would of course have been pruned, in Oliver.
> The finest of the Rowley poems--Eclogues, Ballad of
> Charity, etc., rank absolutely with the finest poetry in
> the language, and gain (not lose) by moderation. As to what
> you say of C.'s want of political sincerity (for I cannot
> see to what other want you can allude), surely a boy up to
> eighteen may be pardoned for exercising his faculty if he
> happens to be the one among millions who can use grown men
> as his toys. He was an absolute and untarnished hero, but
> for that reckless defying vaunt. Certainly that most
> vigorous passage commencing--
>
> "Interest, thou universal God of men," etc.
>
> reads startlingly, and comes in a questionable shape. What
> is the answer to its enigmatical aspect? Why, that he
> meant it, and that all would mean it at his age, who had
> his power, his daring, and his hunger. Still it does,
> perhaps, make one doubt whether his early death were well or
> ill for him. In the matter of Oliver (whom no one
> appreciates more than I do), remember that it was impossible

to have more opportunities than *he* had, or on the other side *fewer* than Chatterton had. Chatterton at seventeen or less said--

"Flattery's a cloak, and I will put it on."
Blake (probably late in life) said--

"Innocence is a winter gown."

... I *have* read the Chatterton article in the review mentioned. If Watts had done it, it would have been immeasurably better. There seems to me, who am very well up in Chatterton, no point whatever made in the article. Why does no one ever even allude to the two attributed portraits of Chatterton--one belonging to Sir H. Taylor, and the other in the Salford Museum? Both seem to be the same person clearly, and a good find for Chatterton, but not conceivably done from him. Nevertheless, I *suspect* there may be a sidelong genuineness in them. Chatterton was acquainted with one Alcock, a miniature painter at Bristol, to whom he addressed a poem. Had A. painted C. it would be among the many recorded facts; but it would be singular even if, in C.'s rapid posthumous fame, A. had never been asked to make a reminiscent likeness of him. Prom such likeness by the miniature painter these *portraits might* derive--both being life-sized oil heads. There is a savour of Keats in them, though a friend, taking up the younger-looking of the two, said it reminded him of Jack Sheppard! And not such a bad Chatterton-compound either! But I begin to think I have said all this before.... Oliver, or "Nolly," as he was always called, was a sort of spread-eagle likeness of his handsome father, with a conical head like Walter Scott. I must confess to you, that, in this world of books, the only one

of his I have read, is **Gabriel Denver**, afterwards
reprinted in its original and superior form as The Black
Swan, but published with the former title in his lifetime.

Rossetti formed no such philosophic estimate of Chatterton's contribution to the romantic movement in English poetry as has been formulated in the essay in Ward's **Poets**. A critic, in the sense of one possessed of a natural gift of analysis, Rossetti assuredly! was not. No man's instinct for what is good in poetry was ever swifter or surer than that of Rossetti. You might always distrust your judgment if you found it at variance with his where abstract power and beauty were in question. Sooner or later you would inevitably find yourself gravitating to his view. But here Rossetti's function as a critic ended. His was at best only the criticism of the creator. Of the gift of ultimate classification he had none, and never claimed to have any, although now and again (as where he says that Chatterton was the day-spring of modern romantic poetry), he seems to give sign of a power of critical synthesis.

Rossetti's interest in Blake, both as poet and painter, dates back to an early period of his life. I have heard him say that at sixteen or seventeen years of age he was already one of Blake's warmest admirers, and at the time in question, 1845, the author of the **Songs of Innocence** had not many readers to uphold him. About four years later, Rossetti made an exceptionally lucky discovery, for he then found in the possession of Mr. Palmer, an attendant at the British Museum, an original manuscript scrap-book of Blake's, containing a great body of unpublished poetry and many interesting designs, as well as three or four remarkably effective profile sketches of the author himself. The Mr. Palmer who held the little book was a relative of the landscape painter of the same name, who was Blake's friend, and hence the authenticity of the manuscript was ascertainable on other grounds than the indisputable ones of its internal evidences. The book was offered to Rossetti for ten shillings, but the young enthusiast was at the time a student of art, and not much in the way of getting or spending even so inconsiderable a sum. He told me, however, that at this period his brother William, who was, unlike himself, engaged in some reasonably profitable occupation, was at all times nothing loath to advance small sums for the purchase of such literary or other treasures as he used to hunt up out of obscure corners: by his help the Blake manuscript was bought, and proved for years a source of infinite pleasure and profit, resulting, as it did, in many very important additions to Blake literature when Gilchrist's **Life and Works** of that author came to be published. It is an interesting fact, mention of which ought not to be omitted, that at the sale of Rossetti's library, which took place a little while after his decease, the scrap-book acquired in the way I describe was sold for one hundred and five guineas.

The sum was a large one, but the little book was undoubtedly the most valuable literary relic of Blake then extant. About the time when a new edition of Gilchrist's **Life** was in the press, Rossetti wrote:

> My evenings have been rather trenched upon lately by helping
> Mrs. Gilchrist with a new edition of the **Life of Blake**....
> I don't know if you go in much for him. The new edition of
> the **Life** will include a good number of additional letters
> (from Blake to Hayley), and some addition (though not great)
> to my own share in the work; as well as much important
> carrying-on of my brother's catalogue of Blake's works. The
> illustrations will, I trust, receive valuable additions
> also, but publishers are apt to be cautious in such
> expenses. I am writing late at night, to fill up a fag-end
> of bedtime, and shall write again on this head.

Rossetti's "own share" in this work consisted of the writing of the supplementary chapter (left by Gilchrist, with one or two unimportant passages merely, at the beginning), and the editing of the poems. When there arose, subsequently, some idea of my reviewing the book, Rossetti wrote me the following letter, full of disinterested solicitude:

> You will be quite delighted with an essay on Blake by Jas.
> Smetham, which occurs in vol ii.; it is a noble thing; and
> at the stupendous design called **Plague** (vol. i.). I have
> extracted a passage properly belonging to the same essay,
> which is as fine as English *can* be, and which I am sorry

to perceive (I think) that Mrs. G. has omitted from the body of the essay because quoted in another place. This essay is no less than a masterpiece. I wrote the supplementary chapter (vol. i.), except a few opening paragraphs by Gilchrist,--and in it have now made some mention of Smetham, an old and dear friend of mine.

You will admire Shields's paper on the wonderful series of Young's *Night Thoughts*. My brother and I both helped in this new edition, but I added little to what I had done before. I brought forward a portentous series of passages about one "Scofield" in Blake's *Jerusalem*, but did not otherwise write that chapter, except as regards the illustrations. However, don't mention what I have done (in case you write on the subject) except so far as the indices show it, and of course I don't wish to be put forward at all. What I do wish is, that you should say everything that can be gratifying to Mrs. G. as to her husband's work. There is a plate of Blake's Cottage by young Gilchrist which is truly excellent.

As I have already said, Rossetti traversed the bypaths of English literature (particularly of English poetry) as few can ever have traversed them. A favourite work with him was Gilfillan's *Less-Read British Poets*, a copy of which had been presented by Miss Boyd. He says:

Did you ever read Christopher Smart's *Song to David*, the only great *accomplished* poem of the last century? The accomplished ones are Chatterton's,--of course I mean earlier than Blake or Coleridge, and without reckoning so exceptional a genius as Burns.... You will find Smart's poem a masterpiece of rich imagery, exhaustive resources, and reverberant sound. It is to be met with in Gilfillan's

Specimens of the Less-Read British Poets (3 vols. Nichol, Edin., 1860)....

I remember your mentioning Gilfillan as having encouraged your first efforts. He was powerful, though sometimes rather "tall" as a writer, generally most just as a critic, and lastly, a much better man, intellectually and morally, than Aytoun, who tried to "do for" him. His notice of Swift, in the volume in question, has very great force and eloquence. His whole edition of the *British Poets* is the best of any to read, being such fine type and convenient bulk and weight (a great thing for an arm-chair reader). Unfortunately, he now and then (in the *Less-Read Poets*) cuts down the extracts almost to nothing, and in some cases excises objectionabilities, which is unpardonable. Much better leave the whole out. Also, the edition includes the usual array of nobodies--Addison, Akenside, and the whole alphabet down to Zany and Zero; whereas a great many of the *less-read* would have been much-read by every worthy reader if they had only been printed in full. So well printed an edition of Donne (for instance) would have been a great boon; but from him Gilfillan only gives (among the *less-read*) the admirable Progress of the Soul and some of the pregnant Holy Sonnets. Do you know Donne? There is hardly an English poet better worth a thorough knowledge, in spite of his provoking conceits and occasional jagged jargon.

The following paragraph on Whitehead is valuable:

Charles Whitehead's principal poem is *The Solitary*, which in its day had admirers. It perhaps most recalls Goldsmith. He also wrote a supernatural poem called *Ippolito*. There was a volume of his poems published about 1848, or perhaps a little later, by Bentley. It is disappointing, on the whole, from the decided superiority of its best points to the rest.... But the novel of ***Richard Savage*** is very remarkable,--a real character really worked out.

To aid me in certain researches I was at the time engaged in making in the back-numbers of almost forgotten periodicals, Rossetti wrote:

The old ***Monthly Mag.*** was the precursor of the New Monthly, which started about 1830, or thereabouts I think, after which the old one ailed, but went on till fatal old Heraud finished it off by editing it, and fairly massacred that elderly innocent. You speak, in a former letter (touching the continuation of ***Christabel***), of "a certain European magazine." Are you aware that it was as old a thing as ***The Gentleman's***, and went on ***ad infinitum?*** Other such were the ***Universal Magazine, the Scots' Magazine***--all endless in extent and beginning time out of mind,--to say nothing of the ***Ladies' Magazine and Wits' Magazine***. Then there was the ***Annual Register***. All these are quarters in which you might prosecute researches, and might happen to find something about Keats. ***The Monthly Magazine*** must have commenced almost as early, I believe. I cannot help thinking there was a similar ***Imperial Magazine***.

The following letter possesses an interest independent of its subject, which to me, however, is interest enough. Mr. William Watson had sent Rossetti a copy of a volume of poems he had just published, and had received a letter in acknowledgment, wherein our friend, with characteristic appreciativeness, said many cordial words of it:

Your young friend Watson [he said in a subsequent letter]
wrote me in a very modest mood for one who can do as he can
at his age. I think I must have hurriedly mis-expressed
myself in writing to him, as he seems to think I wished to
dissuade him from following narrative poetry. Not in the
least--I only wished him to try his hand at clearer dramatic
life. The dreamy romantic really hardly needs more than one
vast Morris in a literature--at any rate in a century. Not
that I think him derivable from Morris--he goes straight
back to Keats with a little modification. The narrative,
whether condensed or developed, is at any rate a far better
impersonal form to work in than declamatory harangue,
whether calling on the stars or the Styx. I don't know in
the least how Watson is faring with the critics. He must not
be discouraged, in any case, with his real and high gifts.

The young poet, in whom Rossetti saw so much to applaud, can scarcely be said
to have fared at all at the hands of the critics.

Here is a pleasant piece of literary portraiture, as valuable from the peep it
affords into Rossetti's own character as from the description it gives of the rustic
poet:

The other evening I had the pleasant experience of meeting
one to whom I have for about two years looked with interest
as a poet of the native rustic kind, but often of quite a
superior order. I don't know if you noticed, somewhere about
the date referred to, in *The Athenaeum*, a review of poems
by Joseph Skipsey. Skip-sey has exquisite--though, as in all
such cases (except of course Burns's) not equal--powers in
several directions, but his pictures of humble life are the
best. He is a working miner, and describes rustic loves and
sports, and the perils and pathos of pit-life with great
charm, having a quiet humour too when needed. His more

ambitious pieces have solid merit of feeling, but are much
less artistic. The other night, as I say, he came here, and
I found him a stalwart son of toil, and every inch a
gentleman. In cast of face he recalls Tennyson somewhat,
though more bronzed and brawned. He is as sweet and gentle
as a woman in manner, and recited some beautiful things of
his own with a special freshness to which one is quite
unaccustomed.

Mr. Skipsey was a miner of North Shields, and in the review referred to much
was made, in a delicate way, of his stern environments. His volume of lyrics is
marked by the quiet humour. Rossetti speaks of, as well as by a rather exasperating
inequality. Perhaps the best piece in it is a poem entitled ***Thistle and Nettle***, treating with peculiar freshness of a country courtship. The coming together of two such
entirely opposite natures was certainly curious, and only to be accounted for on
the ground of Rossetti's breadth of poetic sympathy. It would be interesting to hear
what the impressions were of such a rude son of toil upon meeting with one whose
life must have seemed the incarnation of artistic luxury and indulgence. Later on I
received the following:

Poor Skipsey! He has lost the friend who brought him to
London only the other day (T. Dixon), and who was his only
hold on intellectual life in his district. Dixon died
immediately on his return to the North, of a violent attack
of asthma to which he was subject. He was a rarely pure and
simple soul, and is doubtless gone to higher uses, though
few could have reached, with his small opportunities, to
such usefulness as he compassed here. He was Ruskin's
correspondent in a little book called (I think) Work by
Tyne and Wear. I got a very touching note from Skipsey on
the subject.

From Mr. Skipsey he received a letter only a little while before his death, and to him he addressed one of the last epistles he penned.

The following letter explains itself, and is introduced as much for the sake of the real humour which it displays, as because it affords an excellent idea of Rossetti's view of the true function of prose:

> I don't like your Shakspeare article quite as well as the first ***Supernatural*** one, or rather I should say it does not greatly add to it in my (first) view, though both might gain by embodiment in one. I think there is ***some*** truth in the charge of metaphysical involution--the German element as I should call it--and surely you are strong enough to be English pure and simple. I am sure I could write 100 essays, on all possible subjects (I once did project a series under the title, Essays written in the intervals of Elephantiasis, Hydro-phobia, and Penal Servitude), without once experiencing the "aching void" which is filled by such words as "mythopoeic," and "anthropomorphism." I do not find life long enough to know in the least what they mean. They are both very long and very ugly indeed--the latter only suggesting to me a Vampire or Somnambulant Cannibal. (To speak rationally, would not "man-evolved Godhead" be an English equivalent?) "Euhemeristic" also found me somewhat on my beam-ends, though explanation is here given; yet I felt I could do without Euhemerus; and ***you*** perhaps without the ***humerous***. You can pardon me now; for ***so*** bad a pun places me at your mercy indeed. But seriously, simple English in prose writing and in all narrative poetry (however monumental language may become in abstract verse) seems to me a treasure not to be foregone in favour of German innovations. I know Coleridge went in latterly for as much Germanism as his time could master; but his best genius had then left him.

It seems necessary to mention that I lectured in 1880, on the relation of politics to art, and in printing the lecture I asked Rossetti to accept the dedication of it, but this he declined to do in the generous terms I have already referred to. The letter that accompanied his graceful refusal is, however, so full of interesting personal matter that I offer it in this place, with no further explanation than that my essay was designed to show that just as great artists in past ages had participated in political struggles, so now they should not hold themselves aloof from controversies which immediately concern them:

I must admit, at all hazards, that my friends here consider
me exceptionally averse to politics; and I suppose I must
be, for I never read a parliamentary debate in my life! At
the same time I will add that, among those whose opinions I
most value, some think me not altogether wrong when I
venture to speak of the momentary momentousness and eternal
futility of many noisiest questions. However, you must
simply view me as a nonentity in any practical relation to
such matters. You have spoken but too generously of a sonnet
of mine in your lecture just received. I have written a few
others of the sort (which by-the-bye would not prove me a
Tory), but felt no vocation--perhaps no right---to print
them. I have always reproached myself as sorely amenable to
the condemnations of a very fine poem by Barberino, On
Sloth against Sin, which I translated in the Dante volume.
Sloth, alas! has but too much to answer for with me; and is
one of the reasons (though I will not say the only one), why
I have always fallen back on quality instead of quantity in
the little I have ever done. I think often with Coleridge:

Sloth jaundiced all: and from my graspless hand
Drop friendship's precious pearls like hour-glass sand.
I weep, yet stoop not: the faint anguish flows,
A dreamy pang in morning's feverish doze.

However, for all I might desire in the direction spoken of, volition is vain without vocation; and I had better really stick to knowing how to mix vermilion and ultramarine for a flesh-grey, and how to manage their equivalents in verse. To speak without sparing myself,--my mind is a childish one, if to be isolated in Art is child's-play; at any rate I feel that I do not attain to the more active and practical of the mental functions of manhood. I can say this to you, because I know you will make the best and not the worst of me; and better than such feasible best I do not wish to appear. Thus you see I don't think my name ought to head your introductory paragraph--and there an end. And now of your new lecture, and of the long letter I lately had from you. At some moment I should like to know which pieces among the translations are specially your favourites. Of the three names you leash together as somewhat those of sensualists, Cecco Angiolieri is really the only one--as for the respectable Cino, he would be shocked indeed, though certainly there are a few oddities bearing that way in the sonnets between him and Dante (who is again similarly reproached by his friend Cavalcanti), but I really *do* suspect that in some cases similar to the one in question about Cino (though not Guido and Dante) politics were really meant where love was used as a metaphor.... I assure you, you cannot say too much to me of this or any other work of yours; in fact, I wish that we should communicate about them. I have been thinking yet more on the relations of politics and art. I do think seriously on consideration that not only my own sluggishness, but vital fact itself, must set to a great extent a *veto* against the absolute participation of artists in politics. When has it ever been effected? True, Cellini was a bravo and David a good deal like a murderer, and in these capacities they were not

without their political use in very turbulent times. But
when the attempt was made to turn Michael Angelo into a
"utility man" of that kind, he did (it is true) some
patriotic duty in the fortification of Florence; but it is
no less a fact that, when he had done all that he thought
became him, he retired to a certain trackless and forgotten
tower, and there stayed in some sort of peace (though much
in request) till he could lead his own life again; nor
should we forget the occasion on which he did not hesitate
even to betake himself to Venice as a refuge. Yet M. Angelo
was in every way a patriot, a philosopher, and a hero. I do
not say this to undervalue the scope of your theory. I think
possibilities are generally so much behind desirabilities
that there is no harm in any degree of incitement in the
right *direction*; and that is assuredly mental activity of
all kinds. I judge you cannot suspect *me* of thinking the
apotheosis of the early Italian poets (though surely
spiritual beauty, and not sensuality, was their general aim)
of more importance than the "unity of a great nation." But
it is in my minute power to deal successfully (I feel) with
the one, while no such entity, as I am, can advance or
retard the other; and thus mine must needs be the poorer
part. Nor (with alas, and again alas!) will Italy or another
twice have her day in its fulness.

I happened to have said in speaking of self-indulgence among artists, that there
probably existed those to whom it seemed more important to preserve such a pitiful
possession as the poetical remains of Cecco Angiolieri than to secure the unity of
a great nation. Rossetti half suspected I meant this for a playful backhanded blow
at himself (for Cecco was a great favourite with him), and protested that no such
individual could exist. I defended my charge by quoting Keats's--

... the silver flow
Of Hero's tears, the swoon of Imogen,
Fair Pastorella in the bandit's den,
Are things to brood on with more ardency
Than the death-day of empires.
But Rossetti grew weary of the jest:

I must protest that what you quote from Keats about "Hero's
tears," etc., fails to meet the text. Neither Shakspeare nor
Spenser assuredly was a Cecco; Marlowe may be most meant as
to "Hero," and he perhaps affords the shadow of a parallel
in career though not in work.

The extract from Rosetti's letters with which I shall close this chapter is perhaps the most interesting yet made:

One point I must still raise, viz., that I, for one, cannot
conceive, even as the Ghost of a Flea, the ideal individual
who considers the Poetical Remains of Cecco Angiolieri of
more importance than the unity of a great nation! I think
this would have been better if much modified. Say for
instance--"A thing of some moment even while the contest is
waging for the political unity of a great nation." This is
the utmost reach surely of human comparative valuation. I
think you have brought in Benvenuto and Michael much to the
purpose. Shall I give you a parallel in your own style?

During the months for which poet Coleridge became private
Cumberback (a name in which he said his horse would have
concurred), it seems strange that, in such stirring times,
his regiment should not have been ordered off on foreign
service. In such case that pre-eminent member of the awkward
squad would assuredly have been the very first man killed.

Should we have been more the gainers by his patriotism or the losers by his poetry? The very last man killed in the last *sortie* from Paris during the Prussian siege (he would go behind a buttress to "pot" a Prussian after orders were given to retire, and so got "potted" himself) was Henri Regnault, a painter, whose brilliant work was a guiding beacon on the road of improvement in French methods of art, if not in intellectual force. Who shall fail to honour the noble ardour which drew him from the security of his studies in Tunis to partake his country's danger? Yet who shall forbear to sigh in thinking that, but for this, his progressing work might still yearly be an element in art-progress for Europe? Gerome and others betook themselves to England instead, and are still benefiting the cause for which they were before all things born. It was David who said, "Si on tirait a mitraille sur les artistes, on n'y tuerait pas un seul patriote!" *He* was a patriot homicide, and spoke probably what was true in the sense in which he meant it. As I said, I am glad you turned Ben and Mike to account, but the above is in some respects an open question.

I have, as I say, a further batch of letters to introduce, but as these were, for the most part, written after an event which forms a land-mark in our acquaintance (I mean the occasion of our first meeting), I judge it is best to reserve them for a later section of this book. There are two forms, and, so far as I know, two only, in which a body of letters can be published with justice to the writer. Of these the first and most obvious form is to offer them chronologically *in extenso* or with only such eliminations as seem inevitable, and the second is to tabulate them according to subject-matter, and print them in the order not of date but substance. There are advantages attending each method, and corresponding disadvantages also. The temptation to adopt the first of these was, in this case of Rossetti's letters, almost insurmountable, for nothing can be more charming in epistolary style than the easy grace with which the writer passes from point to point, evolving one idea out of another, interlinking subject with subject, and building up a fabric of which the meaning is everywhere inwoven. In this respect Rossetti's letters are almost as perfect as anything that ever left his hand; and, in freedom of phrase, in power of throwing off parenthetical reflections always faultlessly enunciated, in play of humour, often in eloquence (never becoming declamatory, and calling on "Styx or Stars"), sometimes in pathos, Rossetti's letters are, in a word, admirable. They are comparable in these respects with the best things yet done in English,--as pleasing and graceful as Cowper's letters, broader in range of subject than the letters of Keats, easier and more colloquial than those of Coleridge, and with less appearance of being intended for the public eye than is the case with the letters of Byron and of Shelley. Rossetti's letters have, moreover, a value quite apart from the merits of their epistolary style, in so far as they contain almost the only expression extant of his opinions on literary questions. And this is the circumstance that has chiefly weighed with me to offer them in fragmentary form interspersed with elucidatory comment bearing principally upon the occasions that called them forth.

Such then as I have described was the nature of my intercourse with Rossetti during the first year and a half of our correspondence, and now the time had come when I was to meet my friend for the first time face to face. The elasticity of sympathy by which a man of genius, surrounded by constant friends, could yet bend to a new-comer who was a stranger and twenty-five years his junior, and think and feel with him; the generous appreciativeness by which he could bring himself to consider the first efforts of one quite unknown; and then the unselfishness that seemed always to prefer the claims of others to his own great claims, could command only the return of unqualified allegiance. Such were the feelings with which I went forth to my first meeting with Rossetti, and if at any later date, the ardour of my regard for him in any measure suffered modification, be sure when the time comes to touch upon it I shall make no more concealment of the causes that led to such a change than I have made of those circumstances, however personal in primary interest, that generated a friendship so unusual and to me so serious and important.

CHAPTER VII.

It was in the autumn of 1880 that I saw Rossetti for the first time. Being then rather reduced in health I contemplated a visit to the sea-side and wrote saying that in passing through London I should avail myself of his oft-repeated invitation to visit him. I gave him this warning of my intention, remembering his declared dread of being taken unawares, but I came to know at a subsequent period that for one who was within the inner circle of his friends the necessity to advise him of a visit was by no means binding. His reception of my intimation of an intention to call upon him was received with an amount of epistolary ceremony which I recognise now by the light of further acquaintance as eminently characteristic of the man, although curiously contradictory of his unceremonious habits of daily life. The fact is that Rossetti was of an excessively nervous temperament, and rarely if ever underwent an ordeal more trying than a first meeting with any one to whom for some time previously he had looked forward with interest. Hence by return of the post that bore him my missive came two letters, the one obviously written and posted within an hour or two of the other. In the first of these he expressed courteously his pleasure at the prospect of seeing me, and appointed 8.30 p.m. the following evening as his dinner hour at his house in Cheyne Walk. The second letter begged me to come at 5.30 or 6 p.m., so that we might have a long evening. "You will, I repeat," he says, "recognise the hole-and-cornerest of all existences in this big barn of mine; but come early and I shall read you some ballads, and we can talk of many things." An hour later than the arrival of these letters came a third epistle, which ran: "Of course when I speak of your dining with me, I mean tete-a-tete and without ceremony of any kind. I usually dine in my studio and in my painting coat!" I had before me a five hours' journey to London, so that in order to reach Chelsea at 6 P.M., I must needs set out at mid-day, but oblivious of this necessity, Rossetti had actually posted a fourth letter on the morning of the day on which we were to meet begging me not on any account to talk, in the course of our interview, of a certain personal matter upon which we had corresponded. This fourth and final message came to hand the morning after the meeting, when I had the satisfaction to reflect that (owing more perhaps to the plethora of other subjects of interest than to any suspicion of its being tabooed) I had luckily eschewed the proscribed topic.

Cheyne Walk was unknown to me at the time in question, except as the locality in and near which many men and women eminent in literature resided. It seems hard to realise that this was the case as recently as two years ago, now that so short an interval has associated it in one's mind with memories which seem to cover a large part of one's life. The Walk is not now exactly as picturesque as it appears in certain familiar old engravings; the new embankment and the gardens that separate it from the main thoroughfare have taken something from its beauty, but it still possesses many attractions, and among them a look of age which contrasts agreeably with the spic-and-span newness of neighbouring places. I found Rossetti's house, No. 16, answering in external appearances to the frank description he gave of it. It stands about mid-way between the Chelsea pier and the new redbrick mansions erected on the Chelsea embankment. It seems to be the oldest house in the Walk, and the exceptional proportions of its gate-piers, and the weight and mass of its gate and railings, suggests that probably at some period it stood alone, and commanded as grounds a large part of the space now occupied by the adjoining residences. Behind the house, during eighteen years of Rossetti's occupancy, there was a garden of almost an acre in extent, covering by much the larger part of the space enclosed by a block of four streets forming a square. At No. 4 Maclise had lived and died; at the same house George Eliot, after her marriage with Mr. Cross, had come to live; at No. 5, in the second street to the westward, Thomas Carlyle was still living, and a little beyond Cheyne Row stood the modest cottage wherein Turner died. Rossetti's house had to me the appearance of a plain Queen Anne erection, much mutilated by the introduction of unsightly bay-windows; the brickwork seemed to be falling into decay; the paint to be in serious need of renewal; the windows to be dull with the accumulation of the dust of years; the sills to bear the suspicion of cobwebs; the angles of the steps and the untrodden flags of the courtyard to be here and there overgrown with moss and weeds; and round the walls and up the reveals of doors and windows were creeping the tangled branches of the wildest ivy that ever grew untouched by shears. Such was the exterior of the home of the poet-painter when I walked up to it on the autumn evening of my first visit, and the interior of the house was at once like and unlike the exterior. The hall had a puzzling look of equal nobility and shabbiness. The floor was paved with beautiful white marble, which however, was partly covered with a strip of worn cocoa-nut matting; the ceiling was in one of its sections gracefully groined, and in each of the walls, which were lofty, there was an arched recess containing a piece of sculpture; an old inlaid rose-wood clock filled a bulkhead on one side facing the door, and on the corresponding side stood a massive gas branch. A mezzotint lithograph by Legros was the only pictorial decoration of the walls, which were plain, and seemed not to have been distempered for many years. Three doors led out of the hall, one at each side, and one in front, and two corridors opened into it, but there was no sign of staircase, nor had it any light except such as was borrowed from the fanlight that looked into the porch. These facts I noted in the few minutes I stood waiting in the hall, but during the many months in which subsequently that house was my own home as well as Rossetti's, I came to see that the changes which the building must have undergone since the period of its erection, had so filled it with crooks and corners as to bewilder the most ingenious observer to account for its peculiarities.

Very soon Rossetti came to me through the doorway in front, which proved to be the entrance to his studio. Holding forth both hands and crying 'Hulloa,' he gave me that cheery, hearty greeting which I came to recognise as his alone, perhaps, in warmth and unfailing geniality among all the men of our circle. It was Italian in its spontaneity, and yet it was English in its manly reserve, and I remember with much tenderness of feeling that never to the last (not even when sickness saddened him, or after an absence of a few days or even hours) did it fail him when meeting with those friends to whom to the last he was really attached. Leading the way into the studio, he introduced me to his brother, who was there upon one of the evening visits, which at intervals of a week he was at that time making, with unfailing regularity. I should have described Rossetti, at this time, as a man who looked quite ten years older than his actual age, which was fifty-two, of full middle height and inclining to corpulence, with a round face that ought, one thought, to be ruddy but was pale, large grey eyes with a steady introspecting look, surmounted by broad protrusive brows and a clearly-pencilled ridge over the nose, which was well cut and had large breathing nostrils. The mouth and chin were hidden beneath a heavy moustache and abundant beard, which grew up to the ears, and had been of a mixed black-brown and auburn, and were now streaked with grey. The forehead was large, round, without protuberances, and very gently receding to where thin black curls, that had once been redundant, began to tumble down to the ears. The entire configuration of the head and face seemed to me singularly noble, and from the eyes upwards, full of beauty. He wore a pair of spectacles, and, in reading, a second pair over the first: but these took little from the sense of power conveyed by those steady eyes, and that "bar of Michael Angelo." His dress was not conspicuous, being however rather negligent than otherwise, and noticeable, if at all, only for a straight sack-coat buttoned at the throat, descending at least to the knees, and having large pockets cut into it perpendicularly at the sides. This garment was, I afterwards found, one of the articles of various kinds made to the author's own design. When he spoke, even in exchanging the preliminary courtesies of an opening conversation, I thought his voice the richest I had ever known any one to possess. It was a full deep barytone, capable of easy modulation, and with undertones of infinite softness and sweetness, yet, as I afterwards found, with almost illimitable compass, and with every gradation of tone at command, for the recitation or reading of poetry. The studio was a large room probably measuring thirty feet by twenty, and structurally as puzzling as the other parts of the house. A series of columns and arches on one side suggested that the room had almost certainly been at some period the site of an important staircase with a wide well, and on the other side a broad mullioned window reaching to the ceiling, seemed certainly to bear record of the occupant's own contribution to the peculiarities of the edifice. The fireplace was at an end of the room, and over and at each side of it were hung a number of fine drawings in chalk, chiefly studies of heads, with here and there a water-colour figure piece, all from Rossetti's hand. At the opposite end of the room hung some symbolic designs in chalk, *Pandora* and *Proserpina* being among the number, and easels of various sizes, some very large, bearing pictures in differing stages of completion, occupied positions on all sides of the floor, leaving room only for a sofa, with a bookcase behind, two old cabinets, two large low easy chairs, and a writing desk and chair at a window at the side, which was heavily darkened by the thick foliage of the trees that grew in the garden beyond.

Dropping down on the sofa with his head laid low and his feet thrown up in a favourite attitude on the back, which must, I imagine, have been at least as easy as it was elegant, he began the conversation by bantering me upon what he called my "robustious" appearance compared with what he had been led to expect from gloomy reports of uncertain health. After a series of playful touches (all done in the easiest conceivable way, and conveying any impression on earth save the right one, that a first meeting with any man, however young and harmless, was little less than a tragic event to Rossetti) he glanced one by one at certain of the topics that had arisen in the course of our correspondence. I perceived that he was a ready, fluent, and graceful talker, with a remarkable incisiveness of speech, and a trick of dignifying ordinary topics in words which, without rising above conversation, were so exactly, though freely enunciated, as would have admitted of their being reported exactly as they fell from his lips. In some of these respects I found his brother William resemble him, though, if I may describe the talk of a dead friend by contrasting it with that of a living one bearing a natural affinity to it, I will say that Gabriel's conversation was perhaps more spontaneous, and had more variety of tone with less range of subject, together with the same precision and perspicuity. Very soon the talk became general, and then Rossetti spoke without appearance of reserve of his two or three intimate friends, telling me, among other things, of Theodore Watts, that he "had a head exactly like that of Napoleon I., whom Watts," he said with a chuckle, "detests more than any character in history; depend upon it," he added, "such a head was not given to him for nothing;" that Frederick Shields was as emotional as Shelley, and Ford Madox Brown, whom I had met, as sententious as Dr. Johnson. I kept no sort of record of what passed upon the occasion in question, but I remember that Rossetti seemed to be playfully battering his friends in their absence in the assured consciousness that he was doing so in the presence of a well-wisher; and it was amusing to observe that, after any particularly lively sally, he would pause to say something in a sobered tone that was meant to convey the idea that he was really very jealous of his friends' reputation, and was merely for the sake of amusement giving rein to a sportive fancy. During dinner (and contrary to his declared habit, we did not dine in the studio) he talked a good deal about Oliver Madox Brown, for whom I had conceived a warm admiration, and to whom I had about that time addressed a sonnet.

"You had a sincere admiration of the boy's gifts?" I asked.

"Assuredly. I have always said that twenty years after his death his name will be a familiar one. *The Black Swan* is a powerful story, although I must honestly say that it displays in its central incident a certain torpidity that to me is painful. Undoubtedly Oliver had genius, and must have done great things had he lived. His death was a grievous blow to his father. I'm glad you've written that sonnet; I wanted you to toss up your cap for Nolly." He spoke of Oliver's father as indisputably one of the greatest of living colourists, inquired earnestly into the progress of his frescoes at Manchester, for one of the figures in which I had sat, and showed me a little water-colour drawing made by Oliver himself when very young. Dinner being now over, I asked Rossetti to redeem his promise to read one of his new ballads; and as his brother, who had often heard it before, expressed his readiness to hear it again, he responded readily, and, taking a small manuscript volume out of a section of the bookcase that had been locked, read us *The White Ship*. I have spoken of the ballad as a poem at an earlier stage, but it remains to me, in this place, to describe the effect produced upon me by the author's reading. It seemed to me that I never heard anything at all matchable with Rossetti's elocution; his rich deep voice lent an added music to the music of the verse: it rose and fell in the passages descriptive of the wreck with something of the surge and sibilation of the sea itself; in the tenderer passages it was soft as a woman's, and in the pathetic stanzas with which the ballad closes it was profoundly moving. Effective as the reading sounded in that studio, I remember at the moment to have doubted if it would prove quite so effective from a public platform. Perhaps there seemed to be so much insistence on the rhythm, and so prolonged a tension of the rhyme sounds, as would run the risk of a charge of monotony if falling on ears less concerned with points of metrical beauty than with fundamental substance. Personally, however, I found the reading in the very highest degree enjoyable and inspiring.

The evening was gone by the time the ballad was ended; and it was arranged that upon my return to London from the house of a friend at the sea-side I should again dine with Rossetti, and sleep the night at Cheyne Walk. I was invited to come early in order to see certain pictures by day-light, and it was then I saw the painter's most important work,--the *Dantes Dream*, which finally (and before

Rossetti was made aware of any steps being taken to that end) I had prevailed with Alderman Samuelson to purchase for the public gallery at Liverpool. At my request, though only after some importunity, Rossetti read again his **White Ship**, and afterwards **Rose Mary**, the latter of which he told me had been written in the country shortly after the appearance of the first volume of poems. He remarked that it had occupied three weeks in the writing, and that the physical prostration ensuing had been more than he would care to go through again. I observed on this head, that though highly finished in every stanza, the ballad had an impetuous rush of emotion, and swift current of diction, suggesting speed in its composition, as contrasted with the laboured deliberation which the sonnets, for example, appeared to denote. I asked if his work usually took much out of him in physical energy.

"Not my painting, certainly," he replied, "though in early years it tormented me more than enough. Now I paint by a set of unwritten but clearly-defined rules, which I could teach to any man as systematically as you could teach arithmetic; indeed, quite recently I sat all day for that very purpose with Shields, who is not so great a colourist as he is a draughtsman: he is a great draughtsman--none better now living, unless it is Leighton or Sir Noel Paton."

"Still," I said, "there's usually a good deal in a picture of yours beside what you can do by rule."

"Fundamental conception, no doubt, but beyond that not much. In painting, after all, there is in the less important details something of the craft of a superior carpenter, and the part of a picture that is not mechanical is often trivial enough. I don't wonder, now," he added, with a suspicion of a twinkle in the eye, "if you imagine that one comes down here in a fine frenzy every morning to daub canvas?"

"I certainly imagine," I replied, "that a superior carpenter would find it hard to paint another **Dante's Dream**, which some people consider the best example yet seen of the English school."

"That is friendly nonsense," rejoined my frank host, "there is now no English school whatever."

"Well," I said, "if you deny the name to others who lay more claim to it, will you not at least allow it to the three or four painters who started with you in life?"

"Not at all, unless it is to Brown, and he's more French than English; Hunt and

Jones have no more claim to the name than I have. As for all the prattle about pre-Raphaelitism, I confess to you I am weary of it, and long have been. Why should we go on talking about the visionary vanities of half-a-dozen boys? We've all grown out of them, I hope, by now."

I remarked that the pre-Raphaelite movement was no doubt a serious one at the beginning.

"What you call the movement was serious enough, but the banding together under that title was all a joke. We had at that time a phenomenal antipathy to the Academy, and in sheer love of being outlawed signed our pictures with the well-known initials." I have preserved the substance of what Rossetti said on this point, and, as far as possible, the actual words have been given. On many subsequent occasions he expressed himself in the same way: assuredly with as much seeming depreciation of the painter's "craft," although certain examples of modern art called forth his warmest eulogies. In serious moods he would speak of pictures by Millais, Watts, Leighton, Burne Jones, and others, as works of the highest genius.

Reverting to my inquiry as to whether his work took much out of him, he remarked that his poetry usually did. "In that respect," he said, "I am the reverse of Swinburne. For his method of production inspiration is indeed the word. With me the case is different. I lie on the couch, the racked and tortured medium, never permitted an instant's surcease of agony until the thing on hand is finished."

It was obvious that what Rossetti meant by being racked and tortured, was that his subject possessed him; that he was enslaved by his own "shaping imagination." Assuredly he was the reverse of a costive poet: impulse was, to use his own phrase, fully developed in his muse.

I made some playful allusion, assuredly not meant to involve Mr. Swinburne, to Sheridan's epigram on easy writing and hard reading; and to the Abbe de Ma-rolles, who exultingly told some poet that his verses cost no trouble: "They cost you what they are worth," replied the bard.

"One benefit I do derive," Rossetti added, "as a result of my method of composition; my work becomes condensed. Probably the man does not live who could write what I have written more briefly than I have done."

Emphasis and condensation, I remarked, were indubitably the characteristics of his muse. He then read me a great body of the new sonnets of ***The House of***

Life. Sitting in that studio listening to his reading and looking up meantime at the chalk-drawings that hung on the walls, I realised how truly he had said, in correspondence, that the feeling pervading his pictures was such as his poetry ought to suggest. The affinity between the two seemed to me at that moment to be complete: the same half-sad, half-resigned view of life, the same glimpses of hope, the same foreshadowings of gloom.

"You doubtless think it odd," he said at one moment, "to hear an old fellow read such love-poetry as much of this is, but I may tell you that the larger part of it, though still unpublished, was written when I was as young as you are. When I print these sonnets, I shall probably affix a note saying, that though many of them are of recent production, not a few are obviously the work of earlier years."

I expressed admiration of the pathetic sonnet entitled *Without Her*.

"I cannot tell you," he said, "at what terrible moment it was wrung from me."

He had read it with tears of voice, subsiding at length into suppressed sobs and intervals of silence. As though to explain away this emotion he said:

"All poetry, that is really poetry, affects me deeply and often to tears. It does not need to be pathetic or yet tender to produce such a result. I have known in my life two men, and two only, who are similarly sensitive--Tennyson, and my old friend and neighbour William Bell Scott. I once heard Tennyson read *Maud*, and whilst the fiery passages were delivered with a voice and vehemence which he alone of living men can compass, the softer passages and the songs made the tears course down his cheeks. Morris is a fine reader, and so, of his kind, though a little prone to sing-song, is Swinburne. Browning both reads and talks well--at least he did so when I knew him intimately as a young man."

Rossetti went on to say that he had been among Browning's earliest admirers. As a boy he had seen something signed by the then unknown name of the author of *Paracelsus*, and wrote to him. The result was an intimacy. He spoke with warmest admiration of *Child Roland*; and referred to Elizabeth Barrett Browning in terms of regard, and, I think I may say, of reverence.

I asked if he had ever heard Ruskin read. He replied:

"I must have done so, but remember nothing clearly. On one occasion, however, I heard him deliver a speech, and that was something never to forget. When we were young, we helped Frederick Denison Maurice by taking classes at the Working

Men's College, and there Charles Kingsley and others made speeches and delivered lectures. Ruskin was asked to do something of the kind and at length consented. He made no sort of preparation for the occasion: I know he did not; we were together at his father's house the whole of the day in question. At night we drove down to the College, and then he made the finest speech I ever heard. I doubted at the time if any written words of his were equal to it! such flaming diction! such emphasis! such appeal!--yet he had written his first and second volumes of **Modern Painters** by that time." I have reproduced the substance of what Rossetti said on the occasion of my return visit, and, by help of letters written at the time to a friend, I have in many cases recalled his exact words. A certain incisiveness of speech which distinguished his conversation, I confess myself scarcely able to convey more than a suggestion of; as Mr. Watts has said in *The Athenaeum*, his talk showed an incisiveness so perfect that it had often the pleasurable surprise of wit. Rossetti had both wit and humour, but these, during the time that I knew him, were only occasionally present in his conversation, while the incisiveness was always conspicuous. A certain quiet play of sportive fancy, developing at intervals into banter, was sometimes observable in his talk with the younger and more familiar of his acquaintances, but for the most part his conversation was serious, and, during the time I knew him, often sad. I speedily observed that he was not of the number of those who lead or sustain conversation. He required to be constantly interrogated, but as a negative talker, if I may so describe him, he was by much the best I had heard. Catching one's drift before one had revealed it, and anticipating one's objections, he would go on from point to point, almost removing the necessity for more than occasional words. Nevertheless, as I say, he was not, in the conversations I have heard, a leading conversationalist; his talk was never more than talk, and in saying that it was uniformly sustained yet never declamatory, I think I convey an idea both of its merits and limitations.

I understood that Rossetti had never at any period of his life been an early riser, and at the time of the interview in question he was more than ever before prone to reverse the natural order of waking and sleeping hours. I am convinced that during the time I was with him only the necessity of securing a certain short interval of daylight, by which it was possible to paint, prevailed with him to rise before noon. Alluding to this idiosyncrasy, he said: "I lie as long, or say as late, as Dr. Johnson used to do. You shall never know, until you discover it for yourself, at what hour I rise." He sat up until four A.M. on this night of my second visit,--no unaccustomed thing, as I afterwards learned. I must not omit the mention of one feature of the conversation, revealing to me a new side of his character, or, more properly, a new phase of his mind, which gave me subsequently an infinity of anxiety and distress. Branching off at a late hour from some entirely foreign topic, he begged me to tell him the facts of some unlucky debate in which I had long before been engaged on a public platform with some one who had attacked him. He had heard a report of what passed at a time when my name was unknown to him, as also was that of his assailant. Being forewarned by William Rossetti of his brother's peculiar sensitiveness to critical attack, and having, moreover, observed something of the kind myself, I tried to avoid a circumstantial statement of what passed. But Rossetti was, as has been said by one who knew him well, "of imagination all compact," and my obvious desire to shelve the subject suggested to his mind a thousand inferences infinitely more damaging than the fact. To avoid such a result I told him all, and there was little in the way of attack to repeat beyond a few unwelcome strictures on his poem *Jenny*. He listened but too eagerly to what I was saying, and then in a voice slower, softer, and more charged, perhaps, with emotion than I had heard before, said it was the old story, which began ten years before, and would go on until he had been hunted and hounded to his grave. Startled, and indeed, appalled by so grave a view of what to me had seemed no more than an error of critical judgment, coupled perhaps, with some intemperance of condemnation, I prayed of him to think no more of the matter, reproached myself with having yielded to his importunity, and begged him to remember that if one man held the opinions I had repeated, many men held contrary ones.

"It was right of you to tell me when I asked you," he said, "though my friends usually keep such facts from my knowledge. As to *Jenny*, it is a sermon, nothing less. As I say, it is a sermon, and on a great world, to most men unknown, though few consider themselves ignorant of it. But of this conspiracy to persecute me--what remains to say but that it is widespread and remorseless--one cannot but feel it."

I assured him there existed no conspiracy to persecute him: that he had ardent upholders everywhere, though it was true that few men had found crueller critics. He shook his head, and said I knew that what he had alleged was true, namely that an organised conspiracy existed, having for its object to annoy and injure him.

Growing a little impatient of this delusion, so tenaciously held, against all show of reason, I told him that it was no more than the fever of an oppressed brain brought about by his reclusive habits of life, by shunning intercourse with all save some half dozen or more friends. "You tell me," I said, "that you have rarely been outside these walls for some years, and your brain has meanwhile been breeding a host of hallucinations, like cobwebs in a dark corner. You have only to go abroad, and the fresh air will blow these things away." But continuing for some moments longer in the same strain, he came to closer quarters and distressed me by naming as enemies three or four men who had throughout life been his friends, who have spoken of him since his death in words of admiration and even affection, and who had for a time fallen away from him or called on him but rarely, from contingencies due to any cause but alienated friendship.

At length the time had arrived when it was considered prudent to retire. "You are to sleep in Watts's room to-night," he said: and then in reply to a look of inquiry he added, "He comes here at least twice a week, talking until four o'clock in the morning upon everything from poetry to the Pleiades, and driving away the bogies, and as he lives at Putney Hill, it is necessary to have a bed for him." Before going into my room he suggested that I should go and look, at his. It was entered from another and smaller room which he said that he used as a breakfast room. The outer room was made fairly bright and cheerful by a glittering chandelier (the property once, he told me, of David Garrick), and from the rustle of trees against the window-pane one perceived that it overlooked the garden; but the inner room was dark with heavy hangings around the walls as well as the bed, and thick velvet curtains before the windows, so that the candles in our hands seemed unable to light it, and our voices sounded thick and muffled. An enormous black oak chimney-piece of curious design, having an ivory crucifix on the largest of its ledges, covered a part of one side and reached to the ceiling. Cabinets, and the usual furniture of a bedroom, occupied places about the floor: and in the middle of it, and before a little couch, stood a small table on which was a wire lantern containing a candle which Rossetti lit from the open one in his hand--another candle meantime lying by its side. I re-marked that he probably burned a light all night. He said that was so. "My curse," he added, "is insomnia. Two or three hours hence I shall get up and lie on the couch, and, to pass away a weary hour, read this book"--a volume of Boswell's ***Johnson*** which I noticed he took out of the bookcase as we left the studio. It did not escape me that on the table stood two small bottles sealed and labelled, together with a little measuring-glass. Without looking further at it, but with a terrible suspicion growing over me, I asked if that were his medicine.

"They say there is a skeleton in every cupboard," he said in a low voice, "and that's mine; it is chloral."

When I reached the room that I was to occupy during the night, I found it, like Rossetti's bedroom, heavy with hangings, and black with antique picture panels, with a ceiling (unlike that of the other rooms in the house), out of all reach or sight, and so dark from various causes, that the candle seemed only to glimmer in it-- indeed to add to the darkness by making it felt. Mr. Watts, as Rossetti told me, was entirely indifferent to these eerie surroundings, even if his fine subjective intellect, more prone to meditate than to observe, was ever for an instant conscious of them; but on myself I fear they weighed heavily, and augmented the feeling of closeness and gloom which had been creeping upon me since I entered the house. Scattered about the room in most admired disorder were some outlandish and unheard-of books, and all kinds of antiquarian and Oriental oddities, which books and oddities I afterwards learnt had been picked up at various times by the occupant in his ram-blings about Chelsea and elsewhere, and never yet taken away by him, but left there apparently to scare the chambermaid: such as old carved heads and gargoyles of the most grinning and ghastly expression, Burmese and Chinese Buddhas in soapstone of every degree of placid ugliness, together, I am bound by force of truth to admit, with one piece of carved Italian marble in bas-relief, of great interest and beauty. Such was my bed-chamber for the night, and little wonder if it threatened to mur-der the innocent sleep. But it was later than 4 A.M., and wearied nature must needs assert herself, and so I lay down amidst the odour of bygone ages.

Presently Rossetti came in, for no purpose that I can remember, except to say that he had enjoyed my visit I replied that I should never forget it. "If you decide to settle in London," he said, "I trust you 'll come and live with me, and then many such evenings must remove the memory of this one." I laughed, for I thought what he hinted at to be of the remotest likelihood. "I have just taken sixty grains of chlo-ral," he said, as he was going out; "in four hours I take sixty more, and in four hours after that yet another sixty."

"Does not the dose increase with you?"

"It has not done so perceptibly in recent years. I judge I've taken more chloral than any man whatever: Marshall says if I were put into a Turkish bath I should sweat it at every pore."

There was something in his tone suggesting that he was even proud of the accomplishment. To me it was a frightful revelation, accounting entirely for what had puzzled and distressed me in his delusions already referred to. And now let me say that whilst it would have been on my part the most pitiful weakness (because the most foolish tearfulness of injuring a great man who was strong enough to suffer a good deal to be discounted from his strength), to attempt to conceal this painful side of Rossetti's mind, I shall not again allude to those delusions, unless it be to show that, coming to him with the drug which blighted half his life, they disappeared when it had been removed.

None may rightly say to what the use of that drug was due, or what was due to it; the sadder side of his life was ever under its shadow; his occasional distrust of friends: his fear of enemies: his broken health and shattered spirits, all came of his indulgence in the pernicious thing. When I remember this I am more than willing to put by all thought of the little annoyances, which to me, as to other immediate friends, were constantly occurring through that cause, which seemed at the moment so vexatious and often so insupportable, but which are now forgotten.

Next morning--(a clear autumn morning)--I strolled through the large garden at the back of the house, and of course I found it of a piece with what I had previously seen. A beautiful avenue of lime-trees opened into a grass plot of nearly an acre in extent. The trees were just as nature made them, and so was the grass, which in places was lying long, dry and withered under the sun, weeds creeping up in damp places, and the gravel of the pathway scattered upon the verges. This neglected condition of the garden was, I afterwards found, humorously charged upon Mr. Watts's "reluctance to interfere with nature in her clever scheme of the survival of the fittest," but I suspect it was due at least equally to the owner's personal indifference to everything of the kind.

Before leaving I glanced over the bookcase. Rossetti's library was by no means a large one. It consisted, perhaps, of 1000 volumes, scarcely more; and though this was not large as comprising the library of one whose reading must have been in two arts pursued as special studies, and each involving research and minute original inquiry, it cannot be considered noticeably small, and it must have been sufficient. Rossetti differed strangely as a reader from the man to whom in bias of genius he was most nearly related. Coleridge was an omnivorous general reader: Rossetti was eclectic rather than desultory. His library contained a number of valuable old works of more interest to him from their plates than letterpress. Of this kind were *Gerard's Herbal* (1626), supposed to be the source of many a hint utilised by the Morris firm, of which Rossetti was a member; *Poliphili Hypnerotomachia* (1467); Heywood's *History of Women* (1624); *Songe de Poliphile* (1561); Bonnard's *Costumes of 12th, 13th, and 14th Centuries; Habiti Antichi* (of which the designs are said to be by Titian)--printed Venice, (1664); *Cosmographia*, a history of the peoples of the world (1572); *Ciceronis Officia* (1534), a blackletter folio, with woodcuts by Burgkmaier; *Jost Amman's Costumes*, with woodcuts coloured by hand; *Cento Novelle* (Venice, 1598); Francesco Barberino's Documenti (d'Amore (Rome, 1640); *Decoda de Titolivio*, a Spanish blackletter, without date, but probably belonging to the 16th century. Besides these were various vellum-bound works relating to Greek and Roman allegorical and mythological subjects, and a number of scrap-books and portfolios containing photographs from nearly all the picture-galleries of Europe, but chiefly of the pictures of the early Florentine and Venetian schools, with an admixture of Spanish art. Of Michael Angelo's designs for the Sistine Chapel there was a fine set of photographs.

These did not make up a very complete ancient artistic library, but Rossetti's collection of the poets was more full and valuable. There was a pretty little early edition of Petrarch, which appeared to have been presented first by John Philip Kemble to Polidori (Rossetti's grandfather) in 1812; then in 1853 by Polidori to his daughter, Rossetti's mother, Frances Rossetti; and by her in 1870 to her son. A splendid edition (1552) of Boccaccio's *Decamerone* contained a number of valuable marginal notes, chiefly by Rossetti, the first being as follows:

This volume contains 40 woodcuts besides many initial letters. The greater number, if not the whole, must certainly be by Holbein. I am in doubt as to the pictures heading the chapters, but think these most probably his, only following the usual style of such illustrations to Boccaccio, and consequently more Italianised than the others. The initial letters present for the most part games of strength or skill.

There were various editions of Dante, including a very large folio edition of the ***Commedia***, dated Florence, 1481, and the works of a number of Dante's contemporaries. Besides two or three editions of Shakspeare (the best being Dyce's, in 9 vols.), there were some of the Elizabethan dramatists. Coming to later poetry, I found a complete set of Gilfillan's ***Poets***, in 45 vols. There was the curious little manuscript quarto (much like a shilling school-exercise book) labelled ***Blake***, and this was, perhaps, by far the most valuable volume in the library. The contents and history of this book have already been given.

There were two editions of Gilchrist's ***Blake***; complete (or almost complete) sets of the works of William Morris and A. C. Swinburne, inscribed in the authors' autographs--the copy of ***Atalanta in Calydon*** being marked by the poet, "First copy; printed off before the dedication was in type." It may be remembered that Robert Brough translated Beranger's songs, and dedicated his volume in affectionate terms to Rossetti. The presentation copy of this book bore the following inscription:--"To D. G. Rossetti, meaning in my ***heart*** what I have tried to say in print. Et. B. Brough. 1856." There were also several presentation copies from Robert Browning, Coventry Patmore, W. B. Scott, Sir Henry Taylor, Aubrey de Vere, Tom Taylor, Westland Marston, F. Locker, A. O'Shaughnessy, Sir Theodore Martin; besides volumes bearing the names of nearly every well-known younger writer of prose or verse.

Five volumes of ***Modern Painters***, together with ***The Seven Lamps of Architecture*** and the tract on ***Pre-Raphaelitism***, bore the author's name and Rossetti's in Mr. Ruskin's autograph. There was a fine copy in ten volumes of Violet-le-Duc's ***Dictionnaire de l'Architecture***, and also of the ***Biographie Generale*** in forty-six volumes, besides several dictionaries, concordances, and the like. There was also a copy of Fitzgerald's ***Calderon***. Rossetti seemed to be a reader of Swedenborg, as White's book on the great mystic testified; also to have been at one time interested in the investigation of the phenomena of Spiritualism. Of one writer of fiction he must have been an ardent reader, for there were at least 100 volumes by Alexandre Dumas. German writers were conspicuously absent, Goethe's ***Faust*** and

Carlyle's translation of **Wilhelm, Meister**, being about the only notable German works in the library. Rossetti did not appear to be a collector of first editions, nor did it seem that he attached much importance to the mere outsides of his books, but of the insides he was master indeed. The impression left upon the mind after a rapid survey of the poet-painter's library was that he was a careful, but slow and thorough reader (as was seen by the marginal annotations which nearly every volume contained), and that, though very far from affected by bibliomania, he was not without pride in the possession of rare and valuable books.

When I left the house at a late hour that morning Rossetti was not yet stirring, and so some months passed before I saw him again. If I had tried to formulate the idea--or say sensation--that possessed me at the moment, I think I should have said, in a word or two, that outside the air breathed freely. Within, the gloom, the mediaeval furniture, the brass censers, sacramental cups, lamps; and crucifixes conspired, I thought, to make the atmosphere heavy and unwholesome. As for the man himself who was the central spirit amidst these anachronistic environments, he had, if possible, attached me yet closer to himself by contact. Before this I had been attracted to him in admiration of his gifts: but now I was drawn to him, in something very like pity, for his isolation and suffering. Not that at this time he consciously made demand of much compassion, and least of all from me. Health was apparently whole with him, his spirits were good, and his energies were at their best. He had not yet known the full bitterness of the shadowed valley: not yet learned what it was to hunger for any cheerful society that would relieve him of the burden of the flesh. All that came later. Rossetti was one of the most magnetic of men, but it was not more his genius than his unhappiness that held certain of his friends by a spell.

CHAPTER VIII.

It was characteristic of Rossetti that he addressed me in the following terms probably before I had left his house: for the letter was, no doubt, written in that interval of sleeplessness which he had spoken of as his nightly visitant:

I forgot to say--Don't, please, spread details as to story of **Rose Mary**. I don't want it to be stale or to get forestalled in the travelling of report from mouth to mouth. I hope it won't be too long before you visit town again,--I will not for an instant question that you would then visit me also.

Six months or more intervened, however, before I was able to visit Rossetti again. In the meantime we corresponded as fully as before: the subject upon which we most frequently exchanged opinions being now the sonnet.

By-the-bye [he says], I cannot understand what you say of Milton's, Keats's, and Coleridge's sonnets. The last, it is true, was *always* poor as a sonnetteer (I don't see much in the *Autumnal Moon*). My own only exception to this verdict (much as I adore Coleridge's genius) would be the ludicrous sonnet on *The House that Jack built*, which is a masterpiece in its way. I should not myself number the one you mention of Keats's among his best half-dozen (many of his are mere drafts, strange to say); and cannot at all enter into your verdict on those of Milton, which seem to me to be every one of exceptional excellence, though a few are even finer than the rest, notably, of course, the one you name. Pardon an egotistic sentence (in answer to what you say so generously of *Lost Days*), if I express an opinion

that **Known in Vain** and **Still-born Love** may perhaps be
said to head the series in value, though **Lost Days** might
be equally a favourite with me if I did not remember in what
but too opportune juncture it was wrung out of me. I have a
good number of sonnets for *The House of Life* still in MS.,
which I have worked on with my best effort, and, I think,
will fully sustain their place. These and other things I
should like to show you whenever we meet again. The MS. vol.
I proposed to send is merely an old set of (chiefly)
trifles, about which I should like an opinion as to whether
any should be included in the future.
I had spoken of Keats's sonnet beginning

To one who has been long in city pent,
with its exquisite last lines--

E'en like the passage of an angel's tear
That falls through the clear ether silently,
reminding one of a less spiritual figure--

Kings like a golden jewel
Down a golden stair.

After his bantering me, as of old he had done, on the use of long and crabbed
words, I hinted that he was in honour bound to agree at least with my disparaging
judgment upon *Tetrachordon*, if only because of the use of words that would "have
made Quintillian stare."

I further instanced--

"Harry whose tuneful and well-measured song;" and
"Lawrence, of virtuous father virtuous son,"
as examples of Milton at his weakest as a sonnet-writer. He replied:

I am sorry I must still differ somewhat from you about Milton's sonnets. I think the one on *Tetrachordon* a very vigorous affair indeed. The one to Mr. H. Lawes I am half disposed to give you, but not altogether--its close is sweet. As to *Lawrence*, it is curious that my sister was only the other day expressing to me a special relish for this sonnet, and I do think it very fresh and wholesomely relishing myself. It is an awful fact that sun, moon, or candlelight once looked down on the human portent of Dr. Johnson and Mrs. Hannah More convened in solemn conclave above the outspread sonnets of Milton, with a meritorious and considerate resolve of finding out for him "why they were so bad." This is so stupendous a warning, that perhaps it may even incline one to find some of them better than they are.

Coming to Coleridge, I must confess at once that I never meet in any collection with the sonnet on Schiller's Robbers without heading it at once with the words "unconscionably bad." The habit has been a life-long one. That you mention beginning--"Sweet mercy," etc., I have looked for in the only Coleridge I have by me (my brother's cheap edition, for all the faults of which *he* is not at all answerable), and do not find it there, nor have I it in mind.

To pass to Keats. The ed. of 1868 contains no sonnet on the Elgin Marbles. Is it in a later edition? Of course that on Chapman's *Homer* is supreme. It ought to be preceded[12] in

---

12   I pointed out that it was written later than the one on Chapman's Homer (notwithstanding its first line) and therefore should follow after it, not go before.

all editions by the one **To Homer**,

"Standing aloof in giant ignorance," etc.
which contains perhaps the greatest single line in Keats:

"There is a budding morrow in midnight."

Other special favourites with me are--"Why did I laugh to-night?"--" As Hermes once,"--"Time's sea hath been," and the one **On the Flower and, Leaf**.

It is odd that several of these best ones seem to have been early work, and rejected by Keats in his lifetime, while some of those he printed are absolutely sorry drafts.

I had admired Coleridge's sonnet on Schiller's **Robbers** for the perhaps minor excellence of bringing vividly before the mind the scenes it describes. If the sonnet is unconscionably bad so perhaps is the play, the beautiful scene of the setting sun notwithstanding. Eventually, however, I abandoned my belligerent position as to Milton's sonnets: the army of authorities I found ranged against the modest earth-works within which I had entrenched myself must of itself have made me quail. My utmost contention had been that Milton wrote the most impassioned sonnet (Avenge, O Lord), the two most nobly pathetic sonnets (When I consider and **Methought I saw**), and one of the poorest sonnets (Harry, whose tuneful, etc.) in English poetry.

At this time (September 1880) Mr. J. Ashcroft Noble published an essay on **The Sonnet in England** in The Contemporary Review, and relating thereto Rossetti wrote:

I have just been reading Mr. Noble's article on the sonnet. As regards my own share in it, I can only say that it greets me with a gratifying ray of generous recognition. It is all the more pleasant to me as finding a place in the very Review which years ago opened its pages to a pseudonymous attack on my poems and on myself. I see a passage in the article which seems meant to indicate the want of such a work on the sonnet as you are wishing to supply. I only trust that you may do so, and that Mr. Noble may find a field for continued poetic criticism. I am very proud to think that, after my small and solitary book has been a good many years published and several years out of print, it yet meets with such ardent upholding by young and sincere men.

With the verdicts given throughout the article, I generally sympathise, but not with the unqualified homage to Wordsworth. A reticence almost invariably present is fatal in my eyes to the highest pretensions on behalf of his sonnets. Reticence is but a poor sort of muse, nor is tentativeness (so often to be traced in his work) a good accompaniment in music. Take the sonnet on Toussaint L'Ouverture (in my opinion his noblest, and very noble indeed) and study (from Main's note) the lame and fumbling changes made in various editions of the early lines, which remain lame in the end. Far worse than this, study the relation of the closing lines of his famous sonnet The World is too much with us, etc., to a passage in Spenser, and say whether plagiarism was ever more impudent or manifest (again I derive from Main's excellent exposition of the point), and then consider whether a bard was likely to do this once and yet not to do it often. Primary vital impulse was surely not fully developed in his muse.

I will venture to say that I wish my sister's sonnet work
had met with what I consider the justice due to it. Besides
the unsurpassed quality (in my opinion) of her best sonnets,
my sister has proved her poetic importance by solid and
noble inventive work of many kinds, which I should be proud
indeed to reckon among my life's claims.

I have a great weakness myself for many of Tennyson-Turner's
sonnets, though of course what Mr. Noble says of them is in
the main true, and he has certainly quoted the very finest
one, which has a more fervent appeal for me than I could
easily derive from Wordsworth in almost any case.

Will you give my thanks to Mr. Noble for his frank and
outspoken praise?

Let me hear of your doings and intentions.

Ever sincerely yours.

Three names notably omitted in the article are those of Dobell, W. B. Scott, and Swinburne.

The allusion in the foregoing letter to the work on the Sonnet which I was aiming to supply, bears reference to the anthology subsequently published under the title of **Sonnets of Three Centuries**. My first idea was simply to write a survey of the art and history of the sonnet, printing only such examples as might be embraced by my critical comments. Rossetti's generous sympathy was warmly engaged in this enterprise.

It would really warm me up much [he writes] to know of
your editing a sonnet book You would have my best
cooperation as to suggesting examples, but I certainly think
that English sonnets (original and exceptionally translated

ones, the latter only *perhaps*) should be the sole scheme.
Curiously enough, some one wrote me the other day as to a
projected series of living sonneteers (other collections
being only of those preceding our time). I have half
committed myself to contributing, but not altogether as yet.
The name of the projector, S. Waddington, is new to me, and
I don't know who is to publish.... Really you ought to do
the sonnet-book you aspire to do. I know but of one London
critic (Theodore Watts) whom I should consider the leading
man for such a purpose, and I have tried to incite him to it
so often that I know now he won't do it; but I have always
meant *a complete* series in which the dead poets must, of
course, predominate. As to a series of the living only, I
told you of a Mr. Waddington who seems engaged on such a
supplementary scheme. What his gifts for it may be I know
not, but I suppose he knows it is in requisition. However,
there need not be but one such if you felt your hand in for
it. His view happens to be also (as you suggest) about 160
sonnets. In reply to your query, I certainly think there
must be 20 living writers (male and female--my sister a
leader, I consider) who have written good sonnets such as
would afford an interesting and representative selection,
though assuredly not such as would all take the rank of
classics by any means. The number of sonnets now extant,
written by poets who did not exist as such a dozen years
ago, I believe to be almost infinite, and in sufficiently
numerous instances good, however derivative. One younger
poet among them, Philip Marston, has written many sonnets
which yield to few or none by any poet whatever; but he has
printed such a large number in the aggregate, and so unequal
one with the other, that the great ones are not to be found
by opening at random. "How are they (the poets) to be
approached?--" you innocently ask. Ye heavens! how does the

cat's-meat-man approach Grimalkin?--and what is that relation in life when compared to the ***rapport*** established between the living bard and the fellow-creature who is disposed to cater to his caterwauling appetite for publicity? However, to be serious, I must at least exonerate the bard, I am sure, from any desire to appropriate an "interest in the proceeds." There are some, I feel certain, to whom the collector might say with a wink, "What are you going to stand?"

I do not myself think that a collection of sonnets inserted at intervals in an essay is a good form for the purpose. Such a book is from one chief point a book of instantaneous reference,--it would only, perhaps, be read ***through*** once in a life-time. For this purpose a well-indexed current series is best, with any desirable essay prefixed and notes affixed.... I once conceived of a series, to be entitled,

THE ENGLISH CASTALY: A QUINTESSENCE:
BEING A COLLECTION OF ALL THAT IS BEST IN ALL ENGLISH POETS,
EXCEPTING WORKS OF GREAT LENGTH.

I still think this a good idea, but, of course, it would be an extensive undertaking.

Later on, he wrote:

I have thought of a title for your book. What think you of this?

A SONNET SEQUENCE
FROM ELDER TO MODERN WORK,
WITH FIFTY HITHERTO UNPRINTED SONNETS BY
LIVING WRITERS.

That would not be amiss. Tell me if you think of using the

title *A Sonnet Sequence*, as otherwise I might use it in
the *House of Life*…. What do you think of this
alternative title:

THE ENGLISH SONNET MUSE
FROM ELIZABETH'S REIGN TO VICTORIA'S.

I think *Castalia* much too euphuistic, and though I
shouldn't like the book to be called simply still I have a
great prejudice against very florid titles for such
gatherings. *Treasury* has been sadly run upon.

I did not like *Sonnet Sequence* for such a collection, and relinquished the title;
moreover, I had had from the first a clearly defined scheme in mind, carrying its
own inevitable title, which was in due course adopted. I may here remark that I
never resisted any idea of Rossetti's at the moment of its inception, since resistance
only led to a temporary outburst of self-assertion on his part. He was a man of so
much impulse,--impulse often as violent as lawless--that to oppose him merely provoked anger to no good purpose, for as often as not the position at first adopted with
so much pertinacity was afterwards silently abandoned, and your own aims quietly
acquiesced in. On this subject of a title he wrote a further letter, which is interesting from more than one point of view:

I don't like *Garland* at all C. Patmore collected a
Children's Garland. I think

ENGLISH SONNET'S
PRESENT AND PAST, WITH--ETC.,

would be a good title. I think I prefer *Present and Past*,
or *of the P. and P.,* to *New and Old* for your purpose;
but I own I am partly influenced by the fact that I have

settled to call my own vol. ***Poems New and Old***, and don't
want it to get staled; but I really do think the other at
least as good for your purpose--perhaps more dignified.
Again, in reply to a proposal of my own, he wrote:

I think ***Sonnets of the Century*** an excellent idea and
title. I must say a mass of Wordsworth over again, like
Main's, is a little disheartening,--still the ***best***
selection from him is what one wants. There is some book
called ***A Century of Sonnets***, but this, I suppose, would
not matter....

I think sometimes of your sonnet-book, and have formed
certain views. I really would not in your place include old
work at all: it would be but a scanty gathering, and I feel
certain that what is really in requisition is a supplement
to Main, containing living writers (printed and un-printed)
put together under their authors' names (not separately) and
rare gleanings from those more recently dead.

I fear I did not attach importance to this decision, for I now knew my correspondent too well to rely upon his being entirely in the same mind for long. Hence
I was not surprised to receive the following a day or two later:

I lately had a conversation with Watts about your sonnet-
book, and find his views to be somewhat different from what
I had expressed, and I may add I think now he is right. He
says there should be a very careful selection of the elder
sonnets and of everything up to present century. I think he
is right.

The fact is, that almost from the first I had taken a view similar to Mr. Watts's
as to the design of my book, and had determined to call the anthology by the title

it now bears. On one occasion, however, I acted rather without judgment in sending Rossetti a synopsis of certain critical tests formulated by Mr. Watts in a letter of great power and value.

In the letter in question Mr. Watts seemed to be setting himself to confute some extremely ill-considered remarks made in a certain quarter upon the structure of the sonnet, where (following Macaulay) the critic says that there exists no good reason for requiring that even the conventional limit as to length should be observed, and that the only use in art of the legitimate model is to "supply a poet with something to do when his invention fails." I confess to having felt no little amazement that one so devoid of a perception of the true function of the sonnet should have been considered a proper person to introduce a great sonnet-writer; and Mr. Watts (who, however, made no mention of the writer) clearly demonstrated that the true sonnet has the foundation of its structure in a fixed metrical law, and hence, that as it is impossible (as Keats found out for himself) to improve upon the accepted form, that model--known as the Petrarchian--should, with little or no variation, be worked upon. Rossetti took fire, however, from a mistaken notion that Mr. Watts's canons, as given in the letter in question, and merely reported by me, were much more inflexible than they really proved.

> Sonnets of mine ***could not appear*** in any book which
> contained such rigid rules as to rhyme, as are contained in
> Watts's letter. I neither follow them, nor agree with them
> as regards the English language. Every sonnet-writer should
> show full capability of conforming to them in many
> instances, but never to deviate from them in English must
> pinion both thought and diction, and, (mastery once proved)
> a series gains rather than loses by such varieties as do not
> lessen the only absolute aim--that of beauty. The English
> sonnet too much tampered with becomes a sort of bastard
> madrigal. Too much, invariably restricted, it degenerates
> into a Shibboleth.

Dante's sonnets (in reply to your question--not as part of the above point) vary in arrangement. I never for a moment thought of following in my book the rhymes of each individual sonnet.

If sonnets of mine remain admissible, I should prefer printing the two **On Cassandra to The Monochord** and Wine of Circe.

I would not be too anxious, were I you, about anything in choice of sonnets except the brains and the music.
Again he wrote:

I talked to Watts about his letter. He seems to agree with me as to advisable variation of form in preference to transmuting valuable thought. It would not be afc all found that my best sonnets are always in the mere form which I think the best. The question with me is regulated by what I have to say. But in truth, if I have a distinction as a sonnet-writer, it is that I never admit a sonnet which is not fully on the level of every other.... Again, as to this blessed question, though no one ever took more pleasure in continually using the form I prefer when not interfering with thought, to insist on it would after a certain point be ruin to common sense.

As to what you say of **The One Hope**--it is fully equal to the very best of my sonnets, or I should not have wound up the series with it. But the fact is, what is peculiar chiefly in the series is, that scarcely one is worse than any other. You have much too great a habit of speaking of a special octave, sestette, or line. Conception, my boy, fundamental brainwork, that is what makes the difference

in all art. Work your metal as much as you like, but first
take care that it is gold and worth working. A Shakspearean
sonnet is better than the most perfect in form, because
Shakspeare wrote it.

As for Drayton, of course his one incomparable sonnet is the
Love-Parting. That is almost the best in the language, if
not quite. I think I have now answered queries, and it is
late. Good-night!

Rossetti had somewhat mistaken the scope of the letter referred to, and when
he came to know exactly what was intended, I found him in warm agreement with
the views therein taken. I have said at an earlier stage that Rossetti's instinct for
what was good in poetry was unfailing, whatever the value of his opinions on critical principles, and hence I felt naturally anxious to have the benefit of his views on
certain of the elder writers. He said:

I am sorry I am no adept in elder sonnet literature. Many of
Donne's are remarkable--no doubt you glean some. None of
Shakspeare's is more indispensable than the wondrous one on
Last (129). Hartley Coleridge's finest is

"If I have sinned in act, I may repent."

There is a fine one by Isaac Williams, evidently on the
death of a worldly man, and he wrote other good ones. To
return to the old, I think Stillingfleet's ***To Williamson***
very fine....

I would like to send you a list of my special favourites
among Shakspeare's sonnets--viz.:--

15, 27, 29, 30, 36, 44, 45, 49, 50, 52, 55, 56, 59, 61, 62,

64, 65, 66, 68, 71, 73, 76, 77, 90, 93, 94, 97, 98, 99, 102,
107, 110, 116, 117, 119, 120, 123, 129, 135, 136, 138, 144,
145.

I made the selection long ago, and of course love them in
varying degrees.

There should be an essential reform in the printing of
Shakspeare's sonnets. After sonnet 125 should occur the
words ***End of Part I***. The couplet-piece, numbered 126,
should be called ***Epilogue to Part I.***. Then, before 127,
should be printed Part II. After 152, should be put End of
Part II.--and the two last sonnets should be called Epilogue
to Part II. About these two last I have a theory of my own.

Did you ever see the excellent remarks on these sonnets in
my brother's ***Lives of Famous Poets?*** I think a simple point
he mentions (for first time) fixes Pembroke clearly as the
male friend. I am glad you like his own two fine sonnets. I
wish he would write more such. By the bye, you speak with
great scorn of the closing couplet in sonnets. I do not
certainly think that form the finest, but I do think this
and every variety desirable in a series, and have often used
it myself. I like your letters on sonnets; write on all
points in question. The two last of Shakspeare's sonnets
seem to me to have a very probable (and rather elaborate)
meaning never yet attributed to them. Some day, when I see
you, we will talk it over. Did you ever see a curious book
by one Brown (I don't mean Armitage Brown) on Shakspeare's
sonnets? By the bye, he is not the source of my notion as
above, but a matter of fact he names helps in it. I never
saw Massey's book on the subject, but fancy his views and
Brown's are somewhat allied. You should look at what my

brother says, which is very concise and valuable. I hope I am not omitting to answer you in any essential point, but my writing-table is a chaos into which your last letters have, for the moment, sunk beyond recovery.

I consider the foregoing, perhaps, the most valuable of Rossetti's letters to me. I cannot remember that we ever afterwards talked over the two last sonnets of Shakspeare; if we did so, the meaning attached to them by him did not fix itself very definitely upon my memory.

In explanation of my alleged dislike of the closing couplet, I may say that a rhymed couplet at the close of a sonnet has an effect upon my ear similar to that produced by the couplets at the ends of some of the acts of Shakspeare's plays, which were in many instances interpolated by the actors to enable them to make emphatic exits.

I must now group together a number of short notes on sonnets:

I think Blanco White's sonnet difficult to overrate in thought--probably in this respect unsurpassable, but easy to overrate as regards its workmanship. Of course there is the one fatally disenchanting line:

While fly and leaf and insect stood revealed.

The poverty of vision which could not see at a glance that fly and insect were one and the same, is, as you say, enough to account for its being the writer's only sonnet (there is one more however which I don't know).

I'll copy you overpage a sonnet which I consider a very fine one, but which may be said to be quite unknown. It is by Charles Whitehead, who wrote the very admirable and exceptional novel of **Richard Savage**, published somewhere about 1840.

Even as yon lamp within my vacant room
With arduous flame disputes the doubtful night,
And can with its involuntary light
But lifeless things that near it stand illume;
Yet all the while it doth itself consume,
And ere the sun hath reached his morning height
With courier beams that greet the shepherd's sight,
There where its life arose must be its tomb:--
So wastes my life away, perforce confined
To common things, a limit to its sphere,
It gleams on worthless trifles undesign'd,
With fainter ray each hour imprison'd here.
Alas to know that the consuming mind
Must leave its lamp cold ere the sun appear!

I am sure you will agree with me in admiring **that**. I quote from memory, and am not sure that I have given line 6 quite correctly....

I have just had Blanco White's only other sonnet (On being called an Old Man at 50) copied out for you. I do certainly think it ought to go in, though no better than so-so, as you say. But it is just about as good as the former one, but for the leading and splendid thought in the latter. Both are but proseman's diction.

There is a sonnet of Chas. Wells's **On Chaucer** which is not

worthy of its writer, but still you should have it. It
occurs among some prefatory tributes in Chaucer
Modernised, edited by E. H. Home. I don't know how you are
to get a copy, but the book is in the British Museum Reading
Room. The sonnet is signed C. W. only.

The sonnet by Wells seemed to me in every respect poor, and
as it was no part of my purpose (as an admirer of Wells) to
advertise what the poet could not do, I determined--against
Rossetti's judgment--not to print the sonnet.

You certainly, in my opinion, ought to print Wells's sonnet.
Certainly nothing so disjointed ever gave itself the name
before, but it ought to be available for reference, and I do
not agree with you in considering it weak in any sense
except that of structure.

There is a sonnet by Ebenezer Jones, beginning "I never
wholly feel that summer is high," which, though very jagged,
has decided merit to warrant its insertion.

As for Tennyson, he seems to have given leave for a sonnet
to appear in Main's book. Why not in yours? But I have long
ceased to know him, nor is any friend of mine in
communication with him.... My brother has written in his
time a few sonnets. Two of them I think very fine--
especially the one called ***Shelley's Heart***, which he has
lately worked upon again with immense advantage.... You do
not tell me from whom you have received sonnets. The reason
which prevents my coming forward, in such a difficulty, with
a new sonnet of my own, is this:--which indeed you have
probably surmised: I know nothing would gratify malevolence,
after the controversy which ensued on your lecture, more

than to be able to assert, however falsely, that we had been working in concert all along, that you were known to me from the first, and that your advocacy had no real spontaneity.... When you first entered on the subject, and wrote your lecture, you were a perfect stranger to me, and that fact greatly enhanced my pleasure in its enthusiastic tone. I hope sincerely that we may have further and close opportunities of intercourse, but should like whatever you may write of me to come from the old source of intellectual affinity only. That you should think the subject worthy of further labour is a pleasure to me, but I only trust it may not be a disadvantage to your book in unfriendly eyes, particularly if that view happened to be the proposed publisher's, in which case I should much prefer that this section of your work were withdrawn for a more propitious occasion.... I am very glad Brown is furthering your sonnet-book--he knows so many bards. Of course if I were you, I should keep an eye on the mouths even of gift-horses; but were a creditable stud to be trotted out, of course I should be willing; as were I one among many, the objection I noted would not exist. I do not mean for a moment to say that many very fine sonnets might not be obtained from poets not yet known or not widely known; but known names would be the things to parry the difficulty.

Later he wrote:

As you know, I want to contribute to your volume if I can do so without fear of the consequences hinted at in a former letter as likely to ensue, so I now enclose a sonnet of my own. If you are out in March 1881, you may be before my new edition, but I am getting my stock together. Not a word of this however, as it mustn't get into gossip paragraphs at present. *The House of Life* is now a hundred sonnets--all

lyrics being removed. Besides this series, I have forty-five
sonnets extra. I think, as you are willing, I shall use the
title I sent you--A Sonnet Sequence. I fancy the
alternative title would be briefer and therefore better as

OUR SONNET-MUSE
PROM ELIZABETH TO VICTORIA

I could not be much concerned about the unwillingness to give me a new sonnet
which Rossetti at first exhibited, for I knew full well that sooner or later the sonnet
would come. Not that I recognised in him the faintest scintillation of the affectation so common among authors as to the publication of work. But the fear of any
appearance of collusion between himself and his critics was, as he said, a bugbear
that constantly haunted him. Owing to this, a stranger often stood a better chance
of securing his ready and open co-operation than the most intimate of friends. I frequently yielded to his desire that in anything that I might write his name should not
be mentioned--too frequently by far, to my infinite vexation at the time, and now
to my deep and ineradicable regret. The sonnet-book out of which arose much of
the correspondence printed in this chapter, contains in its preface and notes hardly
an allusion to him, and yet he was, in my judgment, out of all reach and sight, the
greatest sonnet-writer of his time. The sonnet first sent was **Pride of Youth**, but as
this formed part of **The House of Life** series, it was withdrawn, and **Raleigh's Cell
in the Tower** was substituted The following hitherto unpublished sonnet was also
contributed but withdrawn at the last moment, because of its being out of harmony
with the sonnets selected to accompany it:

ON CERTAIN ELIZABETHAN REVIVALS.

O ruff-embastioned vast Elizabeth,
Bush to these bushel-bellied casks of wine,
Home-growth, 'tis true, but rank as turpentine,--
What would we with such skittle-plays at death %
Say, must we watch these brawlers' brandished lathe,

Or to their reeking wit our ears incline,
Because all Castaly flowed crystalline
In gentle Shakspeare's modulated breath!
What! must our drama with the rat-pit vie,
Nor the scene close while one is left to kill!
Shall this be poetry % And thou--thou--man
Of blood, thou cannibalic Caliban,
What shall be said to thee?--a poet?--Fie!
"An honourable murderer, if you will"

I mentioned to you [he says] William Davies, author of
Songs of a Wayfarer (by the bye, another man has since
adopted his title). He has many excellent sonnets, and is a
valued friend of mine. I shall send you, on his behalf, a
copy of the book for selection of what you may please.... It
is very unequal, but the best truly excellent. The sonnets
are numerous, and some good, though the best work in the
book is not among them. There are two poems--The Garden,
and another called, I think, *On a dried-up Spring*, which
are worthy of the most fastidious collections. Many of the
poems are unnamed, and the whole has too much of a Herrick
air. . . .

It is quite refreshing to find you so pleased with my good
friend Davies's book, and I wish he were in London, as I
would have shown him what you say, which I know would have
given him pleasure. He is a man who suffers much from moods
of depression, in spite of his philosophic nature. I have
marked fifty pieces of different kinds throughout his book,
and of these twenty-nine are sonnets. Had those fifty been
alone printed, Davies would now be remembered and not
forgotten: but all poets now-a-days are redundant except
Tennyson. ...

I am this evening writing to Davies, who is in Rome, and could not resist enclosing what you say, with so much experimental appreciativeness of his book, and of his intention to fill it with moral sunshine. I am sure he 'll send a new sonnet if he has one, but I fancy his bardic day is over. I should think he was probably not subject to melancholy when he wrote the *Wayfarer*. However, he tells me that his spirits have improved in Italy. One other little book of Herrickian verse he has written, called The Shepherd!s Garden, but there are no sonnets in it. Besides this, he published a volume containing a record of travel of a very interesting kind, and called The Pilgrimage of the Tiber. This is well known. It is illustrated, many of the drawings being by himself, for he is quite as much painter as poet. He also wrote in *The Quarterly Review* an article on the sonnet (I should think about 1870 or so), and, a little later, one which raised great wrath, on the English School of Painting. These I have not seen. He "lacks advancement," however; having fertile powers and little opportunity, and being none the luckier (I think) for a small independence which keeps off *compulsion* to work, though of willingness he has abundance in many directions.

There is an admirable but totally unknown living poet named Dixon. I will send you two small vols, of his which he gave me long ago, but please take good care of them, and return them as soon as done with. I value them highly. I forgot till to-day that he had written any sonnets, but I see there are three in one vol. and one in another. I have marked my two favourites. He should certainly be represented in your book. If I live, I mean to write something about him in some quarter when I can. His finest passages are as fine as any living man can do. He was a canon of Carlisle Cathedral, and at present has a living somewhere. If you wanted to ask him for an original sonnet, you might mention my name, and address him at Carlisle with *Please forward*. Of course he is a Rev.

You will be sorry to hear that Davies has abandoned the hope of producing a new sonnet to his own satisfaction. I have again, however, urged him to the onslaught, and told him how deserving you are of his efforts.

Swinburne, who is a vast admirer of my sister's, thinks the Advent perhaps the noblest of all her poems, and also specially loves the *Passing Away*. I do not know that I quite agree with your decided preference for the two sonnets of hers you signalise,--the *World* is very fine, but the other, *Dead before Death*, a little sensational for her. I think *After Death* one of her noblest, and the one After Communion. In my own view, the greatest of all her poems is that on France after the siege--To-Day for Me. A very splendid piece of feminine ascetic passion is The Convent Threshold.

I have run the sonnet you like, *St. Luke the Painter*, into a sequence with two more not yet printed, and given the three a general title of *Old and New Art*, as well as special titles to each. I shall annex them to The House of Life.

Have you ever read Vaughan? He resembles Donne a good deal as to quaintness, but with a more emotional personality.

I have altered the last line of octave in *Lost Days*. It

now runs--

"The undying throats of Hell, athirst alway."

I always had it in my mind to make a change here, as the
in standing in the line in its former reading clashed with
in occurring in the previous line. I have done what I
think is a prime sonnet on the murdered Czar, which I
enclose, but don't show it to a soul.

Theodore Watts is going to print a very fine sonnet of his
own in *The Athenaeum*. It is the first verse he ever put in
print, though he wrote much (when a very young man). Tell me
how you like it. I think he is destined to shine in that
class of poetry.

I knew you must like Watts's sonnets. They are splendid
affairs. I am not sure that I agree with you in liking the
first the better of the two: the second (Natura Maligna)
is perhaps the deeper and finer. I have asked Watts to give
you a new sonnet, and I think perhaps he will do so, or at
all events give you permission to use those he has printed.
He has just come into the room, and says he would like to
hear from you on the subject.

From one rather jocular sentence in your note I judge you
may include some sonnets of your own. I see no possible
reason why you should not. You are really now, at your
highest, among our best sonnet-writers, and have written two
or three sonnets that yield to few or none whatever. I am
forced, however, to request that you will not put in the one
referring to myself, from my constant bugbear of any
appearance of collusion. That sonnet is a very fine one--my

brother was showing it me again the other day. It is not my personal gratification alone, though that is deep, because I know you are sincere, which leads me to the conclusion that it is your best, and very fine indeed. I think your Cumberland sonnet admirable. The sonnet on Byron is extremely musical in flow and the symbolic scenery of exceptional excellence. The view taken is the question with me. Byron's vehement directness, at its best, is a lasting lesson: and, dubious monument as ***Don Juan*** may be, it towers over the century. Of course there is truth in what you say; but ***ought*** it to be the case? and is it the case in any absolute sense? You deal frankly with your sonnets, and do not shrink from radical change. I think that on Oliver much better than when I saw it before. The opening phrases of both octave and sestette are very fine; but the second quatrain and the second terzina, though with a quality of beauty, both seem somewhat to lack distinctness. The word ***rivers*** cannot be used with elision--the v is a hard pebble in the flow, and so are the closing consonants. You must put up with ***streams*** if you keep the line.

You should have Bailey's dedicatory sonnet in ***Festus***.

I am enclosing a fine sonnet by William Bell Scott, which I wished him to let me send you for your book. It has not yet been printed. I think I heard of some little chaffy matter between him and you, but, doubtless, you have virtually forgotten all about it. I must say frankly that I think the day when you made the speech he told me of must have been rather a wool-gathering one with you.... I suppose you know that Scott has written a number of fine sonnets contained in his vol of ***Poems*** published about 1875, I think.

I directed the attention of Mr. Waddington (whom, however, I don't know personally) to a most noble sonnet by Fanny Kemble, beginning, "Art thou already weary of the way?" He has put it in, and several others of hers, but she is very unequal, and I don't know if the others should be there, but you should take the one in question. It sadly wants new punctuation, being vilely printed just as I first saw it when a boy in some twopenny edition.

In a memoir of Gilchrist, appended now by his widow to the Life of Blake, there is a sonnet by G., perhaps interesting enough, as being exceptional, for you to ask for it; but I don't advise you, if you don't think it worth.

I have received from Mrs. Meynell, a sister of Eliz. Thompson, the painter, a most genuine little book of poems containing some sonnets of true spiritual beauty. I must send it you.

This book had just then been introduced to Rossetti with much warmth of praise by Mr. Watts, and he took to it vastly.

This closes Rossetti's interesting letters on sonnet literature. In reprinting his first volume of **Poems** he had determined to remove the sonnets of **The House of Life** to the new volume of **Ballads and Sonnets**, and fill the space with the fragment of a poem written in youth, and now called **The Bride's Prelude**. He sent me a proof. The reader will remember that as a narrative fragment it is less remarkable for striking incident (though never failing of interest and picturesqueness) than for a slow and psychical development which ultimately gained a great hold of the sympathies. The poem leaves behind it a sense as of a sultry day. Judging first of its merits as a song (using the word in its broad and simple sense), the poem flows on the tongue with unbroken sweetness and with a variety of cadence and light and shade of melody which might admit of its pursuing its meanderings through five times its less than 50 pages, and still keeping one's senses awake to the constantly recurring advent of new and pleasing literary forms. The story is a striking one, with a great wealth of highly effective incident,--notably the episode of the card-playing, and of the father striking down the sword which Raoul turns against the breast of the bride. Almost equally memorable are the scenes in which the lover appears, and the occasional interludes of incident in which, between the pauses of the narrative, the bridegroom's retinue are heard sporting in the courtyard without.

The whole atmosphere of the poem is saturated in a medievalism of spirit to which no lapse of modernism does violence, and the spell of romance which comes with that atmosphere of the middle ages is never broken, but preserved in the minutest most matter-of-fact details, such as the bowl of water that stood amidst flowers, and in which the sister Amelotte "slid a cup" and offered it to Aloyse to drink. But the one great charm of the poem lies in its subtle and most powerful psychical analysis, seen foreshadowed in the first mention of the bride sitting in the shade, but first felt strongly when she begs her sister to pray, and again when she tells how, at God's hint, she had whispered something of the whole tale to her sister who slept

The dread introspection pictured after the sin is in the highest degree tragic, and affects one like remorse in its relentlessness, although less remorse than fear of discovery. The sickness of the following condition, with its yearnings, longings, dizziness, is very nobly done, and delicate as is the theme, and demanding a touch of unerring strength, yet lightness, the part of the poem concerned with it contains certain of the most beautiful and stirring things. The madness (for it is not less than such) in which at the sea-side, believing Urscelyn to be lost, the bride tells the whole tale, whilst her curse laughed within her to see the amazement and anger of her brothers and of her father, is doubtless true enough to the frenzied state of her mind; but my sympathies go out less to that part of the poem than to the subsequent part, in which the bride-mother is described as leaning along in thought after her child, till tears, not like a wedded girl's, fall among her curls. Highly dramatic, too, is the passage in which she fears to curse the evil men whose evil hands have taken her child, lest from evil lips the curse should be a blessing.

The characterisation seemed to be highly powerful, and, so far as it went, finely contrasted. I could almost have wished that the love for which the bride suffers so much had been more dwelt upon, and Urscelyn had been made somehow more worthy of such love and sacrifice. The only point in which the poem struck me, after mature reflection, as less admirable than certain others of the author's, lay in the circumstance that the narrative moves slowly, but, of course, it should be remembered that the poem is one of emotion, not incident. There are most magical flashes of imagery in the poem, notably in the passage beginning

> Her thought, long stagnant, stirred by speech,
> Gave her a sick recoil;
> As, dip thy fingers through the green
> That masks a pool, where they have been,
> The naked depth is black between.

Rossetti wrote a valuable letter on his scheme for the completion of ***The Bride's Prelude***:

> I was much pleased with your verdict on The Bride's
> Prelude. I think the poem is saved by its picturesqueness,
> but that otherwise the story up to the point reached is too
> purely repellent. I have the sequel quite clear in my mind,
> and in it the mere passionate frailty of Aloyse's first love
> would be followed by a true and noble love, rendered
> calamitous by Urscelyn, who then (having become a powerful
> soldier of fortune) solicits the hand of Aloyse. Thus the
> horror which she expresses against him to her sister on the
> bridal morning would be fully justified. Of course, Aloyse
> would confess her fault to her second lover whose love
> would, nevertheless, endure. The poem would gain so greatly
> by this sequel that I suppose I must set to and finish it
> one day, old as it is. I suppose it would be doubled, but
> hardly more. I hate long poems.

I quite think the card-playing passage the best thing--as a unit--in the poem: but your opinion encourages my own, that it fails nowhere of good material. It certainly moves slowly as you say, and this is quite against the rule I follow. But here was no life condensed in an episode; but a story which had necessarily to be told step by step, and a situation which had unavoidably to be anatomised. If it is not unworthy to appear with my best things, that is all I hope for it. You have pitched curiously upon some of my favourite touches, and very coincidently with Watts's views.
Early in 1881, he wrote:

I am writing a ballad on the death of James I. of Scots. It is already twice the length of *The White Ship*, and has a good slice still to come. It is called *The King's Tragedy*, and is a ripper I can tell you!

The other day I got from Italy a paper containing a really excellent and exceptional notice of my poems, written by the author of a volume also sent me containing, among other translations from the English, *Jenny, Last Confession*, etc.

I have been re-reading, after many years, Keats's Otho the Great, and find it a much better thing than I remembered, though only a draft.

I am much exercised as to what you mention as to a Michael Scott scheme of Coleridge's. Where does he speak of it, and what is it? It is quite new to me; but curiously enough, I have a complete scheme drawn up for a ballad, to be called Michael Scott's Wooing, not the one I proposed beginning now--and also have long designed a picture under the same title, but of quite different motif! Allan Cunningham wrote a romance called **Sir Michael Scott**, but I never saw it.

I have heard from Walter Severn about a subscription proposed to erect a gravestone to his father beside that of Keats. I should like you to copy for me your sonnet on Severn. I hear it is in **The Athenaeum**, but have not seen it. I was asked to prepare an inscription, which I send you. Nothing would be so good as Severn's own words.

I strongly urge you to go on with your book on the Supernatural. The closing chapter should, I think, be on the **weird** element in its perfection, as shown by recent poets in the mess--i.e. those who take any lead. Tennyson has it certainly here and there in imagery, but there is no great success in the part it plays through his **Idylls**. The Old Romaunt beats him there. The strongest instance of this feeling in Tennyson that I remember is in a few lines of The Palace of Art:

And hollow breasts enclosing hearts of flame;
And with dim-fretted foreheads all
On corpses three months old at morn she came
That stood against the wall.

I won't answer for the precise age of the corpses--perhaps I have staled them somewhat.

CHAPTER IX.

It is in the nature of these Recollections that they should be personal, and it can hardly occur to any reader to complain of them for being that which above all else they purport to be. I have hitherto, however, been conscious of a desire (made manifest to my own mind by the character of my selections from the letters written to me) to impart to this volume an interest as broad and general as may be. But my primary purpose is now, and has been from the first, to afford the best view at my command of Rossetti as a man; and more helpful to such purpose than any number of critical opinions, however interesting, have often been those passages in his letters where the writer has got closest to his correspondent in revealing most of himself. In the chapter I am now about to write I must perforce set aside all limitations of reserve if I am to convey such an idea of Rossetti's last days as fills my mind; I must be content to speak almost exclusively of my personal relations to him, to the enforced neglect of the more intimate relations of others.

About six months after my first visit, Rossetti invited me to spend a week with him at his house, and this I was glad to be able to do. I found him in many important particulars a changed man. His complexion was brighter than before, and this circumstance taken alone might have been understood to indicate improved bodily health, but in actual fact it rather denoted in his case a retrograde physical tendency, as being indicative chiefly of some recent excess in the use of his pernicious drug. He was distinctly less inclined to corpulence, his eyes were less bright, and had more frequently than formerly the appearance of gazing upon vacancy, and when he walked to and fro in the studio, as it was his habit to do at intervals of about an hour, he did so with a more laboured sidelong motion than I had previously noticed, as though the body unconsciously lost and then regained some necessary control and command at almost every step. Half sensible, no doubt, of a reduced condition, or guessing perhaps the nature of my reflections from a certain uneasiness which it baffled my efforts to conceal, he paused for an instant one evening in the midst of these melancholy perambulations and asked me how he struck me as to health. More frankly than judiciously I answered promptly, Less well than formerly. It was a luckless remark, for Rossetti's prevailing wish at that moment was to conceal even from himself his lowered state, and the time was still to come when he should crave the questionable sympathy of those who said he looked even more ill than he felt. Just before this, my second visit, he had completed his ***King's Tragedy***, and I had heard from his own lips how prostrate the emotional strain involved in the production of the poem had first left him. Casting himself now on the couch in an attitude indicative of unusual exhaustion, he said the ballad had taken much out of him. "It was as though my life ebbed out with it," he said, and in saying so much of the nervous tension occasioned by the work in question he did not overstate the truth as it presented itself to other eyes. Time after time while the ballad was in course of production, he had made effort to read it aloud to the friend to whose judgment his poetry was always submitted, but had as frequently failed to do so from the physical impossibility of restraining the tears that at every stage welled up out of an overwrought nature, for the poet never existed perhaps who, while at work, lived so vividly in the imagined situation. And the weight of that work was still upon him when we met again. His voice seemed to have lost much in quality, and in compass too to have diminished: or if the volume of sound remained the same, it appeared to have retired (so to express it) inwards, and to convey, when he spoke, the idea of a man speaking as much to himself as to others. More than ever now the scene of his life lacked for me some necessary vitality: it breathed an atmosphere of sorrow: it was like the dream of a distempered imagination out of which there came no welcome awakening, to say it was not true. On the side of his intellectual life Rossetti was obviously under less constraint with me than ever before. Previously he had seemed to make a conscious effort to speak generously of all contemporaries, and cordially of every friend with whom he was brought into active relations; and if, by force of some stray impulse, he was ever led to say a disparaging word of any one, he forthwith made a palpable, and sometimes amusing, effort so to obliterate the injurious impression as to convey the idea that he wished it to appear that he had not said anything at all. But now this restraint was thrown aside.

I perceived that the drug by which he was enslaved caused what I may best characterise as intermittent waves of morbid suspiciousness as to the good faith of every individual, including his best, oldest, and truest friends, as to whom the most inexplicable delusions would suddenly come, and as suddenly go. He would talk in the gravest and most earnest way of the wrongs he had suffered at the hands of a dear friend, and then the moment his eloquence had drawn from me an exclamation of sympathy for him, he would turn round and heap upon the same individual an extravagance of praise for his fidelity and good faith. And now, he so classed his contemporaries as to leave no doubt that he was duly sensible of his own place amongst them, preserving, meantime, a dignified reticence as to the extent of his personal claims.

His life was an anachronism. Such a man should have had no dealings with the nineteenth century: he belonged to the sixteenth, or perhaps the thirteenth, and in Italy not in England. It would, nevertheless, be wrong to say that he was wholly indifferent to important political issues, of which he took often a very judicial view. In dismissing further mention of this second and prolonged meeting with Rossetti, it only remains to me to say (as a necessary, if strictly personal, explanation of much that will follow), that on the evening preceding my departure, he asked me, in the event of my deciding to come to live in London, to take up my quarters at his house. To this proposal I made no reply: and neither his speech nor my silence needs any comment, and I shall offer none.

A month or two later my own health gave way, and then, a change of residence being inevitable, Rossetti repeated his invitation; but a London campaign, under such conditions as were necessarily entailed by pitching one's tent with him, got further and further away, until I seemed to see it through the inverse end of a telescope whereof the slides were being drawn out, out, every day further and further. I determined to spend half a year among' the mountains of Cumberland, and went up to the Vale of St. John. Scarcely had I settled there when Rossetti wrote that he must himself soon leave London: that he was wearied out absolutely, and unable to sleep at night, that if he could only reach that secluded vale he would breathe a purer air mentally as well as physically. The mood induced by contemplation of the tranquillity of my retreat over-against the turmoil and distractions of the city *in* which, though not *of* which, he was, added to the deepening exhaustion which had already begun when I left him, had prevailed with him, he said, to ask me to come down to London, and travel back with him. "Supposing," he wrote, "I were to ask you to come to town in a fortnight's time from now--I returning with you for a while into the country--would that be feasible to you?"

Once unsettled in the environments within which for years he had moved contentedly, a thousand reasons were found for the contemplated step, and simultaneously a thousand obstacles arose to impede the execution of it. "They have at length taken my garden," he said, "as they have long threatened to do, and now they are really setting about building upon it. I do not in the least know what my plans may be." And again: "It seems certain that I must leave this house and seek another. Is there any house in the neighbourhood of the Vale of St. John with a largish room one could paint in (to N. or NE.)?" The idea of his taking up his permanent abode so far out of the market circle was, I well knew, just one of those impracticable notions which, with Rossetti, were abandoned as soon as conceived, so I was not surprised to hear from him as follows, by the succeeding post: "In what I wrote yesterday I said something as to a possibility of leaving town, but I now perceive this is not practicable at present; therefore need not trouble you to take note of neighbouring houses." Presently he wrote again: "Bedevilments thicken: the garden is ploughed up, and I 've not stirred out of the house for a week: I must leave this place at once if I am to leave it alive."[13]

"My present purpose is to take another house in London. Could you not come down and beat up agents for me? I know you will not deny me your help. I hear of a house at Brixton, with a garden of two acres, and only L130 a year." In a day or two even this last hope had proved delusive: "I find the house at Brixton will not do, and I hear of nothing else.... I am anxious as to having become perfectly deaf on the right side of my head. Partial approaches to this have sometimes occurred to me and passed away, so I will not be too much troubled at it." A little later he wrote: "Now

---

13   It is but just to say that, although Rossetti wrote thus
      peevishly of what was quite inevitable,--the yielding up of
      his fine garden,--he would at other times speak of the great
      courtesy and good-nature of Messrs. Pemberton, in allowing
      him the use of the garden after it had been severed from the
      property he hired.

my housekeeper is leaving me, her mother being very ill. Can you not come to my assistance? Come at once and we will set sail in one boat." I appear to have replied to this last appeal in a tone of some little scepticism as to his remaining long in the same mind relative to our mutual housemating, for subsequently he says: "At this writing I can see no likelihood of my not remaining in the mind that, in case of your coming to London, your quarters should be taken up here. The house is big enough for two, even if they meant to be strangers to each other. You would have your own rooms and we should meet just when we pleased. You have got a sufficient inkling of my exceptional habits not to be scared by them. It is true, at times my health and spirits are variable, but I am sure we should not be squabbling. However, it seems you have no intention of a quite immediate move, and we can speak farther of it." I readily consented to do whatever seemed feasible to help him out of his difficulties, which existed, however, as I perceived, much more in his own mind than in actual fact. I thought a brief holiday in the solitude within which I was then located would probably be helpful in restoring a tranquil condition of mind, and as his brother, Mr. Scott, Mr. Watts, Mr. Shields, and other friends in London, were of a similar opinion, efforts were made to induce him to undertake the journey which he had been the first to think of. His oldest friend, Mr. Madox Brown (whose presence would have been as valuable now as it had proved to be on former occasions), was away at Manchester, and remained there throughout the time of his last illness. His moods at this time were too variable to be relied upon three days together, and so I find him writing:

> Many thanks for the information as to your Shady Vale, which
> seems a vision--a distant one, alas!--of Paradise. Perhaps I
> may reach it yet.... I am now thinking of writing another
> ballad-poem to add at the end of my volume. It is romantic,
> not historical I have a clear scheme for it and believe your
> scenery might help me much if I could get there. When you
> hear that scheme, you will, I believe, pronounce it
> precisely fitted to the scenery you describe as now
> surrounding you. That scenery I hope to reach a little
> later, but meantime should much like to see you in London

and return with you.

The proposed ballad was to be called *The Orchard Pits* and was to be illustrative of the serpent fascination of beauty, but it was never written. Contented now to await the issue of events, he proceeded to write on subjects of general interest:

Keats (page 154, vol. i., of Houghton's Life, etc.) mentions
among other landscape features the Vale of St. John. So you
may think of him in the neighbourhood as well as (or, if you
like, rather than) Wordsworth.

I have been reading again Hogg's Shelley. S. appears to have
been as mad at Keswick as everywhere else, but not madder;--
that he could not compass.

At this juncture some unlooked-for hitch in the arrangements then pending for the sale of the *Dante's Dream* to the Corporation of Liverpool rendered my presence in London inevitable, and upon my arrival I found that Rossetti had fitted out rooms for my reception, although I had never down to that moment finally decided to avail myself of an offer which upon its first being broached, appeared to be too one-sided a bargain (in which of course the sacrifice seemed to be Rossetti's) to admit of my entertaining it. In this way I drifted into my position as Rossetti's housemate.

The letters and scraps of notes I have embodied in the foregoing will probably convey a better idea of Rossetti's native irresolution, as it was made manifest to me in the early part of 1881, than any abstract definition, however faithful and exact, could be expected to do. Irresolution was indubitably his most noticeable quality at the time when I came into active relation with him; and if I be allowed to have any perception of character and any acquaintance with the fundamental traits that distinguish man from man, I shall say unhesitatingly (though I well know how different is the opinion of others) that irresolution with melancholy lay at the basis of his nature. I have heard Mr. Swinburne speak of a cheerfulness of deportment in early life, which imparted an idea as of one who could not easily be depressed. I have heard Mr. Watts speak of the days at Kelmscott Manor House, where he first knew him, and where Rossetti was the most delightful of companions. I have heard Canon Dixon speak of a determination of purpose which yielded to no sort of obstacle, but carried its point by the sheer vehemence with which it asserted it. I can only say that I was witness to neither characteristic. Of traits the reverse of these, I was constantly receiving evidence; but let it be remembered that before I joined Rossetti (which was only in the last year of his life) in that intimate relation which revealed to my unwilling judgment every foible and infirmity of character, the whole nature of the man had been vitiated by an enervating drug. At my meeting with him the brighter side of his temperament had been worn away in the night-troubles of his unrestful couch; and of that needful volition, which establishes for a man the right to rule not others but himself, only the mockery and inexplicable vagaries of temper remained. When I knew him, Rossetti was devoid of resolution. At that moment at which he had finally summoned up every available and imaginable reason for pursuing any particular course, his purpose wavered and his heart gave way. When I knew him, Rossetti was destitute of cheerfulness or content. At that instant, at which the worst of his shadowy fears had been banished by some fortuitous occurrence that lit up with an unceasing radiation of hope every prospect of life, he conjured out of its very brightness fresh cause for fear and sadness. True, indeed, these may have been no more than symptoms of those later phenomena which came of disease, and foreshadowed death. Other minds may reduce to a statement of cause and effect what I am content to offer as fact.

Upon settling with Rossetti in July 1881, I perceived that his health was weaker. His tendency to corpulence had entirely disappeared, his feebleness of step had become at certain moments painfully apparent, and his temper occasionally betrayed signs of bitterness. To myself, personally, he was at this stage as genial as of old, or if for an instant he gave vent to an unprovoked outburst of wrath, he would far more than atone for it by a look of inexpressible remorse and some feeling words of regret, whereof the import sometimes was--

I wish you were indeed my son, for though then I should still have no right to address you so, I should at least have some right to expect your forgiveness.

In such moods of more than needful solicitude for one's acutest sensibilities, Rossetti was absolutely irresistible.

As I have said, the occupant of this great gloomy house, in which I had now become a resident, had rarely been outside its doors for two years; certainly never afoot, and only in carriages with his friends. Upon the second night of my stay, I announced my intention of taking a walk on the Chelsea embankment, and begged him to accompany me. To my amazement he yielded, and every night for a week following, I succeeded in inducing him to repeat the now unfamiliar experience. It was obvious enough to himself that he walked totteringly, with infinite expenditure of physical energy, and returned in a condition of exhaustion that left him prostrate for an hour afterwards. The root of all this evil was soon apparent. He was exceeding with the chloral, and little as I expected or desired to exercise a moral guardianship over the habits of this great man, I found myself insensibly dropping into that office.

Negotiations for the sale of the Liverpool picture were now complete; the new volume of poems and the altered edition of the old volume had been satisfactorily passed through the press; and it might have been expected that with the anxiety occasioned by these enterprises, would pass away the melancholy which in a nature like Rossetti's they naturally induced. The reverse was the fact, He became more and more depressed as each palpable cause of depression was removed, and more and more liable to give way to excess with the drug. By his brother, Mr. Watts, Mr. Shields, and others who had only too frequently in times past had experience of similar outbreaks, this failure in spirits, with all its attendant physical weakness, was said to be due primarily to hypochondriasis. Hence the returning necessity to get him away (as Mr. Madox Brown had done at a previous crisis) for a change of air and scene. Once out of this atmosphere of gloom, we hoped that amid cheerful surroundings his health would speedily revive. Infinite were the efforts that had to be made, and countless the precautions that had to be taken before he could be induced to set out, but at length we found ourselves upon our way to Keswick, at nine p.m., one evening in September, in a special carriage packed with as many artist's trappings and as many books as would have lasted for a year.

We reached Penrith as the grey of dawn had overspread the sky. It was six o'clock as we got into the carriage that was to drive us through the vale of St. John to our destination at the Legberthwaite end of it. The morning was now calm, the mountains looked loftier, grander, and yet more than ever precipitous from the road that circled about their base. Nothing could be heard but the calls of the awakening cattle, the rumble of cataracts far away, and the rush and surge of those that were near. Rossetti was all but indifferent to our surroundings, or displayed only such fitful interest in them as must have been affected out of a kindly desire to please me. He said the chloral he had taken daring the journey was upon him, and he could not see. At length we reached the house that was for some months to be our home. It stood at the foot of a ghyll, which, when swollen by rain, was majestic in volume and sound. The little house we had rented was free from all noise other than the occasional voice of a child or bark of a dog. Here at least he might bury the memory of the distractions of the city that vexed him. Save for the ripple of the river that flowed at his feet, the bleating of sheep on Golden Howe, the echo of the axe of the woodman who was thinning the neighbouring wood, and the morning and evening mail-coach horn, he might delude himself into forgetfulness that he belonged any longer to this noisy earth.

Next day Rossetti was exceptionally well, and astounded me by the proposal that we should ascend Golden Howe together--a little mountain of some 1000 feet that stands at the head of Thirlmere. With never a hope on my part of our reaching the summit, we set out for that purpose, but through no doubt the exhilarating effect of the mountain air, he actually compassed the task he had proposed to himself, and sat for an hour on that highest point from whence could be seen the Skiddaw range to the north, Haven's Crag to the west, Styx Pass and Helvellyn to the east, and the Dunmail Raise to the south, with the lake below. Rossetti was struck by the variety of configuration in the hills, and even more by the variety of colour. But he was no great lover of landscape beauty, and the majestic scene before us produced less effect upon his mind than might perhaps have been expected. He seemed to be almost unconscious of the unceasing atmospheric changes that perpetually arrest and startle. the observer in whom love of external nature in her grander moods has not been weakened by disease. The complete extent of the Vale of St. John could be traversed by the eye from the eminence upon which we sat. The valley throughout its three-mile length is absolutely secluded: one has only the hills for company, and to say the truth they are sometimes fearful company too. Usually the landscape wears a cheerful aspect, but at times long fleecy clouds drive midway across the mountains, leaving the tops visible. The scenery is highly awakening to the imagination. Even the country people are imaginative, and the country is full of ghostly legend. I was never at any moment sensible that these environments affected Rossetti: assuredly they never agitated him, and no effort did he make to turn them to account for the purposes of the romantic ballad he had spoken of as likely to grow amidst such surroundings.

Being much more than ordinarily cheerful during the first evenings of our stay in the North, he talked sometimes of his past life and of the men and women he had known in earlier years. Carlyle's **Reminiscences** had not long before been published. Mrs. Carlyle, therein so extravagantly though naturally belauded, he described as a bitter little woman, with, however, the one redeeming quality of unostentatious charity: "The poor of Chelsea," he said, "always spoke well of her." "George Eliot," whose genius he much admired, he had ceased to know long before her death, but he spoke of the lady as modest and retiring, and amiable to a fault when the outer crust of reticence had been broken through. Longfellow had called upon him whilst he was painting the **Dante's Dream**. The old poet was Courteous and complimentary in the last degree; he seemed, however, to know little or nothing about painting as an art, and also to have fallen into the error of thinking that Rossetti the painter and Sossetti the poet were different men; in short, that the Dante of that name was the painter, and the William the poet. Upon leaving the house, Longfellow had said: "I have been glad to meet you, and should like to have met your brother; pray, tell him how much I admire his beautiful poem, **The Blessed Damozel**" Giving no hint of the error, Rossetti said he had answered, "I will tell him." He painted a little during our stay in the North, for it was whilst there that he began the beautiful replica of his **Proserpina**, now the property of Mr. Valpy. I found it one of my best pleasures to watch a picture growing under his hand, and thought it easy to see through the medium of his idealised heads, cold even in their loveliness, unsubstantial in their passion, that to the painter life had been a dream into which nothing entered that was not as impalpable as itself. Tainted by the touch of melancholy that is the blight that clings to the purest beauty, his pictured faces were, in my view, akin to his poetry, every line of which, as he sometimes recited it, seemed as though it echoed the burden of a bygone sorrow--the sorrow of a dream rather than that of a life, or of a life that had been itself a dream. I also then realised what Mr. Theodore Watts has said in a letter just now written to me from Sark, that, "apart from any ques-

Recollections of Dante Gabriel Rossetti   211

tion of technical shortcomings, one of Rossetti's strongest claims to the attention of posterity was that of having invented, in the three-quarter-length pictures painted from one face, a type of female beauty which was akin to none other,--which was entirely new, in short,--and which, for wealth of sublime and mysterious sugges-tion, unaided by complex dramatic design, was unique in the art of the world."

On one occasion the talk turned on the eccentricities and affectations of men of genius, and I did my best to-ridicule them unsparingly, saying they were a purely modern extravagance, the highest intellects of other times being ever the sanest, Shakspeare, Cervantes, Goethe, Coleridge, Wordsworth; the root of the evil had been Shelley, who was mad, and in imitation of whose madness, modern men of ge-nius must many of them be mad also, until it had come to such a pass-that if a gifted man conducted himself throughout life with probity and propriety we instantly began to doubt the value of his gifts. Rossetti evidently thought that in all this I was covertly hitting out at himself, and cut short the conversation with an unequivocal hint that he had no affectations, and could not account himself an authority with respect to them.

With such talk a few of our evenings were spent, but too soon the insatiable craving for the drug came with renewed force, and then all pleasant intercourse was banished. Night after night we sat up until eleven, twelve, and one o'clock, watch-ing the long hours go by with heavy steps; waiting, waiting, waiting for the time at which he could take his first draught, and drop into his pillowed place and snatch a dreamless sleep of three or four hours' duration.

In order to break the monotony of nights such as I describe I sometimes read from Fielding, Richardson, and Sterne, but more frequently induced Rossetti to recite. Thus, with failing voice, he would again and again attempt, at my request, his **Cloud Confines**, or passages from **The King's Tragedy**, and repeatedly, also, Poe's **Ulalume** and **Raven**. I remember that, touching the last-mentioned of these poems, he remarked that out of his love of it while still a boy his own **Blessed Damozel** originated. "I saw," he said, "that Poe had done the utmost it was possible to do with the grief of the lover on earth, and so I determined to reverse the condi-tions, and give utterance to the yearning of the loved one in heaven." At that time of the year the night closed in as early as seven or eight o'clock, and then in that little house among the solitary hills his disconsolate spirit would sometimes sink beyond solace into irreclaimable depths of depression.

It was impossible that such a condition of things should last, and it was with unspeakable relief that I heard Rossetti express a desire to return home. Mr. Watts, who at that time was at Stratford-upon-Avon, had promised to join us, but now wrote to say that this was impossible. Had it been otherwise, Rossetti would willingly have remained, but now he longed to get back to London. His life had lost its joys. The success of his Liverpool picture was almost as nothing to him, and the enthusiastic reception given to his book gave him not more than a passing pleasure, though he was deeply touched by the sympathetic and exhaustive criticism published by Professor Dowden in *The Academy*, as well as by Professor Colvin's friendly monograph in *The World*. At length one night, a month after our arrival, we set out on our return, and well do I remember the pathos of his words as I helped him (now feebler than ever) into his house. "Thank God! home at last, and never shall I leave it again!"

Very natural was the deep concern of his friends, especially of his brother and Mr. Shields, at finding him return even less well than he had set out. With deeper reliance on past knowledge of the man, Mr. Watts still took a hopeful view, attributing the physical prostration to hypochondriasis, which might, in common with all similar nervous ailments, impose as much pain upon the victim as if the sufferings complained of had a real foundation in positive disease, but might also give way at any moment when the victim could be induced to take a hopeful view of life. The cheerfulness of Mr. Watts's society, after what I well know must have been the lugubrious nature of my own, had at first its usual salutary effect upon Rossetti's spirits, and I will not forbear to say that I, too, welcomed it as a draught of healing morning air after a month-long imprisonment in an atmosphere of gloom. But I was not yet freed of my charge. The sense of responsibility which in the solitude of the mountains had weighed me down, was now indeed divided with his affectionate family and the friends who were Rossetti's friends before they were mine, and who came at this juncture with willing help, prompted chiefly, of course, by devotion to the great man in sore trouble, but also--I must allow myself to think--in one or two cases by desire to relieve me of some of the burden of the task that had fallen so unexpectedly upon me. Foremost among such disinterested friends was of course the friend I have spoken of so frequently in these pages, and for whom I now felt a growing regard arising as much out of my perception of the loyalty of his comradeship as the splendour of his gifts. But after him in solicitous service to Rossetti, at this moment of great need, came Frederick Shields (the fine tissue of whose highly-strung nature must have been sorely tried by the strain to which it was subjected), Mr. W. B. Scott, whose visits were never more warmly welcomed by Rossetti than at this season, the good and gifted Miss Boyd, and of course Rossetti's brother, sister, and mother, to each of whom he was affectionately attached. Strange enough it seemed that this man who, for years had shunned the world and chosen solitude when he might have had society, seemed at last to grow weary of his loneliness. But so it was. Rossetti became daily more and more dependent upon his friends for company that should not fail him, for never for an hour now could he endure to be alone. Remembering this, I almost doubt if by nature he was at any time a solitary. There are men who feel more deeply the sense of isolation amidst the busiest crowds than within the narrowest circle of intimates, and I have heard from Rossetti reminiscences of his earlier life that led me to believe that he was one of the number. Perhaps, after all, he wandered from the world rather from the dread than with the hope of solitude. In such pleasant intercourse as the visits of the friends I have named afforded, was the sadness of the day in a measure dissipated, but when night came I never failed to realise that no progress whatever had been made. I tried to check the craving for chloral, but I could as easily have checked the rising tide: and where the lifelong assiduity of older friends had failed to eradicate a morbid, ruinous, and fatal thirst, it was presumptous if not ridiculous to imagine that the task could be compassed by a frail creature with heart and nerves of wax. But the whole scene was now beginning to have an interest for me more personal and more serious than I have yet given hint of. The constant fret and fume of this life of baffled effort, of struggle with a deadly drug that had grown to have an objective existence in my mind as the existence of a fiend, was not without a sensible effect upon myself. I became ill for a few days with a low fever, but far worse than this was the fact that there was creeping over me the wild influence of Rossetti's own distempered imaginings.

Once conscious of such influence I determined to resist it, but how to do so I knew not without flying utterly away from an atmosphere in which my best senses seemed to stagnate, and burying the memory of it for ever.

The crisis was pending, and sooner than we expected it came. A nurse was engaged. One evening Dr. Westland Marston and his son Philip Bourke Marston came to spend a few hours with Rossetti, For a while he seemed much cheered by their bright society, but later on he gave those manifestations of uneasiness which I had learned to know too well. Removing restlessly from seat to seat, he ultimately threw himself upon the sofa in that rather awkward attitude which I have previously described as characteristic of him in moments of nervous agitation. Presently he called out that his arm had become paralysed, and, upon attempting to rise, that his leg also had lost its power. We were naturally startled, but knowing the force of his imagination in its influence on his bodily capacity, we tried playfully to banish the idea. Raising him to his feet, however, we realised that from whatever cause, he had lost the use of the limbs in question, and in the utmost alarm we carried him to his bedroom, and hurried away for Mr. Marshall It was found that he had really undergone a species of paralysis, called, I think, loss of co-ordinative power. The juncture was a critical one, and it was at length decided by the able medical adviser just named, that the time had come when the chloral, which was at the root of all this mischief, should be decisively, entirely, and instantly cut off. To compass this end a young medical man, Mr. Henry Maudsley, was brought into the house as a resident to watch and manage the case in the intervals of Mr. Marshall's visits. It is not for me to offer a statement of what was done, and done so ably at this period. I only know that morphia was at first injected as a substitute for the narcotic the system had grown to demand; that Rossetti was for many hours delirious whilst his body was passing through the terrible ordeal of having to conquer the craving for the former drug, and that three or four mornings after the experiment had been begun he awoke calm in body, and clear in mind, and grateful in heart. His delusions and those intermittent suspicions of his friends which I have before alluded to, were now gone, as things in the past of which he hardly knew whether in actual fact they had or had not been. Christmas Day was now nigh at hand, and, still confined to his room, he begged me to promise to spend that day with him; "otherwise," he said, "how sad a day it must be for me, for I cannot fairly ask any other." With a tenderness of sympathy I shall not forget, Mr. Scott had asked me to dine that day at his more cheerful house; but I reflected that this was to be my first Christmas in London and it might be Rossetti's last, so I put by pleasanter considerations. We dined alone, but, somewhat later, William Rossetti, with true brotherly affection, left the guests at his own house, and ran down to spend an hour with the invalid. We could hear from time to time the ringing of the bells of the neighbouring churches, and I noticed that Rossetti was not disturbed by them as he had been formerly. Indeed, the drug once removed, he was in every sense a changed man. He talked that night brightly, and with more force and incisiveness, I thought, than he had displayed for months. There was the ring of affection in his tone as he said he had always had loyal friends; and then he spoke with feeling of Mr. Watts's friendship, of Mr. Shields's, and afterwards he spoke of Mr. Burne Jones who had just previously visited him, as well as of Mr. Madox Brown, and his friendship of a lifetime; of Mr. Swinburne, Mr. Morris, Mr. Stephens, Mr. Boyce, and other early friends. He said a word or two of myself which I shall not repeat, and then spoke with emotion of his mother and sister, and of his sister who was dead, and how they were supported through their sore trials by religious resignation. He asked if I, like Shields, was a believer, and seemed altogether in a softer and more spiritual mood than I remember to have noticed before.

With such talk we passed the Christmas night of 1881. Rossetti recovered power in some measure, was able to get down to the studio, and see the friends who called--Mr. F. E. Leyland frequently, Lord and Lady Mount Temple, Mrs. Sumner, Mr. Boyce, Mr. F. G. Stephens, Mr. Gilchrist, Mr. and Mrs. Virtue Tebbs, Mrs. Stillman, Mrs. Coronio, and Mr. C. and Mr. A. Ionides occasionally, as well as those previously named. A visit from Dr. Hueffer of the *Times* (of whose gifts he had a high opinion), enlivened him perceptibly. But he did not recover, and at the end of January 1882 it was definitely determined that he should go to the sea-side. I was asked to accompany him, and did so. At the right juncture Mr. J. P. Seddon very hospitably tendered the use of his handsome bungalow at Birchington-on-Sea, a little watering-place four miles west of Margate. There we spent nine weeks. At first going out he was able to take short walks on the cliffs, or round the road that winds about the churchyard, but his strength grew less and less every day and hour. We were constantly visited by Mr. Watts, whose devotion never failed, and Rossetti would brighten up at the prospect of one of his visits, and become sensibly depressed when he had gone. Mr. William Sharp, too (a young friend of whose gifts as a poet Rossetti had a genuine appreciation, and by whom he had been visited at intervals for some time), came out occasionally and cheered up the sufferer in a noticeable degree. Then his mother and sister came and stayed in the house during many weeks at the last. How shall I speak of the tenderness of their solicitude, of their unwearying attentions, in a word of their ardent and reciprocated love of the illustrious son and brother for whom they did the thousand gentle offices which they alone could have done! The end was drawing on, and we all knew the fact. Rossetti had actually taken to poetical composition afresh, and had written a facetious ballad (conceived years before) of the length of *The White Ship*, called *Jan Van Hunks*, embodying an eccentric story of a Dutchman's wager to smoke against the devil. This was to appear in a miscellany of stories and poems by himself and Mr. Watts, a project which had been a favourite one of his for some years, and in which he now, in his last moments, took a revived interest strange and strong.

About this time he derived great gratification from reading an article on him and his works in *Le Livre* by Mr. Joseph Knight, an old friend to whom he was deeply attached, and for whose gifts he had a genuine admiration. Perhaps the very last letter Rossetti penned was written to Mr. Knight upon the subject of this article.

His intellect was as powerful as in his best days, and freer than ever of hallucinations. But his bodily strength grew less and less. His sight became feebler, and then he abandoned the many novels that had recently solaced his idler hours, and Miss Rossetti read aloud to him. Among other books she read Dickens's *Tale of Two Cities*, and he seemed deeply touched by Sidney Carton's sacrifice, and remarked that he would like to paint the last scene of the story.

On Wednesday morning, April 5th, I went into the bedroom to which he had for some days been confined, and wrote out to his dictation two sonnets which he had composed on a design of his called *The Sphinx*, and which he wished to give, together with the drawing and the ballad before described, to Mr. Watts for publication in the volume just mentioned. On the Thursday morning I found his utterance thick, and his speech from that cause hardly intelligible. It chanced that I had just been reading Mr. Buchanan's new volume of poems, and in the course of conversation I told him the story of the ballad called *The Lights of Leith*, and he was affected by the pathos of it. He had heard of that author's retraction[14] of

14   The retraction, which now has a peculiar literary

the charges involved in the article published ten years earlier, and was manifestly touched by the dedication of the romance **God and the Man**. He talked long and earnestly that morning, and it was our last real interview. He spoke of his love of early English ballad literature, and of how when he first met with it he had said to himself: "There lies your line."

"Can you understand me?" he asked abruptly, alluding to the thickness of his utterance.

"Perfectly."

"Nurse Abrey cannot: what a good creature she is!"

That night we telegraphed to Mr. Marshall, to Mr. W. M. Rossetti, and Mr.

---

interest, was made in the following verses, and should, I think, be recorded here:

To an old Enemy.

I would have snatch'd a bay-leaf from thy brow,
Wronging the chaplet on an honoured head;
In peace and charity I bring thee now
A lily-flower instead.
Pure as thy purpose, blameless as thy song,
Sweet as thy spirit, may this offering be;
Forget the bitter blame that did thee wrong,
And take the gift from me!

In a later edition of the romance the following verses are added to the dedication:

To Dante Gabriel Rossetti:

Calmly, thy royal robe of death around thee,
Thou Bleekest, and weeping brethren round thee stand--
Gently they placed, ere yet God's angel crown'd thee,
My lily in thy hand!
I never knew thee living, O my brother!
But on thy breast my lily of love now lies;
And by that token, we shall know each other,
When God's voice saith "Arise!"

Watts, and wrote next morning to Mr. Shields, Mr. Scott, and Mr. Madox Brown. It had been found by the resident medical man, Dr. Harris, that in Rossetti's case kidney disease had supervened. His dear mother and I sat up until early morning with him, and when we left him his sister took our place and remained with him the whole of that and subsequent nights. He sat up in bed most of the time and said a sort of stupefaction had removed all pain. He crooned over odd lines of poetry. "My own verses torment me," he said. Then he half-sang, half-recited, snatches from one of Iago's songs in ***Othello***. "Strange things," he murmured, "to come into one's head at such a moment." I told him his brother and Mr. Watts would be with him to-morrow. "Then you really think that I am dying? At ***last*** you think so; but ***I*** was right from the first."

Next day, Good Friday, the friends named did come, and weak as he was, he was much cheered by their presence. The following day Mr. Marshall arrived.

That gentleman recognised the alarming position of affairs, but he was not without hope. He administered a sort of hot bath, and on Sunday morning Rossetti was perceptibly brighter. Mr. Shields had now arrived, and one after one of his friends, including Mr. Leyland, who was at the time staying at Ramsgate, and made frequent calls, visited him in his room and found him able to listen and sometimes to talk. In the evening the nurse gave a cheering report of his condition, and encouraged by such prospects, Mr. Watts, Mr. Shields, and myself, gave way to good spirits, and retired to an adjoining room. About nine o'clock Mr. Watts left us, and returning in a short time, said he had been in the sickroom, and had had some talk with Rossetti, and found him cheerful. An instant afterwards we heard a scream, followed by a loud rapping at our door. We hurried into Rossetti's room and found him in convulsions. Mr. Watts raised him on one side, whilst I raised him on the other; his mother, sister, and brother, were immediately present (Mr. Shields had fled away for the doctor); there were a few moments of suspense, and then we saw him die in our arms. Mrs. William Rossetti arrived from Manchester at this moment.

Thus on Easter Day Rossetti died. It was hard to realise that he was actually dead; but so it was, and the dreadful fact had at last come upon us with a horrible suddenness. Of the business of the next few days I need say nothing. I went up to London in the interval between the death and burial, and the old house at Chelsea, which, to my mind, in my time had always been desolate, was now more than ever so, that the man who had been its vitalising spirit lay dead eighty miles away by the side of the sea. It was decided to bury the poet in the churchyard of Birchington. The funeral, which was a private one, was attended by relatives and personal friends only, with one or two well-wishers from London.

Next day we saw most of the friends away by train, and, some days later, Mr. Watts was with myself the last to leave. I thought we two were drawn the closer each to each from the loss of him by whom we were brought together. We walked one morning to the churchyard and found the grave, which nestles under the south-west porch, strewn with flowers. The church is an ancient and quaint early Gothic edifice, somewhat rejuvenated however, but with ivy creeping over its walls. The prospect to the north is of sea only: a broad sweep of landscape so flat and so featureless that the great sea dominates it. As we stood there, with the rumble of the rolling waters borne to us from the shore, we felt that though we had little dreamed that we should lay Rossetti in his last sleep here, no other place could be quite so fit. It was, indeed, the resting-place for a poet. In this bed, of all others, he must at length, after weary years of sleeplessness, sleep the only sleep that is deep and will endure. Thinking of the incidents which I have in this chapter tried to record, my mind reverted to a touching sonnet which the friend by my side had just printed; and then, for the first time, I was struck by its extraordinary applicability to him whom we had laid below. In its printed form it was addressed to Heine, and ran:

> Thou knew'st that island far away and lone
> Whose shores are as a harp, where billows break
> In spray of music and the breezes shake
> O'er spicy seas a woof of colour and tone,
> While that sweet music echoes like a moan
> In the island's heart, and sighs around the lake
> Where, watching fearfully a watchful snake,
> A damsel weeps upon her emerald throne.
>
> Life's ocean, breaking round thy senses' shore,
> Struck golden song as from the strand of day:

For us the joy, for thee the fell foe lay--
Pain's blinking snake around the fair isle's core,
Turning to sighs the enchanted sounds that play
Around thy lovely island evermore.

"How strangely appropriate it is," I said, "to Rossetti, and now I remember how deeply he was moved on reading it."

"He guessed its secret; I addressed it, for disguise, to Heine, to whom it was sadly inapplicable. I meant it for *him*."

The Codes Of Hammurabi And Moses
W. W. Davies

QTY

The discovery of the Hammurabi Code is one of the greatest achievements of archaeology, and is of paramount interest, not only to the student of the Bible, but also to all those interested in ancient history...

Religion   **ISBN:** *1-59462-338-4*   **Pages:**132
                                                 MSRP $12.95

The Theory of Moral Sentiments
Adam Smith

QTY

This work from 1749. contains original theories of conscience amd moral judgment and it is the foundation for systemof morals.

Philosophy **ISBN:** *1-59462-777-0*   **Pages:**536
                                                 MSRP $19.95

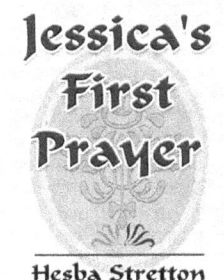

Jessica's First Prayer
Hesba Stretton

QTY

In a screened and secluded corner of one of the many railway-bridges which span the streets of London there could be seen a few years ago, from five o'clock every morning until half past eight, a tidily set-out coffee-stall, consisting of a trestle and board, upon which stood two large tin cans, with a small fire of charcoal burning under each so as to keep the coffee boiling during the early hours of the morning when the work-people were thronging into the city on their way to their daily toil...

Childrens   **ISBN:** *1-59462-373-2*   **Pages:**84
                                                 MSRP $9.95

My Life and Work
Henry Ford

QTY

Henry Ford revolutionized the world with his implementation of mass production for the Model T automobile. Gain valuable business insight into his life and work with his own auto-biography... "We have only started on our development of our country we have not as yet, with all our talk of wonderful progress, done more than scratch the surface. The progress has been wonderful enough but..."

Biographies/ **ISBN:** *1-59462-198-5*   **Pages:**300
                                                 MSRP $21.95

The Art of Cross-Examination
Francis Wellman

I presume it is the experience of every author, after his first book is published upon an important subject, to be almost overwhelmed with a wealth of ideas and illustrations which could readily have been included in his book, and which to his own mind, at least, seem to make a second edition inevitable. Such certainly was the case with me; and when the first edition had reached its sixth impression in five months, I rejoiced to learn that it seemed to my publishers that the book had met with a sufficiently favorable reception to justify a second and considerably enlarged edition. ..

Reference   ISBN: *1-59462-647-2*

Pages:412

MSRP $19.95

On the Duty of Civil Disobedience
Henry David Thoreau

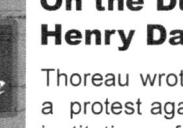

Thoreau wrote his famous essay, On the Duty of Civil Disobedience, as a protest against an unjust but popular war and the immoral but popular institution of slave-owning. He did more than write—he declined to pay his taxes, and was hauled off to gaol in consequence. Who can say how much this refusal of his hastened the end of the war and of slavery ?

Law   ISBN: *1-59462-747-9*

Pages:48

MSRP $7.45

Dream Psychology Psychoanalysis for Beginners
Sigmund Freud

Sigmund Freud, born Sigismund Schlomo Freud (May 6, 1856 - September 23, 1939), was a Jewish-Austrian neurologist and psychiatrist who co-founded the psychoanalytic school of psychology. Freud is best known for his theories of the unconscious mind, especially involving the mechanism of repression; his redefinition of sexual desire as mobile and directed towards a wide variety of objects; and his therapeutic techniques, especially his understanding of transference in the therapeutic relationship and the presumed value of dreams as sources of insight into unconscious desires.

Dream Psychology
Psychoanalysis for Beginners

Sigmund Freud

Pages:196

Psychology   ISBN: *1-59462-905-6*   *MSRP $15.45*

The Miracle of Right Thought
Orison Swett Marden

Believe with all of your heart that you will do what you were made to do. When the mind has once formed the habit of holding cheerful, happy, prosperous pictures, it will not be easy to form the opposite habit. It does not matter how improbable or how far away this realization may see, or how dark the prospects may be, if we visualize them as best we can, as vividly as possible, hold tenaciously to them and vigorously struggle to attain them, they will gradually become actualized, realized in the life. But a desire, a longing without endeavor, a yearning abandoned or held indifferently will vanish without realization.

Pages:360

Self Help   ISBN: *1-59462-644-8*   *MSRP $25.45*

The Rosicrucian Cosmo-Conception Mystic Christianity *by Max Heindel* ISBN: *1-59462-188-8* **$38.95**
The Rosicrucian Cosmo-conception is not dogmatic, neither does it appeal to any other authority than the reason of the student. It is: not controversial, but is: sent forth in the, hope that it may help to clear... New Age/Religion Pages 646

Abandonment To Divine Providence *by Jean-Pierre de Caussade* ISBN: *1-59462-228-0* **$25.95**
"The Rev. Jean Pierre de Caussade was one of the most remarkable spiritual writers of the Society of Jesus in France in the 18th Century. His death took place at Toulouse in 1751. His works have gone through many editions and have been republished... Inspirational/Religion Pages 400

Mental Chemistry *by Charles Haanel* ISBN: *1-59462-192-6* **$23.95**
Mental Chemistry allows the change of material conditions by combining and appropriately utilizing the power of the mind. Much like applied chemistry creates something new and unique out of careful combinations of chemicals the mastery of mental chemistry... New Age Pages 354

The Letters of Robert Browning and Elizabeth Barret Barrett 1845-1846 vol II ISBN: *1-59462-193-4* **$35.95**
by Robert Browning and Elizabeth Barrett Biographies Pages 596

Gleanings In Genesis (volume I) *by Arthur W. Pink* ISBN: *1-59462-130-6* **$27.45**
Appropriately has Genesis been termed "the seed plot of the Bible" for in it we have, in germ form, almost all of the great doctrines which are afterwards fully developed in the books of Scripture which follow... Religion/Inspirational Pages 420

The Master Key *by L. W. de Laurence* ISBN: *1-59462-001-6* **$30.95**
In no branch of human knowledge has there been a more lively increase of the spirit of research during the past few years than in the study of Psychology, Concentration and Mental Discipline. The requests for authentic lessons in Thought Control, Mental Discipline and... New Age/Business Pages 422

The Lesser Key Of Solomon Goetia *by L. W. de Laurence* ISBN: *1-59462-092-X* **$9.95**
This translation of the first book of the "Lernegton" which is now for the first time made accessible to students of Talismanic Magic was done, after careful collation and edition, from numerous Ancient Manuscripts in Hebrew, Latin, and French... New Age/Occult Pages 92

Rubaiyat Of Omar Khayyam *by Edward Fitzgerald* ISBN:*1-59462-332-5* **$13.95**
Edward Fitzgerald, whom the world has already learned, in spite of his own efforts to remain within the shadow of anonymity, to look upon as one of the rarest poets of the century, was born at Bredfield, in Suffolk, on the 31st of March, 1809. He was the third son of John Purcell... Music Pages 172

Ancient Law *by Henry Maine* ISBN: *1-59462-128-4* **$29.95**
The chief object of the following pages is to indicate some of the earliest ideas of mankind, as they are reflected in Ancient Law, and to point out the relation of those ideas to modern thought. Religion/History Pages 452

Far-Away Stories *by William J. Locke* ISBN: *1-59462-129-2* **$19.45**
"Good wine needs no bush, but a collection of mixed vintages does. And this book is just such a collection. Some of the stories I do not want to remain buried for ever in the museum files of dead magazine-numbers an author's not unpardonable vanity..." Fiction Pages 272

Life of David Crockett *by David Crockett* ISBN: *1-59462-250-7* **$27.45**
"Colonel David Crockett was one of the most remarkable men of the times in which he lived. Born in humble life, but gifted with a strong will, an indomitable courage, and unremitting perseverance... Biographies/New Age Pages 424

Lip-Reading *by Edward Nitchie* ISBN: *1-59462-206-X* **$25.95**
Edward B. Nitchie, founder of the New York School for the Hard of Hearing, now the Nitchie School of Lip-Reading, Inc, wrote "LIP-READING Principles and Practice". The development and perfecting of this meritorious work on lip-reading was an undertaking... How-to Pages 400

A Handbook of Suggestive Therapeutics, Applied Hypnotism, Psychic Science ISBN: *1-59462-214-0* **$24.95**
by Henry Munro Health/New Age/Health/Self-help Pages 376

A Doll's House: and Two Other Plays *by Henrik Ibsen* ISBN: *1-59462-112-8* **$19.95**
Henrik Ibsen created this classic when in revolutionary 1848 Rome. Introducing some striking concepts in playwriting for the realist genre, this play has been studied the world over. Fiction/Classics/Plays 308

The Light of Asia *by sir Edwin Arnold* ISBN: *1-59462-204-3* **$13.95**
In this poetic masterpiece, Edwin Arnold describes the life and teachings of Buddha. The man who was to become known as Buddha to the world was born as Prince Gautama of India but he rejected the worldly riches and abandoned the reigns of power when... Religion/History/Biographies Pages 170

The Complete Works of Guy de Maupassant *by Guy de Maupassant* ISBN: *1-59462-157-8* **$16.95**
"For days and days, nights and nights, I had dreamed of that first kiss which was to consecrate our engagement, and I knew not on what spot I should put my lips..." Fiction/Classics Pages 240

The Art of Cross-Examination *by Francis L. Wellman* ISBN: *1-59462-309-0* **$26.95**
Written by a renowned trial lawyer, Wellman imparts his experience and uses case studies to explain how to use psychology to extract desired information through questioning. How-to/Science/Reference Pages 408

Answered or Unanswered? *by Louisa Vaughan* ISBN: *1-59462-248-5* **$10.95**
Miracles of Faith in China Religion Pages 112

The Edinburgh Lectures on Mental Science (1909) *by Thomas* ISBN: *1-59462-008-3* **$11.95**
This book contains the substance of a course of lectures recently given by the writer in the Queen Street Hall, Edinburgh. Its purpose is to indicate the Natural Principles governing the relation between Mental Action and Material Conditions... New Age/Psychology Pages 148

Ayesha *by H. Rider Haggard* ISBN: *1-59462-301-5* **$24.95**
Verily and indeed it is the unexpected that happens! Probably if there was one person upon the earth from whom the Editor of this, and of a certain previous history, did not expect to hear again... Classics Pages 380

Ayala's Angel *by Anthony Trollope* ISBN: *1-59462-352-X* **$29.95**
The two girls were both pretty, but Lucy who was twenty-one who supposed to be simple and comparatively unattractive, whereas Ayala was credited, as her Bombwhat romantic name might show, with poetic charm and a taste for romance. Ayala when her father died was nineteen... Fiction Pages 484

The American Commonwealth *by James Bryce* ISBN: *1-59462-286-8* **$34.45**
An interpretation of American democratic political theory. It examines political mechanics and society from the perspective of Scotsman James Bryce Politics Pages 572

Stories of the Pilgrims *by Margaret P. Pumphrey* ISBN: *1-59462-116-0* **$17.95**
This book explores pilgrims religious oppression in England as well as their escape to Holland and eventual crossing to America on the Mayflower, and their early days in New England... History Pages 268

www.bookjungle.com *email: sales@bookjungle.com fax: 630-214-0564 mail: Book Jungle PO Box 2226 Champaign, IL 61825*

QTY

The Fasting Cure *by Sinclair Upton*   ISBN: *1-59462-222-1*   **$13.95**
*In the Cosmopolitan Magazine for May, 1910, and in the Contemporary Review (London) for April, 1910, I published an article dealing with my experi-
ences in fasting. I have written a great many magazine articles, but never one which attracted so much attention... New Age/Self Help/Health Pages 164*

Hebrew Astrology *by Sepharial*   ISBN: *1-59462-308-2*   **$13.45**
*In these days of advanced thinking it is a matter of common observation that we have left many of the old landmarks behind and that we are now pressing
forward to greater heights and to a wider horizon than that which represented the mind-content of our progenitors...   Astrology Pages 144*

Thought Vibration or The Law of Attraction in the Thought World   ISBN: *1-59462-127-6*   **$12.95**
by William Walker Atkinson   *Psychology/Religion Pages 144*

Optimism *by Helen Keller*   ISBN: *1-59462-108-X*   **$15.95**
*Helen Keller was blind, deaf, and mute since 19 months old, yet famously learned how to overcome these handicaps, communicate with the world, and
spread her lectures promoting optimism. An inspiring read for everyone...   Biographies Inspirational Pages 84*

Sara Crewe *by Frances Burnett*   ISBN: *1-59462-360-0*   **$9.45**
*In the first place, Miss Minchin lived in London. Her home was a large, dull, tall one, in a large, dull square, where all the houses were alike, and all the
sparrows were alike, and where all the door-knockers made the same heavy sound...   Childrens/Classic Pages 88*

The Autobiography of Benjamin Franklin *by Benjamin Franklin*   ISBN: *1-59462-135-7*   **$24.95**
*The Autobiography of Benjamin Franklin has probably been more extensively read than any other American historical work, and no other book of its kind
has had such ups and downs of fortune. Franklin lived for many years in England, where he was agent...   Biographies History Pages 332*

Name	
Email	
Telephone	
Address	
City, State ZIP	

☐ **Credit Card**   ☐ **Check / Money Order**

Credit Card Number	
Expiration Date	
Signature	

*Please Mail to: Book Jungle
PO Box 2226
Champaign, IL 61825
or Fax to: 630-214-0564*

ORDERING INFORMATION

web: *www.bookjungle.com*
email: *sales@bookjungle.com*
fax: *630-214-0564*
mail: *Book Jungle PO Box 2226 Champaign, IL 61825*
or PayPal *to sales@bookjungle.com*

Please contact us for bulk discounts

DIRECT-ORDER TERMS

**20% Discount if You Order
Two or More Books**
Free Domestic Shipping!
Accepted: Master Card, Visa,
Discover, American Express

www.ingramcontent.com/pod-product-compliance
Lightning Source LLC
Chambersburg PA
CBHW080902020726
47502CB00008B/2315